Published by Dreamspinner Press
www.dreamspinnerpress.com

Readers love the Carlisle
series by Andrew Grey

Fire and Water

"All of Andrew ...... k I just
found a new ......

......Bytes

Fire and I...

"This is a story that touches the heart as well as heats the blood. I hope we see more of the Carlisle Cops in the future!"

—House of Millar

Fire and Snow

"*Fire and Snow* by Andrew Grey gave me exactly what I want out of a romance. It was an amazing love story."

—Two Chicks Obsessed

Fire and Hail

"I absolutely LOVE this series and this newest addition is without a doubt a wonderful welcome."

—Diverse Reader

Fire and Fog

"It ...... Carlisle
Co ...... w Grey
co ...... od mix
of ......

......proach

By ANDREW GREY

Published by DREAMSPINNER PRESS
www.dreamspinnerpress.com

By ANDREW GREY

Published by DREAMSPINNER PRESS
www.dreamspinnerpress.com

FIRE AND RAIN
ANDREW GREY

Published by
DREAMSPINNER PRESS

5032 Capital Circle SW, Suite 2, PMB# 279,
Tallahassee, FL 32305-7886 USA
www.dreamspinnerpress.com

This is a work of fiction. Names, characters, places, and incidents either
are the product of author imagination or are used fictitiously, and any
resemblance to actual persons, living or dead, business establishments,
events, or locales is entirely coincidental.

Fire and Rain
© 2016, 2019 Andrew Grey

Cover Art
© 2018, 2019 Kanaxa
Cover content is for illustrative purposes only and any person depicted
on the cover is a model.

Digital ISBN: 978-1-63476-850-4
Mass Market Paperback ISBN: 978-1-64108-193-1
Trade Paperback ISBN: 978-1-63476-849-8
Library of Congress Control Number: 2015918428
Mass Market Paperback published August 2019
v. 1.0

Printed in the United States of America
∞
This paper meets the requirements of
ANSI/NISO Z39.48-1992 (Permanence of Paper).

To police officers everywhere, for doing a difficult job
helping to keep our communities safe.

CHAPTER 1

"I CAN'T take this anymore!" Jeffrey shrilled loudly enough to send a jolt up Kip Rogers's spine like nails on a blackboard.

"Then don't. It isn't like you actually live here," Kip countered. This shit was starting already, and Jeffrey had just gotten in the door an hour ago. "You breeze into town once or twice a month and can't figure out why I can't just take off work and spend my time with you."

"I come here on weekends," Jeffrey countered as though he were stating the most obvious thing in the world. After all, Jeffrey kept lawyer's hours; in his world, no one worked weekends. "I know you have to work and all, but it's a weekend and I gave you notice."

Three days. "You told me Tuesday, and I can't get my schedule changed that fast. Besides, you had plenty to keep you busy while I was at work." Kip was trying to be civil, but even his patience was quickly coming to an end.

"I came here to be with you." Jeffrey stormed into the bedroom and returned with his roller suitcase behind him, swinging his hips like a 1960s TWA stewardess. All he was missing was the updo and the scarf around his neck.

"No. You came here because you wanted some attention and because you were horny. That's all, and you're angry because I can't spend all my time with you even though I cleared the rest of my weekend schedule and put off going out with friends because you called." Kip paused, contemplating giving Jeffrey another chance, but he'd had enough. There was only so much stomping a man's pride could take, and he had reached his limit. He walked to the front door and pulled it open. "Let me help you."

Jeffrey blinked a few times, and then crocodile tears began filling his ice-blue eyes. "You really want me to leave?" He turned slightly to the side. What the hell was this? Jeffrey had to be on something to flip from anger to seduction in two seconds flat. Kip thought back and realized this was his game, the way he got what he wanted. Anger followed by forgiveness and then sex. He should have seen through this shit before, but he'd been too busy thinking with his dick to look any deeper. Right now his dick was asleep, and from the looks of things, it wasn't waking up anytime soon—not for Jeffrey.

"Yes," Kip answered forcefully. "Go back to Mommy and Daddy and all those friends of yours who are in denial. How the hell they don't know you're gay, with the way you prance around like a frilled-up peacock, is beyond me. They must be dumb as a box of rocks." Kip waited while the tears instantly dried and enticement turned to rage.

"I'm not coming back once I go through that door," Jeffrey warned.

"What are you, six? Go on and get the hell out of here. Oh, and I suggest that you get out of town."

"Is that a warning, Officer?" Jeffrey asked seductively.

Kip blinked, and then it hit him: Jeffrey thought this was some kind of game. He knew Jeffrey liked playing games—role-playing in bed, head games out of bed. That was his forte.

"No. Your car is parked illegally, and if you're not gone in two minutes, I'll call someone to ticket it. I wonder how many outstanding tickets and violations they're going to find when they run your plates. Maybe you'll even end up in jail. I can see to it that you get a couple of very large roommates. Maybe guys who have been there a little longer than they should have been." Kip waved his hand toward the door. "This isn't a game, Jeffrey. I've had more than enough game playing in my life." He held his gaze steady, as cold as he could possibly make it. "It's time for you to go and find someone else to play with. I'm through." God, he was so over all of this.

"You're shitting me!" Jeffrey screeched. "This is for real?"

"Oh, yeah. Looks like you overplayed your hand." Kip crossed his arms over his chest. "I'm done. I don't know what's one of your damn games and when you're being serious anymore, and frankly I don't care. You're selfish, hurtful, and a pain in the ass all the time, so it doesn't matter. I'm not a toy." That felt so good to say.

Jeffrey took a few steps. "Fine," he said, jutting his nose into the air. He walked past Kip and out onto the porch. "You were just a bit of fun, you know. A pretty good lay and nothing more."

"You were a selfish lay and managed to be a demanding pain in the ass from the bottom." As soon as Jeffrey's suitcase crossed the threshold, Kip closed the door and threw the lock. A clap of thunder rolled over the house, and Mother Nature chose that minute to open the skies. Rain had been threatening all day, though it had held off until now. Kip pulled the curtains aside and watched as Jeffrey hurried to his Porsche. He popped open the hood and dropped his bag inside. By the time he scurried to open his car door, Jeffrey was nearly soaked. Kip thought about taking pity on him but couldn't bring himself to do it. If he had to listen to Jeffrey screech one more time about his work schedule or how Kip's house wasn't as grand as the ones Jeffrey's other closet-case friends had.... It was time to make a clean break and give his self-respect a little boost.

Why it had taken him so damn long to figure out Jeffrey was only using him for some occasional weekend fun was beyond him. He was a police officer—he should have been able to take a closer look and see what Jeffrey really was: a user and a manipulator. Hell, he had the credit card bills to prove the manipulator part. Every time Jeffrey came to town, they went out to expensive restaurants that Jeffrey made the reservations for, but when the check arrived he'd bat his eyes, and Kip would pay to avoid a scene. He did that same thing in stores. The last weekend Jeffrey had spent nearly $500 on food and drinks alone. This was for the best.

Kip watched Jeffrey pull away and speed off down the street. He wasn't sure where he was going, but Jeffrey was an adult and needed to take care of himself. Hopefully he'd just head home to Pittsburgh and leave the midstate alone for a while. But more likely, he'd head downtown and wait for the clubs to open so he could try to pick up another guy, another sucker, to sponge off of.

Kip released a sigh of relief, and the tension that had been building for days flowed out of him. God, it was good to be able to relax again. Jeffrey was wound so tight that he always filled Kip with so much anxiety that it took days after he left for him to decompress. With a second sigh, he turned and headed through the entrance hall to the stairs, climbing them slowly and then making his way to the master bedroom. Kip still felt off sometimes using that room. It had been his parents' bedroom when he was growing up, and after they passed away and left the house to him, he'd moved in because he couldn't bear to see it empty.

The house was way too big for him alone: massive kitchen, a living room and a dining room, a formal parlor, and four bedrooms upstairs as well as what had once been a maid's quarters on the third floor. It had been built a century ago and was more solid than anything built today. Friends had advised him to sell it when his father passed away, but once he'd gotten a job in Carlisle, it seemed stupid to sell a house that was paid for and had been in his family. The best homes in town rarely came on the market. They sold privately or stayed in families, and Kip had a great house. Granted, it took a lot of his spare time to keep it up, and as he went into his bedroom to get ready for work, he noticed that the paint in the hallway and bedroom needed refreshing. Another project to add to the list.

Kip shucked his jeans and shirt in favor of one of his police uniforms. He pulled off the plastic wrap from the cleaners and got dressed. He liked the way he looked in his uniform. Jeffrey had told him once that it made his ass look great and that he was very sexy in it. Of course, Kip wasn't sure if that was real or just another one of Jeffrey's games.

He left the bedroom and went down to the kitchen. He made himself some food for his meal break. With the second shift rotation he was on, he didn't know whether to call it lunch or dinner. All he knew was that he was always hungry when the time rolled around. Once he had everything he needed, Kip locked the house and hurried to his car, thankful the rain had let up a little.

Steady rain made for a miserable shift, and that was what Kip knew he was in for as he drove to the station. It was only afternoon, but it felt like much later in the day, the low thick clouds more indicative of late fall than September, along with the chill in the air. Usually this weather held off for a few weeks at least.

Kip parked in the lot and went into the station. "Hey, Red," he called with a smile, and he got one in return. Red smiled more often now. Kip used to avoid him, but now he liked talking to him. "How's Terry?"

"Training every chance he gets. He has his heart set on the Olympics, and he's qualified for the team, so next summer he and I will be going to Rio." Red's grin was extraordinary. "He wants to qualify for a number of events, so he's working hard on different strokes." Red's partner, Terry, was a swimmer, and a damn good one, judging by all the success he'd had.

"You know I'll be cheering him on." Kip wished he could go someplace exciting like Rio to watch the Olympics. But the closest he was ever likely to get to something like that was his television.

Red nodded. "Are you just coming on shift?"

"Yeah." Kip continued through with Red, and they both clocked in, then went in for their assignments. Kip had been on the force a few years, but he wasn't one of the senior guys, so he still got mostly patrol duty. That was fine, and on a night like this, at least he was inside a car as opposed to walking one of the neighborhoods.

"Me too. I hate working second."

Kip nodded. He hated it mostly because it meant he never saw any of his friends. His schedule was too opposite theirs. Thankfully this was his last week on second shift, and then he'd rotate to first shift for a while. He needed a little normalcy in his life. "When do you rotate off?"

"Got a little more than a week," Red answered, and they sat down, waiting for the captain to brief them on what was happening and what they should look out for. Mostly it was the usual stuff: reports of dealing, unruly kids, some vandalism. Drugs were making their way back into town, but they'd had a reprieve after Red had helped take down one of the leaders and they'd been able to round up much of the organization.

"There have been reports of dealing after dark in Thornwald Park, so if you're on patrol in that area, be sure to pass through. Not that there's likely to be activity on a night like this, but if the rain lets up, there will be. Are there any questions?"

Kip raised his hand. "At the corner of the alley behind Ridge, there's a brush pile that's acting as a dead drop. One of my neighbors told me what he saw this morning."

"That's pretty bold," the captain said. He looked out over the assemblage. "Good, let's get going." He stepped down, and Kip retrieved the keys to his patrol car and began his shift, signing on to his computer and letting dispatch know he was on the job.

Kip was relieved he hadn't been put on traffic duty. He hated spending an entire shift sitting in one place waiting for drivers to speed by just a little too fast. Yes, it was done in the interest of public safety, but it was boring as all get-out.

He'd been assigned the north side of town, so he began his patrol, making a police presence visible. He answered calls and helped a couple whose car had broken down. He also broke up a domestic dispute. He wished the woman had been willing to press charges. Domestic disputes were the worst, because Kip knew another officer would end up paying them a visit again, but until charges were filed there was little he could do. It was one of the most frustrating parts of the job, knowing someone was being hurt, and would be again, but not being able to help. Kip stopped back at the station on his break and ate his late dinner before heading out again.

With the continuing bad weather, traffic was light and there were few people out on the sidewalks, even in the busier areas of town like outside the theater and restaurants. Darkness came early with the cloud cover, and Kip resumed his patrol. He took the back streets, watching for trouble. The streetlights came on, and Kip was thankful everyone was indoors. He wasn't looking forward to traipsing around in the rain.

"A report of someone sleeping in the doorway of Hansen's Men's Wear" came through his radio from Dispatch.

"I'll take it," Kip said, answering the call and making the turn back toward the main street of town. With the weather like this and the fact that the store was one of those old-fashioned ones with the deep display windows, someone was bound to try to take shelter there. Kip made his final turn and came up on the store. He passed by but didn't see anything, so he went around the block and pulled to a stop. The trees that lined the street cast shadows over the windows. Kip groaned as he pulled on his hat and raincoat before getting out of the car and tugging them tight around him. The cold and wet went right through the coat as the swirling wind blew water in all directions.

He took it slow and placed his hand on his gun as he approached the front of the store. Sure enough, a dark figure lay pressed back against the door of the closed business. It was covered in a dark blanket. As Kip got closer, he heard something he didn't expect: singing. It barely reached his ears over the noise of the rain and water dripping off eaves and tumbling through drainpipes, but it was there. A lullaby, most definitely.

"I'm sorry. You need to move on," Kip said as gently as he could. He didn't want to frighten them. He pulled out his flashlight, shining it around. The blanket lowered, revealing a pair of haunted blue eyes. Kip was careful not to shine the light in his face, but he needed to see the man. "This is private property and you can't stay here. There's the Salvation Army a few blocks down. They have a shelter."

"They're already full," the man said, though he sounded like a kid. "We got turned away from there a few hours ago."

Kip's suspicion rose. We? What exactly was going on under that blanket? Kip waited, and the man lowered the blanket farther until a small blond head made an appearance. The man—though now that Kip could see him better, he really wasn't much older than a kid, maybe nineteen or twenty—held the young boy closer.

A pair of eyes that closely matched the older kid's looked up at him, and then the boy darted back down, hiding under the blanket. Kip stopped the gasp that rose in his throat. That was quickly followed by anger. "The Salvation Army turned you away?" He wondered if they'd seen that he had a child.

"Yeah. It seems everyone in town tried to get in, and they filled up right away. I knocked, but they said they were full without really looking at me."

Kip stepped back and made a call to Dispatch. "I checked out Hansen's."

"Is it clear?"

"Negative," he answered and waited for a response.

"We're going," the kid said as he slowly got to his feet and then lifted the child, who looked about three, into his arms. He wrapped the child in a blue blanket that had been hidden under the darker one and finally pulled the other blanket over them both. "You don't need to take me in or anything. I wasn't causing any trouble." The kid stepped out into the rain and walked down the street toward the square.

"They've moved on," Kip said, watching from the shelter of the overhang. Then he turned and shone the light into the store. Something glinted on the stoop when the beam passed over it. Kip stepped over and bent down, lifting up a gold chain with a coin on it. He didn't know if it was real gold or not. Kip turned and hurried back to the sidewalk, but the kid was no longer in sight.

Kip got in his car and pulled into traffic. They couldn't have gone very far. At the square he turned and saw the kid huddled under an overhang with the child in his arms. He pulled into a parking spot so he wouldn't spook them, scrolled through his phone, and made a call. "Carter, it's Rogers from work."

"Hey. What's going on?"

"I need a favor, or at least…."

"What is it?"

"I got a call about one of the usual homeless hang-outs. Hansen's Men's Wear. When I got there, it was a guy about twenty and a kid, maybe three or four. They were under this blanket and…." He tried not to let his voice break, but it did anyway. "Now I think I know how you felt when you found Alex last year."

"You can take just about anything, but when it's kids…."

"It rips your heart out," Kip finished. "Yeah. I'm hoping you could get in touch with Donald. When I talked to him, the guy said the Salvation Army had turned them away. They need a dry place for the night and probably longer. They're in a bad way, and the situation on the street is only going to get worse as the weather turns."

"Let me call him. Can I use this number?"

"Sure. I have them in sight. Right now they're standing under one of the bank awnings on High Street. They're dry for now, but the guy looks about ready to collapse, like he's had about all he can take…. Shit." Kip saw the guy slide down the wall and end up in a heap on the sidewalk, the youngster still in his arms. The little kid was crying as Kip approached.

"I'm okay," the older kid said, and he tried to get up but ended up sitting on the sidewalk with the kid curled in his lap.

"Jos, open your eyes. Don't go like Mama." The younger kid began to cry, and Kip lifted him into his arms.

"It's all right. I'm not going to hurt you," Kip told him as he gently rubbed his back. The guy got to his feet but wobbled and seemed drunk, except there wasn't the faintest scent of alcohol on him. "I'm not going to hurt you either." Kip took his arm with his free hand and led him to the car. "Just get inside. It's warm and we can talk. I'm not arresting you, and I won't hurt you. I promise." It took him a few minutes to coax Jos into the car, and once he was seated, Kip placed the boy in his arms. Kip left the door open and popped the trunk, grabbed a large umbrella, and held it over all of them.

A call came in and Kip explained that he was already busy. He heard one of the other patrols take it. Then he opened the front passenger door and grabbed one of his bottles of water. He handed it to Jos, who opened it and gulped like he was dying of thirst.

"When was the last time you ate?"

The guy shrugged at him, eyes blank and a little vacant. Kip got a package of peanut butter cheese crackers that he kept in his bag and handed them to Jos. He looked at the food in disbelief and then opened the package, handing the first two to the kid before eating one himself. The kid nibbled while Jos finished three of the four pieces in three bites.

"Feeling better?" Kip asked, and Jos nodded before sharing the water with the kid, who had finished his crackers and was looking around for more.

"Yes. Thank you. Can we go now?" Jos asked as he finished the bottle of water.

"Just take a few minutes to rest. I've called a friend, and he's seeing if he can help you with a shelter for the night."

Panic rose in Jos's eyes. "I need to go," he said, lifting the kid into his arms. "I'm not letting anyone take Isaac away from me. He's my brother and I'll take care of him. Those vultures will only put him with strangers, and I just need a chance to get on my feet."

"No one is taking anyone," Kip said. "Donald is a friend of mine, and he's trying to find you a place to stay. He can help you if you let him."

Jos shook his head. "I've heard the stories. I know what those people do." He held Isaac tighter and shifted him farther from Kip, probably in case he tried to take him. Kip had no intention of taking anyone anywhere other than to a place that was safe and dry and where they could get food and any help they needed.

"No one is going to take Isaac away from you. I'm just trying to help," Kip said. His phone rang. He pulled it out of his pocket and answered it.

"Every shelter I called is beyond full," Donald explained. "I tried to call in favors, but it did no good. I can give them some supplies if you can bring them to the house. I can also give them a good meal."

"That's a start," Kip said. "I'll be there in a few minutes." He hung up and then called in to Dispatch to explain what had happened and where he'd be. His call was acknowledged, and he was given permission to do whatever he could.

"Nothing, huh," Jos said, and he began sliding along the seat to get out of the car. "No one has been willing to help."

"The shelters are full, but my friend said he'll help you with supplies. He can also give you a good meal."

Jos stood and shifted Isaac away from Kip. "And what does your friend want for his help? My mouth? Maybe my ass? No, thanks."

Jesus, how long had they been on the streets? And what had happened to him? Jos was a combination of bravado and tough guy mixed with the fear that shone in his eyes.

"No," Kip said. "Donald works with child services, and he can help you. He cares enough to have me bring you by his house and to cook for you and Isaac. So if you want a good meal, then come along with me. If you don't, then you're free to go."

Jos got out of the car and wrapped the mostly wet blanket around him and Isaac. Then, without another word, he began shuffling down the sidewalk. Kip knew there was little he could do and was about to get back into his cruiser when he remembered what he'd found. "Jos, is this yours?" he asked. He grabbed the chain and hurried down the sidewalk. Jos turned and his eyes widened. He set Isaac on his feet and patted his pockets. Then he extended his hand, and Kip placed the chain into it.

"Thanks," Jos said and lifted Isaac into his arms again before hurrying off down the sidewalk. Kip didn't know what else to do for them. He picked up the phone once he got back to his car and called Donald.

"They decided to go their own way," Kip said.

"Okay," Donald said with resignation.

"It doesn't surprise you?"

"No. Many of the people on the streets are suspicious of everyone. They've been hurt too much. Some of them have mental issues that, if treated, would allow them to function more fully, but they don't get it and fall further and further from the rest of society. You helped them and that's all you can do short of bringing them in, which would have been even more traumatic."

"What about Isaac, the kid?"

Donald sighed. "That's the tough point. You could turn them in, and then child services could put him in foster care. Truthfully, there's no easy answer there. You end up taking the child away from the family, and then the path for reconnection can be nearly impossible. You made a decision, and I'd say you might have made the best one for now. I don't know."

"Well, thanks for being there," Kip said and disconnected the call. Then he pulled out into traffic and back on patrol. But Jos and Isaac weren't far from his thoughts as he continued his shift.

After answering another call that turned out to be an older lady scared that someone was in her garage, Kip ended up chasing away a feral cat and helping close up a hole in her garage door to keep it from coming back. She thanked him profusely and even offered him coffee, which he declined.

The rain had stopped by the time he left, and Kip was looking forward to the end of his shift. He called in to tell them he was free and decided to make another pass through town. He drove down Hanover and turned west on High in the square. After going a block, he turned left onto Pitt and cruised slowly, watching the sides of the street for anything unusual.

The last house on the first block had been empty for a while, so when Kip saw activity outside, he slowed to a stop. A small figure stood at the side of the porch. Kip recognized him as Isaac and pulled the cruiser to a stop. He got out, forgetting his hat, and hurried up to the porch. Isaac stepped back until he was pressed to the wall of the house, holding his blanket, panic in his eyes, a thumb in his mouth.

"It's okay. Where's Jos?" Kip asked.

Isaac blinked at him a few times and then pointed to the side of the house.

Kip was about to walk around the side when he heard a scuffle of some sort. He called in for backup and then turned to Isaac. "Can you sit over there and make yourself really small?"

Isaac nodded and backed away in the corner of the porch, practically curling into a ball. The scuffing sound came again, followed by a muffled cry. Kip pulled his gun, slowly making his way around the corner.

Two figures were beside the house, and one had the other pressed to the wall.

"Stop right there!" Kip shouted and raised his gun.

"There's nothing to see here," a gruff voice growled back.

"Police. Step back and get on the ground," Kip said.

"It's nothing, officer. My boy and I were just having a conversation."

Kip wished he could pull his flashlight, but he didn't want to break his concentration. "Then let him speak for himself. Is that you, Jos?" He heard a mumble, but that was all. "Let him go. Now!"

"He and I were just having a little fun." The voice was softer now, but Kip wasn't buying it.

"I said back off. I can hit a fly at this distance, so I'll have no problem putting a bullet in your ear. Get on the ground, arms and legs out where I can see them. Now!" Sirens sounded in the distance, and Kip was relieved that backup was on the way. He saw the guy looking in various directions. He was starting to panic now. Kip knew the signs; he was looking for a way out. "You move, you die."

The man released Jos and slowly got down on the ground. Kip saw Jos reach down and realized he was pulling up his pants. Jesus Christ, he hoped like hell he'd gotten there in time. The other man's pants were in place, so he prayed he had. Other cars pulled up, and Kip saw that Jos looked about ready to spook.

"Isaac," Jos said softly.

"He's fine. He's up on the porch. He told me where to find you." Kip got his cuffs and clasped them on the man. "Stay there."

"But it's wet," he grumbled.

"Get up and it's resisting arrest. I'll start by tasing you. That should be a delight." Other officers came into view, and Kip holstered his gun. Thank God one was Red. He told them what was going on and asked them to lead the suspect to the car. Red was reading him his rights clearly and carefully just before they put him in the car.

"Good thing you got here fast," Kip said to Red.

"What about the other one? Did you know there's a kid on the porch too?"

"Yeah. I encountered them during that homeless call I had earlier at Hansen's." Kip looked over at Jos, who was doing his best to comfort Isaac, who held on to him and whimpered.

"Do you think the bruiser got to him?"

Kip wasn't going to shiver in front of his colleague. "I don't know. I hope to hell not. Jos's sole concentration seems to be on watching out for Isaac, and I think if he thought it would keep Isaac safe, he would do just about anything."

"Well, go find out. Because if we want to keep this piece of work off the streets, we have to have something we can charge him with other than trespassing. We'll take him in and get him settled in a nice dry cell. Maybe with him gone, you'll get something out of him." Red motioned with his head to Jos, who stood with Isaac in his arms, singing the same lullaby he had before.

Kip slowly walked over to where the two of them stood. "Jos, what happened?"

He didn't answer, standing taller and staring Kip down. Of course it didn't work, and Kip simply stared back and repeated the question, adding a fierceness to his tone until Jos began to shift from foot to foot.

"Are you going to follow us around all night?"

"If I have to. Now tell me what happened."

"I am not his boy," Jos said defiantly.

Kip waited for him to continue, but he didn't. "What's his name?"

"Tyler Adamson, but I don't know if the name's real or not. He laid claim to me about a week ago, and I've tried to keep Isaac and me away from him. I did good too, until he found me a while ago."

"Did he hurt you?" Kip asked.

"You mean did he manage to fuck me? No. You were in time to stop that."

Kip suppressed a sigh. "Did he hit you or grab you?"

"He pushed me against the house. That hurt. He threatened to hurt Isaac if I didn't do what he wanted. Said he'd cut his... you know off. The guy's a pervert—likes guys and girls, or so I hear, but wants it rough and likes them unwilling, if you know what I mean. Word on the street is that the more they fight, the more he likes it."

"Okay. I need you to come to the station with me so you can tell me what happened. That way I can keep him in jail."

"What about your friend? Is that offer of food still good? Isaac's really hungry, and...."

Kip would make sure they ate. That wasn't optional now, as far as he was concerned. "Here's the deal. I'll make sure you both eat all you want. You need to tell me what happened so I can get your statement."

"Then we can go?"

"Then you need to show up at the police station tomorrow morning so you can identify this Tyler Adamson and formally press charges. I have enough for assault, attempted rape, and I'll see if I can add some more once I have your statement." Kip stepped closer to Jos. "You have to trust me. I'm not going to hurt either of you, and if you let me, I'll try to help."

"Why?" Jos shot back. "Nobody does something for nothing. Never has, never will."

"Maybe I'm doing it because I don't want Isaac sleeping on the street. Isaac's relying on you to take care of him. Are you going to give up a chance for him to be warm and comfortable?"

"Okay, fine. I'll go with you."

Kip nodded and checked the time. His shift was just ending. "Then let's get you in the car. I need to take you to the station so I can punch out and then get my car. I'll call my friend so he can help you. Donald is a good man, and he said he can give you some things for Isaac—clean clothes, things like that."

"You're really going to help me?" Jos asked.

"Yes."

"And you don't want nothing?"

"No. I don't want anything from you other than your honesty. Now let's get in the car so we can get you two fed and then find you a place to sleep, okay?" Kip motioned to the cruiser, and Jos helped Isaac and then got into the back seat without another word.

Kip drove to the station and transferred Jos and Isaac to his car. Then he went inside, clocked out, and left for the night, calling Donald as he went. "Is that offer of dinner still on?"

"What happened?" Donald asked. "And yes. If they need it, you know I'm there. I'll see what I have. Bring them over. Carter is home, so he can help too."

"Thanks," Kip said as he got to his car. Isaac fussed as they rode, and Jos did his best to soothe him, but he couldn't be soothed. Kip figured he was hungry. When he parked in front of Carter and Donald's house, Donald met them and ushered the three of them inside.

"I have food heated up, so come to the table."

"This is Jos, and the little one is Isaac," Kip said. "He's Donald and this is Carter," Kip added as Carter came down the stairs. Isaac stayed plastered to Jos's legs, staring up at the newcomers. "Alex is in bed, I'm sure." Donald and Carter's energetic little boy was a little older than Isaac.

"Yes, and he'll be disappointed that he missed someone he could have played with," Carter said.

"Are you hungry?" Donald asked Isaac, who nodded. "Then come with me. I have macaroni and cheese. Do you like that?" Isaac nodded again and looked up at Jos. "I also have some soup, and I made some sandwiches, so come to the kitchen."

Jos took Isaac's hand and led him to the table. Donald helped Jos put Isaac in a booster chair and then set a plate in front of him. Isaac looked at Jos once again and then began to eat. Donald gave him a sippy cup of milk, but Isaac barely stopped shoveling food into his mouth to notice. Jos sat next to him, and Donald brought him a plate of food as well as a bowl of soup.

Kip sat down, and Donald brought him a sandwich before sitting down next to Carter.

"Will you tell me your full name?" Kip asked. He wasn't sure Jos would, but he hoped rescuing him and helping feed him and Isaac would go a long way.

"Josten Applewhite," he answered between bites.

"How did you end up on the streets?" Donald asked Jos.

"Got kicked out." He barely paused to talk before going back to eat.

Kip shared a glance with Donald and Carter, ate his sandwich, and accepted a cup of coffee, watching both Jos and Isaac eat.

It wasn't long before Isaac began to tire. He ate a large amount of food for a boy his size and drank two glasses of milk. Once he was done, he began falling asleep in his chair. Jos lifted Isaac out of the chair, setting him on his lap, and Isaac put his arms around Jos's waist and his head on Jos's chest and fell asleep. Soon Jos had eaten his fill too, and he sat back in the chair.

"Thank you," he whispered.

Kip was pretty sure Jos was very close to reaching the end of his rope.

"You're welcome," Donald said and then excused himself.

Kip shared a glance with Carter, who nodded, and Kip followed Donald out of the room.

"What should I do?" he asked Donald quietly in the hall. "I can't put them back out on the street, but all the shelters are full to bursting." He hoped Donald would offer to let them stay here. But they had Alex, and Kip wasn't sure they even had room.

"It's nearly midnight. I suggest you take them back to your house and put them to bed for the night. They need a chance to rest. I'll come over in the morning and see what I can do to help." Donald led Kip to a small room off the living room. "Here are some pajamas that should fit Isaac." Donald grabbed a grocery store reusable shopping bag and began putting some things inside. "I've got clean clothes and things for him, as well as some other supplies you'll need. If you don't use it, bring it back."

"Thanks. What about Jos?"

"I'll let you help him. He's closer to your size." Donald grinned and handed Kip the bag. "They're both dead on their feet, so take them home, put them to bed, and I bet you won't hear a peep out of either of them for hours."

"I hope you're right," Kip said and took the bag before returning to the kitchen. Isaac was still asleep, and Jos seemed about ready to fall asleep as well. "Come on. I'm going to take you home so you can both get some sleep." He helped Jos to his feet and carried the things.

"Thank you," Jos said to Donald and Carter as they left the house.

"You'll need a booster seat," Donald said as he rushed to the car and got it installed for Isaac in the back seat. "Can't have you breaking the law, Officer," Donald teased. He stood back as Jos got Isaac strapped in and then got in next to him.

"I appreciate your help," Kip said.

"I'll see you in the morning," Donald called, and Kip waved before closing his door and pulling away from the curb.

He was dog-tired and glad he only had to go to the other side of town. The five-minute drive took most of the energy he had left. Kip parked in front of his house, and Jos got out, gathering Isaac into his arms.

"Is this where you live?" Jos asked.

"Yes. It was my mother's dream house," Kip said, watching Jos stand on the sidewalk, looking up at the large house in front of him.

"I like the porch. I bet it's nice on summer nights. I remember—" Jos stopped cold and shifted Isaac onto his other shoulder, stepping out of the way. Kip locked his car and walked to the front door, then let them in. He turned on the hall lights, but not the ones to the other rooms. Kip intended to get them all up to bed, so he made a direct line to the stairs.

"I'll put both of you in the guest room. I'm assuming Isaac is going to be most comfortable sleeping with you." Kip opened the first door at the top of the stairs and turned on the light. "Get yourselves comfortable." He set the bag on the bed. "There are pajamas for Isaac and some fresh clothes for him to have in the morning."

"Can I take a shower?" Jos asked longingly.

"Sure. I'll get you something to sleep in. The bathroom's right there." Kip opened a door across the hall and got out some towels for Jos. Then he went to his room and found a comfortable T-shirt and some light sweats. They'd be too big, but it was something clean for Jos to wear. "I can throw your clothes in the washer if you want. Just give them to me when you're done, and I'll put them in before I go to bed."

Kip left Jos alone and heard him gently singing to Isaac. Kip went to his room and changed into comfortable clothes. When he returned, Isaac was already in bed, nearly asleep. Jos looked like the walking dead as he shuffled into the bathroom and closed the door. Kip knocked and handed Jos the clean clothes when he cracked the door. Then he left him alone to clean up.

Kip purposely had Jos use that bathroom. There was nothing in there but the basic things for guests. He didn't know him that well and hadn't wanted him to use the other bath, where he kept his various medications. He hoped Jos wasn't using drugs, but he didn't want to provide any temptation.

When Jos was done showering quite a while later, he looked a little revived and smelled a hell of a lot better. Kip took his clothes and carried them all the way to the basement, started the machine, and put in the clothes. He also made a note to remember to see to it that Jos had something to wear for the morning. The clothes he was washing didn't seem as though they'd hold up much longer. When he climbed the stairs, Kip found the guest room door closed and the bathroom door open, towels hung to dry, and the sink and tub clean. Jos was neat—Kip had to give him that.

Kip went to his room and got ready for bed. He climbed between his crisp, clean sheets and realized just how much he took for granted. He didn't want to think about the last time Jos and Isaac slept in a clean bed. Yet he hated it when his sheets were scratchy. Kip rolled onto his side and tried to go to sleep, but he ended up listening to the sounds of the house. Of course he knew he was listening for Jos and Isaac, but they were quiet.

He fell asleep but woke with a start in the middle of the night. Something wasn't right, but he couldn't put his finger on what it was. He stilled and listened, and a soft rustling reached his ears.

Kip got up and left his room. The door to the guest room was closed, and the sound came from there. Kip stepped to the door and stood still. Whimpering—he was hearing soft whimpers. He sighed. It was sobbing, muffled by bedding. Tears someone didn't want heard and was trying his best to keep quiet.

Kip reached for the doorknob but stopped himself. He wasn't going to intrude. Even if he wanted to try to help, there were limits to what he could do other than provide them a place for the night and try to see to it that both of them were safe. He went back to his room and climbed into bed, wondering how much he dared try to do to help.

CHAPTER 2

JOSTEN WOKE with a start. It was still dark, but he was too warm and definitely too comfortable. Something was wrong. When he opened his eyes and saw the street-light-illuminated room with a fireplace and nice curtains, he remembered. Isaac was still asleep, burrowed down into the covers, pressed right against him, but he began to stir. Josten wanted to break into tears, but he'd already done that once and that was enough. He and Isaac had been fed and given a place to sleep that wasn't on the streets or in one of those dormitory rooms with dozens of other people snoring, crying out, or just plain yelling their fear and terror in the middle of the night.

"Josten," Isaac whined from next to him. "I have to go."

"Okay," Jos said and lifted Isaac out of the bed. He quietly opened the door and walked as softly as he could across the upstairs hall to the bathroom, where a nightlight burned. He set him on the potty so he could go.

"I like it here. It's warm and there are no scary people."

"I know."

"Can we stay here? Mr. Policeman seems nice."

"I doubt it," Jos said. This was only for one night, and after Kip gave them some food in the morning, he and Isaac would be on their way. Maybe he could find a way to make some money so the two of them could get to a place where they might have a chance. What he needed was a job and a place to live. He'd had both of those not long ago, but then everything had gone to hell in two days. Two fucking days was all it had taken to pull his life away from him and put both him and Isaac on the streets. He hadn't known it could happen that fast, but it had, and Jos didn't know what to do to fix it. "Are you done?"

Isaac nodded, and Jos helped him off the toilet and helped him wipe. Then Jos pulled up his pajamas and lifted him into his arms. When he opened the door, he found Kip coming up the stairs with a glass of water. Jos smiled and took Isaac back to the bedroom and closed the door. He heard Kip go back to his room, and then the house was still once more.

"This is really nice," Isaac said as he burrowed under the covers.

"I know it is, but we can't get used to it, okay? I don't know where we're going to have to sleep tomorrow, but I'll do my best for you. I can promise you that." Jos hugged Isaac to him. "Now go to sleep, okay?"

"Okay," Isaac said and laid his head on the pillows. They were too soft for the likes of them. It had been longer than Jos wanted to admit since he'd slept someplace as nice as this. His fears for tomorrow kept him awake for a while, but fatigue eventually won out.

JOS WOKE to a rumbling stomach and the scent of food hovering in the air. The next thing he noticed was that he was alone. He threw back the covers and jumped out of the bed, then raced down the stairs in a blind panic. They had come for Isaac after all. Kip had promised nothing would happen to them, and.... He should never have trusted a police officer, no matter how nice he'd seemed on the surface.

Laughter rang from the bottom of the stairs, and Jos slowed a little, making his way toward the sound, which rang out again. "You like that, huh?" he heard Kip say, and damned if the sound of Isaac's laughter didn't spear hard at Jos's heart. He hadn't heard that sound in a long time. "Have some more if you want."

Jos walked into the kitchen and stopped cold. Isaac sat on a stool by the table shoveling bacon into his mouth as he waved another piece in the air.

"I likes bacon," Isaac said when he saw Jos and then extended his hand, offering the piece to him.

"You eat it," Jos said, his stomach protesting because the house smelled good and there was food on the table and on the stove. He'd learned a while ago to avoid restaurants like the plague when he didn't have anything to eat. The scent only made him hungrier, and while food was just a few feet away, none of it was for him... or Isaac.

"Sit down," Kip said, motioning to the table. "I have eggs if you want some."

Jos just nodded, afraid to say anything or he'd.... Fuck, he had no idea how he'd react, and that scared the shit out of him, so he sat down, and Kip put a plate of eggs, toast, and bacon in front of him. He even added a huge glass of juice. "Go ahead."

Jos didn't have to be told twice. He tucked in and ate, his belly not knowing quite what to make of two big meals in a row. "Thanks… for me and for him."

Kip sat down with a cup of coffee. "I ate with him," Kip said, making faces at Isaac that sent him into more peals of laughter. "How long were you and Isaac without food?"

"I take care of him. It's what I'm supposed to do, and I do the best I can." Jos's defenses were instantly high and at the ready.

"Whoa, slow down. I was just asking. Not judging," Kip said, immediately disarming him with his kind tone. "I'm only concerned."

"A day, I guess. I found a dollar so I got Isaac something at that place on Pomfret. They have these cheesy crackers that Isaac likes, and I got him two boxes that he ate," Jos answered quickly. "It came to a dollar and one cent, and the guy behind the counter gave me the penny. You can ask him. I never steal anything."

"I never thought you did, otherwise I wouldn't have let you stay in my home," Kip said.

Jos nodded. "Sorry."

"When was the last time *you* ate?" Kip asked.

Jos shrugged. "Yesterday morning. I had breakfast at the mission shelter, and then they cleared us out for the day. You have to leave, and then you can come back at night for dinner, if you get there fast enough. Last night I wasn't fast enough. Everyone opened early, and Isaac and I were out of luck… until we met you, I guess."

Kip nodded and sipped from his mug, which Jos was grateful for because it gave him time to eat. His stomach kept growling, and when he emptied his plate, Kip filled it again.

"Slow down. There's plenty, and no one is going to take it from you." Kip got up and opened the refrigerator door, then pulled out a huge bowl of strawberries that had Isaac's eyes boggling. Jos knew his half brother loved strawberries, and Isaac reached into the bowl as soon as it came close to him.

"You like those?" Kip asked as Isaac was already shoving one into his mouth, reaching for another. "Take your time, buddy."

Jos finished his second plate, but he didn't reach for a berry. Kip pushed the bowl his way, and Jos watched him, reaching for a berry, expecting the slap or rebuke that always came when he reached for something that they didn't think was for him. Granted, they never said, they only hit, so he never knew when it was coming. Jos bit into the berry and grinned. It was good, cold, and slid easily down his throat. He picked up the bowl and handed it back.

"Don't you want any more?" Kip asked, and Jos blinked a few times. "Eat them—I can get more."

Isaac threw his hands in the air like he'd won a prize and dug in. Soon Jos was doing the same and felt himself smile. Fuck, he must be totally pathetic if a bowl of strawberries could make him this ridiculously happy.

The doorbell rang, and instantly Jos was on his guard. He moved closer to Isaac, who was completely engrossed in what he was eating, and watched the doorway, wondering what was going to happen next.

"Hey, Donald, come on in. We're eating." Kip's voice boomed through the house, and Jos turned his chair slightly so he could see better. The guy from last night came into the kitchen carrying a bag in his arms. He walked closer and handed it to Jos.

"I brought you some things you might need. Toothpaste and stuff like that. There's also some hand sanitizer and an extra change of clothes for Isaac." Donald turned and spoke to someone out of sight. "You can come in too. Don't be shy."

A boy a little older than Isaac came into the room. He stopped next to Donald, staring up at him and then at Isaac, who whined and looked at the floor. Alex walked over to Isaac and started talking. After a few hellos and tentative smiles, Alex asked if Isaac wanted to play Legos, and they were off together.

"Play nice," Donald said gently and sat down at the table.

"Are they going to be okay?" Jos asked.

"Alex just went to get his blocks," Donald said, and sure enough Alex came back into the room with Isaac right behind. He scoped out a section of the floor of the large kitchen, emptied the bag with a crash of Legos, and the boys were off.

Donald leaned over the table and turned his attention to Jos. "I'm with child services here in the county, and the reason I'm here is to try to help you. But in order to do that, I need some information."

Jos wasn't sure he wanted to tell anyone anything about himself or Isaac. "Do I have to?"

"No. You're welcome to go. But if you want to have a chance to take care of Isaac and give him a chance at a life other than on the streets, you need to trust someone and let us help you. I know you've been through a lot—"

"You don't know shit about what I've been through," Jos countered. "You don't know me at all."

"Don't I? You're about twenty. You used to have a job, but it was probably eliminated in some of the recent cuts that were announced. You'd just been hired recently so you were the first to go. You had an apartment, but as soon as the landlord heard you'd lost your job, he kicked you out."

"How?"

"Gordon Powers, right?"

"Yeah."

"The man's a slumlord. He packs as many people as he can into his buildings by renting them tiny apartments, and let me guess, when you first rented, he said he liked you and that you had an honest face, so there was no need for a lease or anything like that. He was your friend, after all."

"Jesus," Jos breathed.

"It's the way he operates. If you ask for a lease, then he says he's just remembered that he rented the apartment the day before and he's sorry you couldn't do business. He's a piece of work, and Kip and his co-workers have been trying to get something on him for years."

"Okay. So you guessed some things."

"Yes, I did. But what I really need to know about is you and Isaac. I need your full names and Social Security numbers, if you have them. I also need to know what happened to Isaac's parents."

"Well, his dad hasn't ever been in the picture. My mom…." Jos shrugged. "She was a loser magnet. If there was a loser within ten miles, she drew him in. I guess my dad was loser number three. Isaac's was loser number six or seven. She died a few months ago after loser number nine or so. I lost track. He shot her and then realized what he'd done and killed himself. I have a wonderful family."

"So you took custody of Isaac?" Donald asked.

"Yeah. There was no one else. Mom had a sister she hadn't talked to in years, and I hardly knew her. There was a will that I begged her to draw up after Isaac was born, and she left custody of Isaac to me. We had to leave the house we were living in because I couldn't afford it. I think she got money from the losers to help pay for it." Jos shrugged. "I knew what the will said, so I got Isaac out."

"Where is the will?"

"It was in the apartment, and when I lost all my stuff…."

"Yeah," Donald said, turning to Kip. "That's another of his tricks. He kicks people out with no notice and then uses their stuff to furnish his apartments so he can get more tenants. This guy's a real piece of work."

"The apartment wasn't much, but it was all I could afford, and I made room for Isaac. I even got him in day care while I was working. I wasn't sure how I was going to pay for it, but I managed."

Donald nodded. "Okay. First thing, I need Isaac's Social Security number and that of his mother. We also need to try to find that will. Kip, maybe you can help with that. Gordon most likely just left the stuff there."

"So if someone hasn't rented it yet, the paperwork might be there?" Kip asked. "Is there another copy of the will? Like with the attorney who drew it up?"

Jos shook his head and shrugged. "Why do we need all this stuff?"

"Because your mom worked, right?"

"Yeah."

"Then if I have the paperwork, I can help you apply for Social Security survivor benefits for Isaac. I can also work with social services to try to get you some assistance and help get both of you off the streets. They can then help you find a job. It isn't hopeless."

"Then why are there so many people out there on the streets?" Jos asked. "They're everywhere."

"The system isn't perfect, and I only work for child services, but because of Isaac I can try to help you too. But you have to trust me and Kip."

Jos wasn't sure he was ready to let go. "Can I think about it?" he asked. He needed time to figure things out.

"At least give me your old address so I can try to find your things," Kip said.

Jos thought about it for a few minutes, then told Kip where the building was. "It's on the third floor, guaranteed to freeze in winter and roast in summer. But it was mine and…."

Isaac must have heard his plaintive tone and hurried across the room, sliding between his knees. "Don't be sad," he said. "I made this for you. It's a horsey." The blob of red and blue Legos looked nothing like a horse, but Jos smiled and hugged Isaac tight.

"Thank you. Why don't you make a corral out of Legos for the horsey to live in?" Jos watched Isaac run back and drop to the floor with Alex. He stared, eyes filling as he wished for so much more. Isaac deserved to have a life like this, where he could play and have friends. He didn't deserve to go hungry and wonder where his next meal was coming from, and he certainly deserved a house instead of living outside and trying to find shelter from the rain in doorways. "I promised I would take care of him," Jos said, half under his breath. "He still misses Mom something terrible, and I've tried to be good to him."

"No one doubts that," Donald told him.

"That lady last week did. She came to the shelter we were staying at and began preaching and wailing against sins of the flesh. Then after she was done telling us how nobody should be having sex because we didn't have homes, she came up to me and said that Isaac would be better off in foster care. At least he'd have a home and food. I told her we'd both be better off without self-righteous bitches like her, but I was just mad, and...." Jos blinked a few times. "Maybe she was right."

"I don't know about that," Donald said. "She probably would have gotten a lot further if she'd offered some help rather than preaching condemnation. But I've heard that plenty of times as well."

"Why?"

"Some people think the homeless are that way because of some internal failing, and that they have no one to blame but themselves. People like that woman who preached at you most likely think being homeless is God's retribution for a sinful life. In my job I've heard all kinds of crap like that." Donald glanced over at Kip. "We can help you, but you have to want to be helped. It takes grit and determination to rebuild your life, and it doesn't come easily. I can help you apply for survivor benefits, but it's the government, so we have to have all the paperwork, and that will is key."

"I'll make a few phone calls," Kip said. "I know there's more than one officer in the department who'd like to get something on our local slumlord."

"Wouldn't he just throw away everything he didn't want?" Jos asked.

"Most likely. But if we don't try, we won't know for sure. Tell me where your mother lived. If the will was drawn up by a lawyer, he might have had it registered with the county there, and that could get us a copy as well."

"But where are we supposed to live while all this is going on?" He'd thought living on the street would be fine, but it hadn't turned out that way. He and Isaac were vulnerable out there, as the attack the night before attested. Jos had done his best to try to stay away from the people he knew were dangerous or just plain crazy, but it wasn't always possible.

"Let me work on that," Donald said and turned to Kip. "You have room here. Can they stay a few days until I can get things rolling?"

Kip didn't answer right away, and Jos got up from the chair. "It's all right. You did what you could, and I don't blame you for not wanting strangers in your house." He walked over to Isaac and gently took his hand. "We need to go upstairs and get our things. It's time for us to go."

Isaac let go of the Legos he was holding and turned to him, lower lip trembling. Jos knew exactly how Isaac felt, but they didn't have any other choice. People said they wanted to help, but that either came with a price or they simply got his hopes up only to dash them once again. He lifted Isaac into his arms and carried him up the stairs. He now had a few bags of things, but he wasn't sure what he was going to do with them. Maybe he could find a shopping cart or something.

"I wanna stay and play Legos," Isaac told him.

"I know you do. But we have to go. It was nice of Kip to give us breakfast and a place to sleep last night. Maybe if we're lucky, we can get into a shelter for a few days." It seemed pathetic that his hopes and dreams had been reduced to trying to find a shelter that would take in the two of them for more than one night. Jos sat on the edge of the bed and held Isaac tight in his arms, ready to burst into tears. This was not how his life was supposed to be, and certainly not what he wanted for Isaac.

"You don't have to go," Kip said from the doorway.

"I saw what you really thought, and I don't need your pity. Isaac and I will be fine. It's still warm and I'm going to try to find a job." How he was going to do that with Isaac along with him he had yet to work out, but he'd figure something out.

"It's not pity, and you need to quit jumping to conclusions. I didn't even answer and you were out of there like a shot. Donald is getting ready to leave, but he needs the information he requested so he can help. Maybe you could let Isaac go down and say good-bye to Alex."

Jos wanted to believe that Kip wanted to help him. Lord knew he wasn't doing all that well on his own. "Go on," he said to Isaac, putting him down. Isaac hurried to the doorway and then ran back to Jos.

"Don't be sad," Isaac said and then hurried away, plodding down the stairs. Jos put on his bravest face, even though he felt like a scared rabbit, and followed Kip down and back into the kitchen. Isaac was helping Alex put the Legos back into the bag, the two of them talking. "I wanna keep my horsey," Isaac said, protecting his group of blocks from going into the bag.

"Those are Alex's blocks," Jos said and gently took them away and put them into the bag. Isaac whimpered and reached for the bag, scattering everything on the floor. The horsey went to pieces, and Isaac sat on the floor, wailing that he'd killed his horsey. Jos picked him up and tried to comfort him, but Isaac was inconsolable, reaching down toward the blocks. Alex put the spilled ones back in the bag while Donald helped him.

"Daddy, why is Isaac sad?" Alex asked as he began scooping up pieces of the horsey. He put it back together and then handed it to Isaac, who took it and clutched it to him.

"Thank you," Jos said to Alex.

"Don't be sad," Alex said and stepped back to Donald, looking up as though he was trying to figure out what had happened. Jos felt the same way, but he had noticed that Isaac tended to get attached to inconsequential things, or things that didn't *seem* important, and held on tight.

"It's all right," Donald said, gently rubbing Isaac's head. "You keep the horsey."

The pity Jos saw in Donald's eyes nearly sent his blood boiling.

Isaac continued clutching the Lego horsey, his cries turning to whimpers, and then he rested his head on Jos's shoulder. "I want Mama," he whispered, and Jos sighed and continued soothing him, having no idea what to say. "Mama," Isaac whispered in his ear over and over, like a wish whispered on a prayer.

"It's okay," Jos said and turned to Kip, who seemed as confused as he was.

"We're going to go," Donald said.

"I need to give you that information." Jos carried Isaac up to the bedroom and found his jacket. He propped Isaac on his hip as he fished inside the lining for the envelope that held his most vital pieces of documentation. It was damp, but the cards inside were dry, and he carried them back down the stairs. "I wasn't able to save much at all. They gave me an hour to get out, and I had to take care of Isaac." He handed over the envelope. "Can you really help us?"

Donald looked at what was inside and smiled. "You have Isaac's birth certificate. That's awesome. It will prove his relationship to your mother. You might have to get a copy of yours to prove common parentage, but we'll see. As long as no one contests that Isaac is with you, then…."

Jos said a silent prayer and let Donald take the documents. "Okay. As long as I get them back." It seemed stupid, but it was all he had of his life—well, that and Isaac. Everything else was gone. Even his mother's necklace, the one Kip had returned, was gone, taken by his attacker.

"You will," Donald said. "Let me do some of my magic so I can see what I can come up with." Donald looked at Kip, who followed him and Alex out. Jos knew they were talking about him, but there was nothing he could do about it.

When Kip came back, he sat at the table and made phone calls. Jos stood with Isaac in his arms, watching and listening. When Kip was done, he turned to Jos. "Did Adamson, umm, Tyler, take anything from you?"

"Yeah," Jos said. "He said I belonged to him and then rummaged around in my pants pockets. He took everything I had in them. I don't know what he did with any of it, though. Was it on him?"

"I need you to come to the station. He had a number of items on him, including one I know was yours because I gave it back to you." Kip got up from his chair. "Let's get you down to the station so you can give your statement and we can press charges. If he has your things, then it will be easier to press assault charges, and we can add theft as well."

The last thing Jos wanted to do was go near a police station, but he had to get his stuff back. He also needed to know that Tyler was going to be off the streets. That guy gave him the creeps completely. "He didn't really hurt me."

"No, but he could have, and if I hadn't gotten there, he would have taken something from you that I don't think you were willing to give."

The thought of being raped was bad enough, but having it happen where Isaac could have seen him…. Jos shivered and swore for the hundredth time in less than a day that he had to be strong for Isaac. He needed him; Jos was all Isaac had. "We should go," Jos said.

"Then you need to get dressed. Go on and use the bathroom upstairs. I'll watch Isaac for you. Then you can get him dressed, and we'll go." Kip stood, looking at him eye to eye. Jos stood stock-still, wondering why he was doing this, and then his mind immediately snapped to the soft kindness in Kip's eyes. Kip could be strong and harsh; he'd seen that in the alley and the way he'd dealt with Tyler. There had been nothing but power and force in his voice and body. But now there was none of that. Yes, Kip was still strong and his arms filled his shirtsleeves, but he was caring and his features were much gentler now. His lips curled up slightly and his broad shoulders were relaxed, the power Jos knew was there resting until it was needed.

"Jos," Isaac said, pulling him out of his thoughts. Jos hoped he hadn't been too obviously checking Kip out.

"Will you go to Kip? He's going to play with you and the horsey. I'm going upstairs to clean up, and then we'll get you dressed, okay?" Isaac nodded, and Jos handed him over to Kip, who began talking to him, asking him what the horsey's name was. Jos wasn't sure how long Isaac would be quiet, so he hurried upstairs and got the kit Donald had given him. He went into the bathroom and, damn, he hadn't remembered how good it felt to brush his teeth, shave properly, and just feel clean and fresh once again. When he was done, he went back into the bedroom and pulled on some of the clothes Donald had brought for him. The jeans and T-shirt were a little big, but that was better than too small. He'd even included a belt for him so he could keep his pants from falling down.

He went back downstairs and found the dishes cleared from the table and Kip playing with Isaac. There was a big smile on Isaac's face as he chattered away about what his horsey was doing.

"Do you have to go?" Jos asked Isaac, and Isaac slid off Kip's lap, telling him all about the adventure they'd had. He took Jos's hand, still holding the horsey in the other, and Jos led him up the stairs to the bathroom.

While Isaac went, Jos got his clothes from the bedroom and then ran some water in the bathtub. Isaac liked taking a bath, and Jos put him in and let him play for a couple of minutes.

"I want the horsey," Isaac said, extending his arm and making a "gimme" hand.

"Okay." Jos handed him the horsey and a washcloth and let Isaac clean himself. "We don't have a lot of time. Mr. Kip needs to get going." Jos just hadn't been able to pass up the chance for Isaac to get clean. When Isaac had washed, he stood, and Jos wrapped him and his horsey in a clean towel, dried him, and then helped him dress in new, clean clothes.

"How long can we stay here?" Isaac asked. "I like it." He smiled. "I'll be good, I promise. Can we stay if I'm good?" Isaac reached for the Lego horse as Jos finally got the squirming youngster into his clothes. He could be a handful at times, and Jos gave him a hug.

"I don't know. Let's go see Mr. Kip so we can get things done with the police." Jos cleaned up the bathroom as best he could, hanging up towels and then rinsing out the tub. Then he opened the door, and Isaac raced to the stairs and started descending.

"Mr. Kip, I have the horsey," he called. Jos followed him, watching. Three steps from the bottom, Isaac slipped. Jos grabbed him to prevent a fall, but the horsey slipped from his hand, then shattered into pieces at the bottom of the stairs. Isaac stared at the individual pieces, then turned to look up at him, lower lip trembling.

Kip hurried in. "It's okay. They're not broken. Now you can make a new horsey with them."

Jos lifted Isaac and waited for the meltdown he was afraid was coming, but Isaac nodded, eyes still watery, and Kip picked up the blocks. He put them in a small bag and handed it to Isaac.

"We have horsey fun-ral like Mama fun-ral," Isaac said.

"How about we get you a different kind of horsey," Kip said right away.

Jos turned away, trying not to let Kip see the pain that must have flashed on his face. His mother had never been much of a parent. Even when he was young, Jos spent a lot of time at his friend Amy's house. She didn't have much more than he did, but Amy's mom was a lion. She made sure Amy got to school and did her homework, something his mom never, ever asked about. Amy's mom told her, and by extension him, that the only way any of them were getting out of the hellhole they lived in was to get smart and learn all they could.

"Yay!" Isaac broke into song and scrambled to get down. Then Isaac did a little dance, wiggling his butt and bouncing up and down. "I'm getting a real horsey, I'm getting a real horsey." He twirled and stomped until he got dizzy and fell down. After a few seconds, he got up and did it again.

"Isaac, where are we going to keep a real horse?" Jos asked. He hated to be a killjoy, but he had to set Isaac straight. Their lives were bleak enough, and Isaac needed to know things like real horses weren't in their future.

"Let him be happy. I know what he means, and we'll get him a 'real' horse, just as soon as we finish at the police station."

Jos looked at him skeptically but nodded. He'd let Isaac be happy for a little while. He'd had too little of that lately. "I'm ready to go when you are."

"Let me get my wallet and shield, and then we can go." Kip scooped Isaac into his arms, making helicopter sounds as he zoomed him into the kitchen. A few seconds later, they zoomed out again, to peals of laughter and giggles from both of them. Jos even allowed himself a smile, although he could already see the heartbreak and hear the crying when all this came to an end and they had to leave.

"Jos is my big brother," Isaac was telling Kip as Jos checked that he had what little he needed. "He's not my whole brother, though, only half."

"Which half, the top half or the bottom half?" Kip said to giggles from Isaac. "Or is it this side or that side?" More giggles from Isaac. "Maybe…," he said dramatically, "it's the back half."

"I'm not Jos's butt brother. That part's stinky," Isaac said, holding his nose, and Jos had to laugh at that. There was no way not to.

"You know," Kip said, turning to him, "you're beautiful when you smile."

Jos didn't know quite what to make of that. "Um, thanks." He smiled slightly.

Isaac tapped Kip on the side of the head to get his attention. "Jos had a boyfriend once. It made Mama mad."

"Isaac," Jos said sternly.

"Why was she mad?" Kip asked Isaac, but he shrugged and made a thinking motion. "She said boys should be with girls." Isaac made a face. "They're yucky, though."

"Come on, let's go," Kip said. He glanced at Jos with a quick wink, and then he carried Isaac out the door. He locked it behind them, and then they went to Kip's car. Jos got Isaac strapped into his seat and then got into the car, and they rode to the police station, Jos's nervousness increasing by the second.

CHAPTER 3

KIP HAD no idea why he'd made the comment about Jos being beautiful when he smiled. He should've known better than to say something like that without thinking. In those few seconds, he'd outed himself to Jos. Granted, he hadn't seemed taken aback and hadn't recoiled, so maybe he hadn't scared Jos off, but he hadn't helped himself either. Jos was handsome enough, with deep eyes and a sculptured nose, and plump lips that would be perfect for kissing and other things he didn't dare think about. Jos was a guy he was trying to help and a witness to a crime. It was a terrible idea for him to have these kinds of thoughts about someone like him. He'd help Jos get the support he needed because it was the right thing to do, and then he'd move on with his life.

Thank God the drive to the station wasn't very long. Even with the air-conditioning on, Kip more than once tugged at his collar, warmth spreading through him. His heart pounded and he was hyperaware of the way Jos's leg bounced nervously as they rode. "It's okay. No one is going to hurt you or try to take anything from you."

"Sure," Jos said. "When Powers kicked me out of the apartment, I knew it was illegal and thought about trying to fight it. But then a policeman showed up and did nothing to stop Powers. They seemed like they were buddy-buddy, and all the policeman said was that it was his property, and without a lease or any paperwork, there was nothing he could do. Then the bastard smiled at me with mock sympathy, got back in his car, and drove off as Isaac and I stood on the sidewalk with nowhere to go. So I'm not feeling really good about going into the police station. What if he's there and makes trouble for me?"

Kip narrowed his gaze. "If he is, you point him out to me." He gripped the steering wheel tightly. He and Aaron Cloud, one of the detectives, had been after Powers for a long time, and if one of the men on the department was helping him, no wonder he always stayed one step ahead. This bastard was feeding him information. Kip made a note to talk to Aaron as soon as he could get the other officer alone. "But wait until we leave. Pretend you don't recognize him if you do see him."

"Okay," Jos agreed, but he still didn't settle down.

"All we need to do is get your statement so we can make our charges stick on Tyler. Then I have some items I need you to look over, and finally I'm going to check if Aaron is on duty so you can talk to him too." Kip pulled into the lot and parked. "Don't worry—he's a good guy, and he'll help you."

"What if he's the one?" Jos asked, and Kip had to stop to think a few seconds. He didn't think Aaron Cloud, one of the senior men on the force, would be involved with Gordon Powers, but Jos was right; he had to be cautious.

"I'll be careful and make sure you see him before he sees you." How he was going to do that, though, he wasn't sure. "Come on inside with me, and we'll go right to one of the interview rooms. They're pretty private." Kip opened his car door and got out, waiting for Jos to follow him with Isaac.

He led them into the station, past the officer on duty, and into one of the interview rooms, where Jos settled into a chair with Isaac on his lap. "I'll be right back." Kip left and went to his work area. He grabbed his laptop and brought it back to the interview room with him. It would be easier to type up the statement as he went than it would be to transcribe it later.

"What's going on, Rogers?" Carter asked, poking his head in the interview room. "Hi, guys."

Isaac smiled and Jos nodded.

"I need to take their statements. Could you get the effects we took off the guy we brought in last night? I think some of it is stolen from Josten here."

"Sure thing," Carter said and left the room.

Kip powered up his computer, pulled up the form, and began gathering the information he needed. Jos was a great witness, remembering details and relaying what happened with as little emotion as possible. That concerned him, though, because he figured Jos was most likely repressing what happened so he could deal with it, but the clear facts were helpful.

Carter returned with an envelope and left the room, then returned again with a bottle of water, which he handed to Jos.

"It's all right. Take your time," Kip said.

Jos opened the bottle, then gulped water quickly. "I don't want to think about what could have happened."

"I know." Kip wanted to take Jos's hand to try to comfort him. He knew relating the events was hard, but this was only the first time, and most likely Jos would have to do it again and again if he had to go to court. It wasn't a pleasant notion. "Just take your time. There's no hurry."

"Is there a place Isaac can sit where he isn't going to hear?"

Kip wasn't sure what to do.

Carter came to the rescue. "I can ask Donald to come down for Isaac. When I talked to him a while ago, he said Alex wanted to know if Isaac was okay."

"I appreciate it," Kip said, and Carter left once again. Kip settled and gave Jos some time, letting him talk about what happened in his own way as best he could. "I heard Tyler say you were his. What did he mean?"

"On the street, bigger people prey on the weaker ones. Tyler wanted me to stay with him and…." Jos paused and looked down at Isaac. "You can figure out what he wanted. He promised to protect Isaac and me, but I didn't believe him. He's a lying snake, and everyone is afraid of him. Some said he killed people, but I don't know if that's true or not." Jos held Isaac tighter on his lap.

"Tyler is bad and he smells," Isaac said, holding his nose. "He needs a bath. Maybe two."

"Yeah, he was smelly," Kip agreed. He let Jos drink his water and calm down. Donald came in after about ten minutes, and Isaac slipped off Jos's lap and went with him and Alex.

"We'll be down in the breakroom. The boys can play Legos some more. Take whatever time you need."

Jos seemed about ready to freak when Isaac left, but then he settled, and Kip walked Jos through what had happened.

"Did he actually rape you?" he asked.

"No. He got my pants down and was about to open his when you showed up and stopped him." Most of the color left Jos's face.

Once he'd finished taking Jos's statement, Kip opened the envelope and pulled out the items inside one by one. They were in evidence bags.

"That's mine, and so is that watch," Jos said. He pointed to his mother's necklace. "You know that's mine too. He said that his protection came at a higher price than just my ass." Jos paused and shivered even though the room was warm. "He's an asshole, and I hope you get him for everything you can."

"We will. Now we can add theft, and we have the items. I wonder where he got the rest."

"I don't know. I tried to stay away from him as much as I could, and usually I could smell him before I saw him."

"All right." Kip stood. "Let me go check the roster and see if Aaron is in. I don't believe he's in league with Powers, but it doesn't hurt to be sure. I'll be a minute." Kip paused. "Do you know what day you were evicted?"

"Three weeks ago yesterday," Jos answered.

"Let me check and see if he was on duty." That was a much safer approach. Kip left and checked the schedules. Aaron was on duty that day. So he found Carter and asked if he could check the call logs for the day of the eviction.

"What are you looking for?" Carter asked as he logged in, bringing up the log.

"A call about an eviction. It would be the area on A Street where Powers has that run of small apartment buildings."

"I don't see it. Who made the call?" Carter printed out the basic call log for him. Kip took it and returned to Jos to ask.

"I didn't call," Jos said. "I was going to, but then he just showed up. I thought one of the neighbors had called...."

"Nope," Kip answered. He began to think. The guy could be someone impersonating a police officer or someone Powers called on to put down any resistance and to make what he was doing easier to complete. "This is a picture of Aaron." Kip showed it to Jos, who shook his head. "Good. I'm going to get him." Kip printed off the statement, got it from the printer, and handed it to Jos. "Go ahead and read it while I'm gone, and then you can sign it if I have everything right." He grabbed his laptop and took it back to his desk before going in search of Aaron.

"Isn't today your day off?" Aaron asked when Kip found him at his desk.

"Yeah. It's a long story, but I have someone who might be able to help with Powers. He was evicted a few weeks ago, and he said there was a police officer there. He isn't sure who it was, but he said the guy told him there was nothing he could do. I checked the records, and Jos confirmed that he never called the police. The police officer was just there, probably at Power's request."

"Okay...."

"So what if Powers has a man inside the department?" Kip asked. "I think you should talk to Jos. But be gentle. This guy has been through a lot, and he's nervous enough being here."

"Is this the man who has a kid that's staying with you?"

God, word sure traveled fast. "Yeah. He needed some help."

"Be careful," Aaron said. "I know you want to help. It's why most of us went into this kind of work. But we can't be all things to everyone, and we have to have a life outside the job." Aaron stood up and came around his desk. "To a degree we're all about the job. It takes over a lot of our lives. Nine-to-five isn't for us, but we also need some part of our lives that's quiet and ours."

"I don't understand."

Aaron clapped him on the back. "Just don't let the job take over everything in your life. Being a police officer cost me a marriage because I didn't know how to let go of things. I brought cases home and even a kid who needed help, like you. But it was too much for Kirsten, and she ended up leaving."

"I'm not married, but I think I understand what you're saying." There wasn't anything he could do about it now because there was no way he'd put Isaac and Jos back on the streets. He just had to help them put their life together again so they could be on their own. "I'll be careful."

Aaron followed him out of his office and down the hall to the interview room where Jos waited, his bouncing leg stilling as soon as Kip returned.

"I'm Detective Cloud." Jos nodded and watched Aaron intently, as though he expected to be attacked at any moment.

"Jos has identified a number of items that we recovered from last night's suspect, so we can add theft to the charges," Kip said.

"When will I get them back?" Jos asked.

Aaron sat down. "This is the crappy part. We need them as evidence, so they have to stay with us until we find out if he's going to fight the charges in court. You could have your items back now, but then the theft charges would have to be dropped. Hopefully we can make all the charges stick, and this helps."

Jos lowered his gaze. "So he steals from me no matter what. He takes my stuff, you get it back, and I lose it anyway because you need it."

"I know how you feel, but the courts require evidence, and it's temporary. Him having your things on him is dead-to-rights proof of theft," Aaron explained. He leaned forward, resting his hands on the table. "I understand you have a complaint to file against Gordon Powers for wrongful eviction."

"I don't know if there's anything you can do. I don't want to go back there ever again, but all my stuff was taken, not that I have any place to keep it."

"Tell him what you told me," Kip said.

"There was a policeman there. He showed up when they were kicking me out. I thought maybe the neighbors had called the police, but I should have known better. Most of the people there don't speak much English, and they aren't going to call attention to themselves if they can help it." Jos seemed defeated. "I'd lost my job, and he didn't even give me the chance to find another one. He just kicked me and Isaac out on the street."

"Was it just you?"

"No. He did it to another family too. I thought it was really strange. The apartment across the way from me was empty. I don't know about the others in the building."

"It had nothing to do with you losing your job. Powers sold that building to a developer who bought the land behind it. The guy needed access and paid Powers a lot, I'm guessing, for the building. Probably made it a condition that the tenants be gone so he could tear it down right away. Powers is a real piece of work."

"There was a policeman there," Jos reiterated.

"We didn't get a call," Kip said and handed Aaron the call logs from that night. "We think he was there because Powers made sure he was."

"Why didn't you call me right away?" Aaron asked as he stared at the log.

Kip kept quiet and hoped Jos would as well.

"Kip?" Aaron pressed and Kip shrugged. "I get it. You thought it was me?"

"I didn't think so, but we had to be sure."

"What did the officer look like?"

"I don't know. I wasn't paying much attention to him. Isaac was crying, and I was scared to death because I didn't have any place to go. I had a little money, but it would be gone in a few days at a hotel, and the weather was warm…. I didn't know what else to do. We managed to get into a shelter, thank God, and I kept what little money I had hidden."

"I need you to think. Try to remember. Did his uniform look like Kip's? Did he have the same patches and his badge in the same place?" Aaron turned to him for a second and then back to Jos. "Was his shirt blue or white?"

"White," Jos answered. "It was definitely white, and he wore a tie."

"South Middleton Township police," Aaron said. "That explains why we don't have a record of a call at all—we didn't get one."

"But he was out of his jurisdiction," Kip said. "He couldn't do anything."

"Yeah, but he kept anyone else from calling the police because they all thought the police were already there. And the building is empty now, I suspect, waiting for demolition."

Kip smiled. "Can we get a warrant? Maybe Jos's things are there, and we can get something out. He has paperwork he needs, and maybe his and Isaac's clothes. He left with practically nothing."

"I'll try," Aaron agreed. "It's hard to get anything on this guy, and the judges are getting pretty demanding because we always seem to come up empty. I might be more successful if I can restrict it just to Josten's apartment."

"Whatever you can do," Kip said.

"I know I don't deserve your help, but thank you," Jos said.

Kip watched as Aaron's mouth dropped open in near total shock. "Of course you deserve my help. Everyone does. That's what we're here for—to help wherever and whomever we can. It doesn't matter who you are or if you're homeless or not—we're here to help." The indignation in Aaron's voice filled the room. "I'll do whatever I can." Aaron stood, and Kip thought he was going to leave the room, but he walked around the table and crouched near Jos. "You have nothing to fear from the police. I know a lot of people on the streets are afraid of us because we make them move on when they find a place to stay, but it isn't personal, and we don't hate the homeless." Aaron stood back up as Isaac bounded into the room. He stopped when he saw Aaron and walked slowly around to Jos.

"Are you done?" he stage-whispered. "Mr. Donald said we could get ice cream when you were done." Isaac danced from foot to foot.

"Almost," Kip told him. He walked over, scooped Isaac into his arms, and blew bubbles on his belly. Isaac laughed at the top of his lungs, and Kip did it again. Isaac continued giggling and squirming. A few seconds later Kip looked up and realized not only were Aaron and Jos looking at him, but half the department was peering in the doorway. "Let's go find Mr. Donald so we can clean up and get ready to go. Jos and Officer Aaron are going to have a talk, and they don't really need us." He carried Isaac into the breakroom, where Donald and Alex were sitting at the table.

"Is he done?" Alex asked.

"Almost." Isaac practically shook with excitement, then turned to look up at him. "Mama used to take me to get ice cream sometimes, but Jos hasn't."

"What was your mama like?" Kip asked. He figured it was better to get Isaac to talk about it than to ignore the fact that his mother was gone.

"Tall—not as tall as you—and pretty. Mama used to dress pretty and go out." Isaac put his arms around Kip's neck and rested his head on his shoulder. "I want my mama," he said softly. "We had fun-ral and she gone, but I want Mama."

Kip's heart leaped and wept at the same time. That Isaac would turn to him and trust him with his heartbreak was both sad and amazing. There had been few times in his life when he'd felt as close to someone as he did to Isaac in those few minutes. Isaac's innocence, and the way he only needed to be cared for, touched something deep inside him.

"You should definitely be a father," Donald said softly. "You were meant for that."

"I don't think so," Kip said.

"It doesn't matter one bit, gay or straight, the kind of father we'll be. I like to think that Carter and I are good fathers."

"I wish I'd have had someone like you as my father." The role model he'd had scared the crap out of him when it came to children. Basically Kip thought about what his father would do and then did the exact opposite. "Mine never held me like this. I don't remember him going to a game or seeing a program at school. I do remember him sitting in his chair, television on, a beer in one hand and the next one ready on the table." Movement caught his attention, and he turned as Jos leaned against the doorframe. Kip put Isaac on his feet, and he rushed over to Jos.

"Ice cream now?"

"Alex, you and Isaac clean up the Legos, and then we'll go get some ice cream." Donald handed Alex the bag, and Isaac hurried over to help put the blocks away.

"Did you tell Aaron what he needed?"

"Yeah. He said if he got the warrant, he'd let me know so I could go over and get my things. He said he was going to say that the apartment contained stolen property. Because it does. Powers stole my stuff from me. He isn't sure he'll be able to make the charges stick because he said Powers will say that I just didn't come back for my things, but hopefully…."

"If you get the papers, it'll help a lot. You could get replacements, but that takes time you don't have right now." Donald pulled Alex up onto his lap, and Jos sat down, letting Isaac climb onto his. The obvious affection between Isaac and Jos was tender and sweet. They even tilted their head the same way when they listened. You could tell they were brothers, although with their age difference, Isaac could be Jos's son.

"I'll try." Jos sighed. "All this is overwhelming, and I can hardly believe you can help me. I half expect all this to end at any second."

"There are limits to what we can do, but of course we'll help," Kip said, stepping behind Jos's chair. He nearly placed his hands on his shoulders but stopped himself just in time. Jos was someone he was trying to help, not his family or his boyfriend.

"Why would you help me?" Jos said. "I mean, I know you're helping for Isaac, but I appreciate it."

Kip knelt next to Jos's chair. "I'd help even if it was just you. This isn't just about Isaac." There would be limited things Donald could do to help if Isaac wasn't involved, but Kip really wanted to think he'd help Jos even if Isaac wasn't around. "Now how about we go get that ice cream, and then we can stop at the store so I can do what I promised and get Isaac a real horsey."

Jos turned to him, smiled slightly, and then nodded. "Okay."

"Yay!" Isaac said. Kip wasn't sure if it was about the ice cream or the horsey, maybe both. He had no idea, and it didn't matter. Isaac was happy, and after a few seconds Jos smiled as well.

"Are you ready?" Kip waited while Jos put Isaac down and took his hand, leading him out of the station. "We'll follow you," Kip told Donald, and he helped Isaac get into his seat. Then he waited for Donald to get ready, following him the few blocks to the Bruster's.

KIP WAS happy, Isaac was full and asleep in the back seat, holding the blond stuffed horse Kip got him at Walmart, and even Jos seemed content as they pulled up in front of Kip's house. As soon as Kip recognized the car parked across the street, he got out. Jeffrey did the same and walked over to him.

"I thought I'd give you some time to cool off and think," Jeffrey said.

"About what?" Kip asked. "Quitting my job so my life fits your schedule?"

Jos got out of the car and helped Isaac.

Jeffrey's expression turned icy. "I see you found someone else." Jeffrey stepped closer. "I see you like them young.... Jailbait, even." He glared at Jos.

"That's enough. Jos is a friend who needs a little help, so he and Isaac are staying with me."

"How close is he staying?" Jeffrey sneered.

"Remember, you were the one who picked a fight and then left. Now you're back and acting pissy. Well, you have no reason to. You were the one who wasn't happy, and yet here you are. But nothing has changed. I still work odd hours, and I won't be able to be available all the time. That's what you wanted." Jeffrey showing up was the last thing he'd have expected.

Jeffrey looked at Jos and then steered Kip away from the car and down the sidewalk. "I had a chance to think about things, and I realized I wasn't being fair. I came into town, and I expected you to change everything because I was here. That wasn't right. We have a lot in common, and we've had some special times together, so I was thinking I would try to get a job here again, and then we could be together." Jeffrey smiled his million-watt smile, the one Kip had come to know as the deal-maker.

"That's nice, but get a job here for you, not for me. I don't want you to change your life because of me. I wouldn't for you," Kip said, staring clear-eyed at Jeffrey, whose lips curled upward in what Kip thought was a smile, but which quickly darkened into a sneer and then a grimace. "I'm not quitting my job, and I can't ask you to do the same."

"Damn you, Kip. I came all this way back because I thought we had something, that you cared."

"I do."

"But not enough. Is that it?" Jeffrey asked, his voice getting louder.

"Enough for what? To stop living my life so you can be happy? That's what you want, isn't it? You want me to stop what I love, stop being a police officer and find some other work that will mean that I'll be home when you want me." Kip caught himself before he began to yell. "I won't do that. I am a police officer—it's an important part of my life, and I'm not going to give that up. I told you that before, and nothing has changed. I can't give up what I love."

"I thought you loved me," Jeffrey said.

Kip glanced back to where Jos and Isaac stood by the car, little Isaac holding the stuffed horse Kip had bought for him, Jos biting his lower lip nervously.

"Are you paying attention to what I'm saying?" Jeffrey said. "I thought you loved me!" He took a step back. "But I guess you didn't love me enough."

"For what? To give up my life and myself for you? Love means building a life together based around what both people want. It isn't about putting your wants ahead of others, but about figuring out what's best for both. You were never interested in that. After you graduated from Dickinson, all you wanted was for me to bend to what you wanted. I tried doing that for a while, and it didn't work." Kip tried to explain as best he could, but he wasn't sure if his meaning was coming across. It was apparent from Jeffrey's expression that he either wasn't listening or didn't care enough to actually give any thought to Kip's feelings.

"So now I'm the selfish one. I drove hours the other day to see you, and I thought you'd trade shifts or whatever, so we could have some time together. But you didn't. We had a fight. So what? People fight sometimes. They don't move on in a few days and decide to play house." Jeffrey motioned toward Jos and Isaac.

Up until then, Kip had been fine letting Jeffrey rant on, but that got under his skin. "They're friends, and that's enough!" he snapped. He saw Isaac flinch and grip his horse tighter. "You don't have any right to tell me how to live my life, any more than I do yours. You live in Pittsburgh, three hours away, and we were friends first and became something more, but you know as well as I do that all this drama is just that—as false as anything on the stage. It isn't backed by any deep feeling for me. You got your ego bruised, and you came back to see if you could soothe it and get a little satisfaction."

"Now you think you're Freud," Jeffrey said sarcastically. "Don't try to analyze me—you hardly have the brain power for it."

"That's enough, Jeffrey. Now please get back in your car and go. This conversation is over."

"Or what?" Jeffrey stepped even closer. "What are you going to do? Call the police?" He grinned. "I bet your friends would like to hear about the big bad cop having to call for reinforcements."

"You're making a fool of yourself," Kip said, not rising to Jeffrey's bait. That was how he worked. It had taken a while before Kip realized that when Jeffrey was losing he always tried to turn his opponent's strength into a weakness somehow.

"Am I?"

"Yes. You certainly are. I'm sorry you drove all this way, but you should have called first. We could have talked on the phone and saved you a trip." Kip pointed to the car and waited. "You might as well go. You aren't going to get me to back down, and throwing a hissy fit isn't going to help either." Kip stood firm, staring Jeffrey down until he turned and took the first steps toward his car.

"You're going to be sorry."

"Oh, please. I know I'm not, and you sound like a bad movie." He watched as Jeffrey finally got in his car and zoomed out of his parking spot, leaving a trail of black behind him. Kip thought about calling the department and having them track and stop him for his driving, but he wanted him gone as quickly as possible.

"Maybe we should go somewhere else," Jos said. "I don't want to come between you and your boyfriend."

Kip shook his head. "He isn't my boyfriend, and he never was. He was…. I don't know what he was." He walked back to where Isaac and Jos stood next to the car. "Why don't we go inside."

"That man yelled," Isaac said. "He was mean and it made his face all scrunchy." Isaac tried to imitate Jeffrey, and Kip laughed because he did a good job.

"Yes, he was a scrunchy-face. But he's gone now, probably for good."

"Are you sorry he's gone?" Jos asked, and Kip shook his head. Jos turned away. "Is it always that easy for you to let people go?"

"No," Kip said. "But it was easy to let Jeffrey go. He and I had a thing. But it was a long-distance, mostly physical thing and little more."

"But he said…," Jos began.

"Jeffrey will say just about anything to get his own way. You saw the car he drives. It costs more than I make in two years. It was a gift from his father, as was much of what Jeffrey has. He's used to being given what he wants, and I wasn't going to be one of those gifts." Kip didn't want to go into this in front of Isaac. "So what are you going to name your horse?" Kip asked Isaac to change the subject.

"Um…." Isaac put his finger in his mouth. "Ice Cream."

"Is that really what you want to name him? Because you can name him anything you want."

"Then Spist…. That ice cream you had."

"Pistachio," Kip said.

"Yeah. That's his name. Spistachio," Isaac said, hugging the horse tight. "Can I play?"

"Sure," Jos said.

"Why don't you play with Pistachio on the porch? That way he won't get too dirty," Kip suggested. "I can get some lemonade, and we can all sit outside for a while." Fresh air would definitely do him good. He led the way, and Isaac went right to one of the wicker lounges, declaring it a corral for "Spistachio." Jos sat rigidly in one of the chairs while Kip went inside. He made up some frozen lemonade and brought a pitcher and cups on a tray out to the porch.

"This is probably going to be one of the last truly nice days of the year," Kip said. "Around here it's like someone flips a switch and spring is here, and then the switch gets flipped again in the fall and winter is upon us."

"I know," Jos said and sat back in his chair, cradling the cup in both hands. He drank every now and then, watched Isaac, and said nothing at all. Kip watched Isaac play for a while, but his gaze kept traveling back to Jos. He was chewing on something. Kip could almost see the wheels in his mind turning something over and over again. He'd sat quietly with people and been perfectly comfortable. This was not one of those times. It seemed like the pressure inside Jos was building by the second.

"What is it?" Kip eventually asked.

"I keep thinking we should go," Jos replied.

Kip sighed. "Where are you going to go? To a shelter? Back on the streets?" It wasn't as though he had a lot of options, but Kip stopped because Jos looked as though he'd hit him. "Dammit, I didn't mean it like that. If I think you need to leave, then I'll tell you. Jeffrey and I were done before I met you, and you didn't break anything up or ruin a relationship, because the one we had was over. He didn't want to accept it. Nothing more. So don't worry."

"But what—"

"Are you scared?" Kip asked. "You look like a rabbit ready to run."

"I'm always scared. I have been for weeks. Mom died and suddenly I'm a parent to a four-year-old. That threw me for a loop, but just as I was getting things under control, everything fell apart with the job and the apartment. Not that I was going to be able to stay in the apartment for very long unless I got a job, but I even had day care for Isaac because they had a small center at work. Since then I've been moving from shelter to shelter. I don't know where our next meal is coming from, I have people telling me that Isaac would be better off with strangers in foster care, and finally you come along and I don't know what the hell to think, because you and Donald are the first people who've really tried to help me other than filling a plate and telling me to move along."

"That was a mouthful."

"I guess, but I can't help thinking that your help is only going to last so long, and then I'll be right back where I was."

"But you won't. If Donald can help Isaac get survivor benefits, then you'll have some support coming in until he's eighteen. It won't be a huge amount, but it will be guaranteed money. Donald's contacts will also try to find you a place to live with a reputable landlord."

"It's hard to let someone do things for me when…." Jos paused and swallowed. Kip watched his delicate throat work and knew he should not be watching Jos that closely. Of course it didn't help that sometimes he was sure he saw Jos watching him.

"It can be hard to trust people," Kip continued. "It's easier to rely on yourself, but you can't do it all, and getting your life back on track is going to require more than you can do alone. And your primary focus needs to be on Isaac."

"But…."

"I'm not going to hurt you, and neither is Donald. Think of it this way: trusting us doesn't have a cost. You can leave if you want, and if what Donald and I are trying to do doesn't work, you're no worse off. But you could be much better off, with a home and support for Isaac. You only have to let us help."

Jos took a drink, the ice cubes rattling in the cup, then said, "But why would you want to? Why would you go to all this trouble for me… us? We're not your family, and you don't know us at all."

"We know you," Kip said. "Both Donald and I see people who need help each and every day. Sometimes they're victims of crime and sometimes just victims of the cruelty of life. All of us try to help. It's why Donald went into social work and why I became a police officer. Sometime I'll tell you how Alex came to live with them. It'll break your heart. I barely knew either Carter or Donald back then, but what they did for Alex opened my eyes, and we became friends."

"So why are you helping us?"

Kip didn't answer right away.

"Really, why?"

"Okay. A year ago I got this call. It was for a domestic disturbance. Turned out we found a woman nearly dead, and she died later. We took the guy into custody. He was a real piece of work, and he made his money having children do what no child should ever have to do." Kip took a few breaths to clear his head and keep focused on the story. Even though he was a cop, there were some things that got to him like nothing else.

"I was on the call with Carter. He's a computer geek, but he followed his nose through the house. He found toys, but no kid. I thought he was crazy, but he went up in the attic, and that was where he found Alex. He was Isaac's age, and that little boy had been through hell. He was messed up, but Carter took care of him. I thought he was crazy to get involved. Let social services do their thing—that way he could stay out of it."

"But he didn't?"

"No. From what he told me later, he goaded Donald into taking Alex. To make a long story short, they fell in love with each other while taking care of Alex. He was their matchmaker."

"Is that what you expect now? That Isaac is going to bring you and me together somehow? That you're going to find love because of him?" Jos asked skeptically.

"No, that's not what I expect. But I realized that if it had been up to me, I probably would have left that house without checking the attic, and little Alex would have stayed up there alone. Hell, he could have died. That was a real eye-opener, and I told myself that if it ever happened again, I'd step in and do what I could to help. So that's what I've tried to do. I should have done it when I first encountered you, but by some miracle, I got a second chance, and thank God I got there in time." Kip sighed. He'd been so damn close to making the same mistake twice. "Sometimes being a police officer and trying to help people isn't enough. There are times when you just have to do something." He sat back. "So I'm doing something."

"And what do you expect to get for it?" Jos asked with a harsh tone.

Isaac took that moment to laugh and pick up Pistachio from his "corral" and start galloping around the porch, making horse noises. Kip followed him with his eyes and smiled.

"Isn't that more than enough?" Kip asked, and Jos nodded with tears in his eyes. "He's happy, and that smile of his...."

"I know," Jos said. "I've tried to make him happy and never seem to be able to. Everything I touch turns to crap, and now he's the one who's paying the price."

"You're both paying for things that are beyond your control, and you're not alone. Do you know how many people are a paycheck or two away from going through what you did? A huge number. You were the one who everything seemed to conspire against. But part of that is because you didn't know there was help available. There should have been a social worker who helped you when you got custody of Isaac. They should have helped you sign up for survivor benefits and explained what your options were and how they could help. Instead, you were left on your own."

"But if I'd been prepared...," Jos said. He got up, lifting Isaac into his arms, then sat down with Isaac in his lap.

"Who's ever prepared for parenthood?" Kip asked. "People usually have nine months, but new parents are almost always overwhelmed at some point. You were trying to make a life for yourself and now you're doing it for two. That adds more challenges. So don't blame yourself, and concentrate on making the best life you can."

Jos nodded.

"Have you thought about trying to get a new job?"

"Yeah. But...."

"I'm not saying right now, but think about what you want to do. I mean *really* want to do. I bet Donald could help you get into school. There are lots of programs and help available. You just need to think about what you want."

"To feed myself, have a house that's mine, and to know that Isaac is safe, fed, and healthy. That's all I really want. Everything else is immaterial," Jos answered. "I can't think beyond that right now. He has to come first."

"I know—"

"No, you don't," Jos interrupted. "I know you're trying to think longer term, but it's the here and now that's the problem. Hopes for the future come after we have enough food." Isaac squirmed, and Jos let him slide off his lap. He ran back to his stuffed horse and began playing again, talking up a storm, telling "Spistachio" everything.

"I used to have dreams. Big dreams. I wanted to be an engineer, the train kind, and then a doctor. I even wanted to be a policeman for a while. Even when I was working at the warehouse, I used to work hard and did my job the best I could in hopes I'd get noticed and promoted. On the streets, everything is immediate. How do I stay out of the rain? Get enough to eat, make sure I don't get robbed, or hurt… maybe worse."

"I was only trying to help," Kip said. "If you aren't willing to look further, then nothing ever changes."

"But I can't think about what I want to do in five years when Isaac doesn't have enough to eat now. That's all I think about. He's fed and happy, which is a relief, so now I'm wondering how I can get him his next meal and make sure he's safe and not going to get sick. That's all I think about, and I know you're going to say that we're going to have dinner here, but what about in a few days or a week? We could be right back out there on the street again." Jos's voice got louder and his eyes wider. He sat back in the chair, gulping for air, on the verge of having a panic attack. Kip jumped to his feet, took the cup and set it aside, then pulled Jos's arms up over his head to stretch his chest and help him fill his lungs.

"It's going to be okay."

Isaac ran over and put Pistachio onto Jos's lap. "I'm okay," Jos said, and Kip released his arms. Jos took Pistachio into his arms and hugged him tight.

Isaac whimpered, and Kip lifted him onto his lap. "Jos is a little upset, but not at you. Go on and play for a while. We'll be right here."

Isaac turned to Jos. He clearly wasn't buying it. Jos forced a smile and handed Pistachio back to Isaac. "Go on and play," he whispered. "I'm fine." Isaac took his horse, and Kip set him down once again.

"First thing, you are not going to end up back on the streets. That isn't an option. Donald is going to help, and so am I." Kip put his hand on Jos's shoulder. He only meant it as a gesture of comfort, but the heat that shot through him was nearly overwhelming. Kip should have pulled his hand away, but he didn't want that to be misinterpreted, so he left it and gently wriggled his fingers.

"I can't stop worrying," Jos said. "What if Tyler had gone after Isaac instead of me?" He began to hyperventilate again.

Kip soothed him as best he could. "He didn't, and you're here where it's safe. And Tyler is behind bars, where he belongs. You don't have to worry about him any longer."

The way Jos tried to curl into the chair made him seem small, like if he curled up as far as he could, he'd disappear completely. "I can't help worrying. Isaac deserves so much more. I need to find a way to make sure this doesn't happen again."

"What you need to do is stop blaming yourself for what happened and try to forgive yourself. Guilt sucks, and we can let it take over our lives."

"What do you have to feel guilty about?" Jos shot back. "You have all this, and you had parents who loved and cared for you. I bet everything was perfect for you."

"Then that's a bet you'd lose," Kip retorted and pulled his hand away. He reached for his glass, wishing like hell there was something stronger than lemonade in it. "We all have things we feel guilty about." Kip stood and went inside the house. He closed the front door and walked through to the kitchen. He set his glass on the counter and placed both hands on the granite counters his mother had installed just before she died. It was his turn not to hyperventilate as anger and long-festering guilt rose to mix together in a soup of blackness.

After a few minutes, he heard the front door open and close, then soft footsteps. Kip pushed away from the counter and opened the freezer door. He needed a pretense, something to cover his actions, and going for more ice seemed to work. He put an extra cube in his glass and then slid the tray home and closed the door.

"I'm sorry," Jos said. "I shouldn't have snapped at you. It's just hard to make people understand some-times, and I got upset, and…." Jos stared at the floor.

"It wasn't your fault." An old wound that had been with him for a very long time had suddenly decided to split open in a big way. "Go back out with Isaac. I'll be right back out."

Jos turned and left, and Kip went upstairs to the spare bedroom on the third floor. The room was air-conditioned and heated, so he used it for storage. Plastic tubs were stacked one on top of the other against the wall. Kip scanned the labels until he found the one he wanted. He moved tubs around until he got to it and pulled it open.

Inside were toys. Kip found a few dolls that had been played with hard. He lifted them out and set them aside. He removed a stuffed bear and put it aside too. Then he found what he'd been looking for: a brown horse with a dark plastic saddle. He lifted it out and stared at it. Then he shook his head, put everything back, and slammed the lid back on the tub before wiping away the tears in his eyes. He pulled out the next tub and lifted the lid. Then he grabbed both of them and left the room, carrying them down the flights of stairs and out to the porch.

He set down the tubs, and Isaac hurried over, peering inside as Kip lifted the lid on the top tub. "These were mine when I was a kid, and I thought you could play with some of them." Kip pulled out various trucks and cars, setting them on the porch floor. Isaac squealed, dropped to the floor, and started pushing the cars around. Kip had needed a chance to clear his head for a few minutes, and getting the toys for Isaac was just the break he needed. And judging by Isaac's reaction, the decision was a good one.

"You're going to spoil him," Jos told him when Kip sat down.

"He deserves to be spoiled for a while, and so do you," Kip countered. He found it difficult to sit still and went back inside, returning a few minutes later with a plate of cheese, crackers, and grapes. He set it on one of the side tables and sat back down.

"You're trying to make me fat," Jos accused even as he placed a slice of cheese on a cracker.

"You're too thin and you know it," Kip said. "So eat and relax. Isaac is happy, and you're both safe." He sat down and leaned back in his chair, letting his eyes drift closed. Of course, as soon as he did, his imagination took over.

"Why that grin?" Jos asked after a few seconds.

Kip shook his head. "Nothing," he lied. There was no way he'd admit that he'd been sitting next to Jos wondering what he'd look like without his clothes on and what he'd feel like under him. His imagination had conjured up the most amazing chorus of soft needy sounds, and Kip leaned forward, hoping like hell he wasn't showing wood. He sure as hell had it, but putting on a display wouldn't be good. "I was just thinking." He needed to stop having those thoughts. It wasn't right and nothing could come of it.

"Kip," Jos said, and Kip colored, wondering what he'd seen. "I see you looking at me sometimes."

The heat in Kip's cheeks rose even higher. "I'm sorry. I look. It doesn't mean that…. I'm not like Tyler, you know." Where had that come from? It seemed hard to believe that Jos had only been staying with him for a day.

"I know that. You'd never do anything like what he tried," Jos said and leaned forward in his chair. "I am gay, just so you know. So you don't have to worry about me being offended by your little daydreams."

Kip swallowed. "Even if I were to confess that they were about you?"

"I figured that," Jos said with a smile and sat back in his chair. Kip did the same, listening to the happy sound of Isaac as he ran cars around the porch. After a while, Isaac went back to playing with his horse, but somehow Pistachio now made the same sounds as a truck.

When Isaac said he was hungry, Kip made lunch and they ate on the porch. It was a late lunch because of their unscheduled ice cream stop, but that was fine. Isaac played the rest of the afternoon on the porch, and Jos watched him. Kip thought he might have relaxed somewhat and even nodded off for a while. Kip took that as a sign of Jos's comfort around him.

When Isaac crawled into Jos's lap and curled next to him later in the afternoon, Kip wondered if something was wrong, but Isaac just rested his head on Jos's shoulder and dozed off.

"Kip," Jos whispered after a while. "I have to go inside. Would you please…?" He stood and gently transferred Isaac. Kip expected Isaac to wake, but he remained asleep and curled against Kip, barely stirring. Jos put Pistachio to Isaac's arm, and he curled it close. "I'll be right back."

Kip nodded and looked at the small body and angelic face resting on his lap, Isaac's usual quiet energy banked for later use. Kip stroked a stray lock of Isaac's hair from his forehead and just watched him sleep. When Jos returned, Kip asked if he wanted him back and was exceedingly happy when Jos shook his head and stretched out on the wicker love seat. "Go ahead and close your eyes if you want. He and I will be fine."

Kip tried to remember the last time he'd spent an afternoon doing nothing. Even when he wasn't at work, he was almost always doing something. The house always needed some kind of attention, and while he sat, he ran through the list of things he should be doing. When he was with Jeffrey, that list of items always seemed so important, but right now, it was secondary to enjoying the peace and quiet of one of those warm fall days that could be the last of the year.

"No!" Jos mumbled and stirred, groaning and then whimpering softly. Kip reached over and gently put his hand on Jos's back and held it there, letting him know he wasn't alone. Jos mumbled some more and then settled quietly once again.

A few minutes later, Isaac woke with a start, whining the way his brother had. "It's okay. It's just Kip." He picked up Pistachio from where he'd tumbled out of Isaac's arms and continued holding him for a few minutes until Isaac squirmed to be let down. "You have to play quietly."

Isaac nodded and put a finger up to his lips, making a "shhh" sound to Pistachio before going to the other end of the porch and the chaise longue corral.

"Where's Isaac?" Jos asked with a start, sitting straight up.

"He's playing with his horse," Kip said levelly, and Jos sighed and turned so his feet were on the floor. "God…. I dreamed someone had taken him, and when I went to get him back, he was gone and I couldn't find him. Faceless people kept saying that he was better off, and after a while I began to believe it, and—"

"It was just a dream. Isaac is right there, and he's fine," Kip said lightly. "None of that is going to happen."

"How do you know?" Jos asked. "I know you bent the rules last night when you didn't call child services when you found us in the doorway. Why do you think I had to get away as fast as I could? I won't let anyone take Isaac away. We're the only family we've got, and I can't leave him alone, not after what happened to Mom."

"Donald and I aren't going to let it happen." Why he was so vehement in his conviction and so trusting of Jos was beyond him. He was a police officer; he should know better than to trust a stranger. He saw things every day that told him he needed to be much more careful, and yet Jos had gotten past his defenses and under his cynical police nature without him even realizing it.

His phone vibrated in his pocket. Kip read the message, then said, "Aaron got the warrant, and they're going over now. He said to come by in half an hour and we should be able to have a look around."

Jos seemed nervous and turned away. Instantly the suspicions he'd just been admonishing himself for pushing aside came rushing forward. "Is there something there that you don't want them to see?"

Jos turned back to him. "How would you like other people going through your stuff?"

"They aren't going to. Aaron got a warrant because there was stolen property on the premises. Yours. He's claiming that in kicking you out illegally, Powers in effect stole your property from you. Hopefully it will stick in court, but Powers will have a bunch of lawyers with a million explanations." Kip's phone buzzed again. "We need to go," he said and got to his feet. "Get Isaac in the car. Powers was already in the process of tearing down the building."

Kip called Aaron. "How could that happen so fast?" he asked when Aaron answered.

"I have someone checking, but it looks like the permit came through today so he wasn't wasting any time. We stopped the work, but the bulldozers have already demolished half the building." Kip pulled open the door to his car and started the engine. As soon as Jos had Isaac in his seat and the doors closed, he zoomed to the other side of town.

"STAY HERE," Kip said. He lowered the windows, then got out and walked to where Aaron was standing. One side wall of the brick structure was gone. "Jesus."

"Tell me about it. That was Josten's apartment," Aaron said, pointing to the undamaged side of the building.

"What do we do?"

"It seems undamaged, and I have them stopped for now."

"Has anyone else complained?" Kip asked.

Aaron nodded. "The units seem mostly empty. When I looked into the ones with the missing wall there were a few pieces of old furniture, but most everything was gone. I haven't been able to look in the unit above, but I'm starting to think that Josten may have been the lone holdout."

"Do you think Jos was lying?"

Aaron shook his head. "I think Powers was. He comes here making a show of force complete with a police officer to make it look really good. He tells everyone in the building that they're being evicted and to get the hell out. The few others get their stuff once the show is over and clear out. Josten doesn't know it's a show, and he has no other place to go, so he grabs what he can and heads to a shelter."

"Son of a bitch," Kip swore.

"The guy is slime. Hell, he's shit in slime. But he got what he wanted. The building is empty and there are no leases, and no one complains because they're scared shitless. He gets a permit, and the building comes down…. Everything is gone, and he can go through with his sale of the land."

"So what do we do?"

"The demolition has stopped, but the building is going to be unstable."

"Can we go inside?"

"Red is already there. He wanted to look around," Aaron explained. Kip turned to the doorway, and Red came out and walked over to them.

"This side of the building seems good for now. The walls and ceiling are intact, and there aren't any cracks. These places were built pretty solidly. I'd say give the tenant an hour to take what's vital, and then we need to condemn the place and let them take it down for safety. I took pictures inside in case the complainant wants to press charges. But the place is now a hazard and the door wasn't locked when I got here, so I'm afraid anything of value has been removed."

Kip sighed. *Another injury to someone who's been kicked around way too much.* "I'll get Jos, and he can decide what he wants to do," Kip said and hurried back to the car. "You can go in and get what's important. The place seems stable for now. I'll stay with Isaac." Kip opened the trunk. "Load up the trunk with whatever you can get."

"Can I use the grocery bags?" Jos asked.

"Whatever you need," Kip said as he saw Red coming over.

"I can help you," Red offered.

"Jos, this is Red. He's an officer and a personal friend."

"Thanks," Jos whispered, clearly overwhelmed. "I don't even know where to start."

"Pictures, papers—whatever is most important to you and Isaac," Kip said, wishing he could help him. But someone needed to stay with Isaac, and a total stranger would freak Isaac out. Jos nodded, and Red led him into the building.

KIP SAT with Isaac, doing his best to entertain him, watching what was left of the building and worrying. Jos came out with his arms full of clothes for him and Isaac. "Can you stay here? I'll just be at the back of the car," Kip told Isaac and left the door open for air. He took the load, and Jos hurried back inside. Kip did his best to fold things and put them into bags and organize the trunk. When Jos came out again, he had a few more bags, and Red was following him.

"That's all," Jos said. "People went through everything." His lips quivered. "The TV and stuff like that was gone. They were old, but somebody still took them."

Red set a bag in the trunk. "I found some pictures and put them in there for you. Some of the glass was broken, but I figured the pictures were what was important."

Jos nodded. He looked about ready to cry. "I found the papers Donald said he needs. They were in a pile of stuff that was thrown on the floor."

"We'll wash all the clothes when we get them home. Did you find any of Isaac's toys?"

Jos shook his head. "I tried to find the bear Mom gave him. He always slept with it. I couldn't find it when we got evicted, so we had to leave without it, and I didn't see it anywhere just now. Why would someone take it?" Jos put his hands over his face. "Why? It was just a stupid bear. It didn't mean anything to anyone except Isaac and me."

"Was there anything else you wanted to get?"

"The furniture were things I got at thrift stores for a few dollars. All I wanted was some of Isaac's things. It was the only stuff worth anything."

"Was there anything of real value left inside?" Aaron asked, and Jos went to pieces when Red shook his head. "I'm sorry."

"Can you roast the bastard?" Jos asked before Kip folded him into his arms. He wasn't in uniform, and he didn't care at that point what the other officers thought. Jos was reaching a breaking point. It seemed like every time the guy turned around, any sort of good news was followed by a bitter disappointment.

"What's going on here?" a rough voice demanded. "This building should be down by now. Why has everything stopped?"

"And you are?" Aaron asked forcefully. "We have a warrant, and in order to fulfill it, we stopped the work."

"Gordon Powers. I own this lot, and I have a demolition permit."

"This building contained property that wasn't yours," Aaron explained.

"That's too bad. The tenants were given ample notice and have had weeks to get their property out. The locks were changed two weeks ago, and we've gotten no requests for access."

"You kicked us out with no notice," Jos said.

"I did no such thing. You were given notice, and then you abandoned the apartment. We sent registered letters that went unanswered. So I'm within my rights to move ahead." Powers turned his considerable girth toward the demolition crews. "Take her down, boys."

He turned back to Aaron. "Unless you have a court order specifically stopping the demolition...."

Kip wanted to slap the smug look off the bastard's face.

"Didn't think so," Powers said and motioned to the men to continue. "I'm not paying you to stand around. Knock it to the ground and start hauling it away." He stepped back, arms crossed across his chest defiantly as the trucks started up and a bulldozer pushed into the building.

"Do you want to watch this?" Kip asked Jos, who shook his head. Kip felt so damned powerless.

Aaron and the other officers moved away as a bulldozer plowed into the other side wall and the weakened structure imploded in on itself, roof falling in followed by the side walls.

Kip moved Jos toward the car and got him inside. Isaac was craning his neck to try to see what was happening, his hands over his ears. "Sorry, buddy," Kip said. "Let's go home and get some dinner, okay?"

"Pizza?" Isaac asked.

"It was Mom's favorite, so we had it a lot," Jos explained.

"Sure. I'll have one delivered," Kip agreed. He drove as fast as he could away from the devastation that had been Jos and Isaac's last home. He fumed for much of the trip. Powers was a total bastard, and Kip didn't believe a thing the man had said, but they couldn't prove otherwise, so they were stuck looking like fools while Powers did what he wanted anyway.

"Did you find Weeble?" Isaac asked, holding Pistachio.

"I'm sorry. I tried to find him."

"He was under my bed. I put him there to save him when the mean men came," Isaac said, and Kip looked to Jos, who held his face in his hands. Kip didn't have to ask to know that Jos hadn't looked there.

"I'm sorry, buddy, but can you take care of Pistachio instead?" Kip had to try to think of a way to make Isaac feel better—and by extension Jos, who once again seemed on the edge of losing it. "He needs you."

"Weeble needs me too," Isaac said, and Kip pulled the car into a driveway and turned it around. He raced back to the devastation and caught Aaron as he was pulling away.

"What is it?" Aaron asked.

"Isaac's bear was under his bed in the apartment," Kip said. "Get them to stop so we can see if we can find it."

"You're kidding," Aaron said.

Kip leaned out his window. "Do you want to tell a four-year-old that we didn't even try to find his bear?" he asked, turning on the guilt. They had to try.

"Okay. Red and I will help." Aaron backed up and flipped on his flashers. The bulldozer came to a stop, and Aaron got out. Kip pulled in next to him and told Jos to stay with Isaac. If Isaac's toy was in there, he was going to find it.

CHAPTER 4

JOS COULDN'T believe Kip was actually doing this.

"Where did he go?" Isaac asked from the back seat.

"To try to find Weeble for you," Jos answered, not taking his eyes off Kip as he stopped the bulldozers from taking down the rest of the building and Aaron threatened to arrest them all on suspicion of something or other. He couldn't hear it all clearly, but there was plenty of yelling, most of it coming from his former landlord.

Jos got out and opened Isaac's door, then helped him out of his seat. Then he lifted his brother into his arms so he could see what was happening. What was left of the building was a jumbled mess. But it was Kip standing toe-to-toe with Powers that was the real attraction. The big, rumbling engines on the equipment grew silent, and Kip's voice carried on the evening breeze.

"I'll tell the media what you did and make sure your ugly mug is plastered all over the evening news as a slumlord. You won't be able to rent an apartment to a flea-infested rat by the time they're done with you."

"Now see here," Powers retorted. "You're a police officer—"

"I'm off duty and I'm here as a private citizen. And I want a chance to look through the wreckage to find something." Kip's chest thrust forward, and he looked even larger than he actually was.

"He looks mad," Isaac said.

"I think he is, but not at us."

"Is he mad at the mean man who took Weeble?" Isaac asked.

It surprised him sometimes just how much Isaac grasped. He was very smart, and Jos knew that once they were settled, he'd get him in some sort of pre-school. "Yes, he is. But it's a good kind of angry. Not the mean kind of angry like Mr. Powers."

Isaac nodded and put his thumb in his mouth. Jos gently pulled it away and shifted Isaac on his hip so he could lean into the car and grab Pistachio for him. That seemed to make Isaac feel better.

"I can't believe he's doing that," Detective Cloud said as he joined them.

"I'm sorry about all this," Jos said, just above a whisper. "It's all my fault. I should have told him to just go home."

"Are you kidding? Seeing Powers frustrated and angry as hell but not able to do anything about it is priceless."

"But won't Kip get into trouble?"

"For what? Red and I haven't seen anything." Aaron smiled, and Red came over to join them.

"I should help," Red said.

"We can't. There isn't any reason for us to be looking in there, and we're on duty. The only reason we're here is because of a dispute between two citizens that has the potential to escalate," Aaron said, watching Kip as he carefully walked over the rubble pile.

"How long is he going to take?" Powers huffed as he walked over. "I pay these men by the hour, and I'll send the bill to the department."

"Go ahead. You taking this building down is suspect, since you knew there was someone else's property inside, so don't give me a bunch of your crap," Aaron said. "I don't believe your story at all. I just can't prove different. But that doesn't mean we can't cause trouble for you. Give him a few minutes. If your men want to help, it will get us out of here all the faster."

Powers stomped away and talked to the drivers. They got down out of their cabs and came over.

"What's he lookin' for?" one of the men asked.

"Weeble," Isaac answered, lower lip shaking, tears welling in his eyes.

"A teddy bear," Jos said. "When Powers kicked us out, it scared Isaac and he hid his bear under his bed. Kip is trying to find it."

"Come on," the driver said to the other man. They walked to the rubble pile. "Which apartment was it?"

"Third floor, this side, that corner of the building." Jos pointed, and they began digging around. Jos watched, but truthfully he wasn't holding out much hope. Kip seemed determined and continued digging through the pile, pulling bricks and parts of wall off and tossing them to the side. The other men joined him.

Jos figured this was a lost cause. "Kip," he called and shook his head. Kip ignored him and continued digging, pulling out part of the wall, which sent up a cloud of dust. Kip jumped back and then began digging around in the hole he'd made. A mattress came up next, and then Kip held his hand high in the air.

"Weeble!" Isaac cried at the top of his lungs. Kip climbed off the pile, and so did the other two men. Kip shook hands with both of them and then jogged to where they waited.

The brown bear was nearly white with dust. Kip bumped him against his hand, knocking a lot of it away. "When we get home, Jos and I will clean him up for you," Kip said when Isaac reached for him. "You can have him then."

"Promise?" Isaac asked.

"Yes. I promise." Kip put Weeble in the back seat, and they all got into their cars. Powers still huffed, but Jos was done with this place. He never wanted to see it again as long as he lived. As Kip pulled away, Jos refused to turn around. Somehow he had to make his life move forward to a better place.

KIP STOPPED for pizza since it was getting late. When they got back to the house, Isaac was nearly asleep, and Jos got him cleaned up and put him in bed with Pistachio. Weeble had been washed and was in the dryer. Kip had been afraid that the dust from the demolition wasn't good for Isaac, but in the morning, he'd have his bear back.

"I can't believe you did that," Jos said as he and Kip sat on the porch in the near darkness.

"Why not? He's been through more pain than anyone his age should ever have to be, and if he wanted his bear, I had to do what I could to get it for him."

Jos reached out to Kip and squeezed his hand. "Thank you. It means a great deal to both of us. I only wish I'd known where it was when I went inside. I could have prevented the extra searching."

"Seeing Powers about ready to explode was worth it. Even his own men weren't happy with him." Kip sat back and put his feet up on the table. "The weather says it's going to get cold again tomorrow and probably stay that way from now on, so we may as well enjoy the last of the warm weather."

Jos agreed and tried to relax, but there were so many things he didn't know. "When do you have to go back to work?"

"Day after tomorrow. This is my weekend, I guess. I rarely get a full Saturday and Sunday off together because I'm one of the lower men on the totem pole, but it doesn't really matter. Two days off together gives me time to do what I need and to rest and get some projects done around here."

"It was quite a day," Jos said as he ran over everything that had happened in his mind.

"Yes, it was. And we should get your things out of the trunk." Kip didn't make any effort to move. "There's a dresser in the guest room that's empty. Go ahead and put your things in there." Kip stretched his arms over his head and his shirt rode up, giving Jos a peek at Kip's flat belly. "I'll help you in a minute. I just need to relax a bit."

It had turned very dark by the time Kip got up to move. He unlocked the trunk and began carrying things into the house. They should have done this before Isaac went to bed, but Kip had a solution and put the bags in the next room.

"At least it's all in and you can take care of things in the morning," Kip told him when they were all done. Jos didn't want to question what Kip had said, and it seemed Kip wanted him and Isaac to stay, at least for a few more days. Jos nodded and dug in one of the bags for some clothes to wear to bed. Then he said good night and went into the bathroom to clean up.

Isaac never moved when Jos came in the room and got into bed with him. He held Pistachio tight and lay curled almost into a ball. Jos wondered what sort of dreams he was having and hoped they were happy ones. Granted, there hadn't been a lot of happiness in their lives lately, but Jos prayed that would change.

JOS WOKE to a scream that cut the night like a knife. He sat up as Isaac thrashed and kicked him, yelling once again. Jos pulled Isaac to him, hugging and soothing him until he woke up and began to cry.

"What happened?" Kip asked as he raced into the room, shirtless and wearing only a pair of shorts.

"Isaac had a nightmare," Jos said. He rubbed Isaac's back, trying to get him calmed down and quiet once again.

"What happened, buddy?" Kip asked.

"The mean man tried to take me away, Jos. He put me in the house and then it fell down and I couldn't find Weeble." Isaac wiped his eyes, and Kip left the room.

"It's okay. You know it was just a dream. It wasn't real."

"I know," Isaac sniffled. When Kip returned, he handed Weeble to Isaac.

"It's all better. You have Weeble now," Jos said and helped Isaac get back under the covers.

"I have to go," Isaac said. Jos got him out of bed and took him to the bathroom. Isaac yawned more than once, and when he was done, he washed his hands and then hurried back into the bedroom, jumped up on the bed, and scrambled under the covers. He held both Weeble and Pistachio, settling easily. Isaac went right back to sleep, but Jos doubted he would. He left the room and met Kip in the hallway outside. Neither said a word; they just walked down to the kitchen and Kip put a kettle on the stove.

"He scared the life out of me," Kip admitted as he sat down at the table.

Jos agreed and managed to sound coherent despite his attention being drawn to Kip's bare chest. He was strong and fit, with defined pecs and big arms. A dusting of hair in the center of his chest trailed off to a line that ran down his ridged belly. "I thought someone was really hurting him." Jos needed to stop staring but found it damn hard.

"I did too."

"I hate that he gets so scared." Jos wiped his eyes. "I know it's all my fault. I should be doing better for him." He rested his elbows on the table and put his head in his hands. "Maybe he would be better off with someone else to care for him. They sure as hell couldn't do worse than I am." He sniffled and looked at Kip.

"Hey, Isaac loves you, and that's what's important." Kip put a hand on his shoulder. "This has been a very difficult few days, and I think you're feeling worn a little thin right now."

"You think?"

"Yeah, I do. Lots of things have come to a head, and you're trying to deal with them all at once."

Jos shook his head. He felt like he was made of glass and was going to shatter into a million pieces at any second. It took all his energy to hold himself together. And he had to for Isaac.

The teakettle whistling pulled him out of his funk and back to the present. Kip got up, and damned if Jos couldn't help following him with his eyes, especially as those gray shorts slid just a little bit lower on his narrow hips with every step. Kip put tea bags into two mugs and poured the water. Then he brought them back to the table and placed one in front of him.

Jos barely noticed. Those shorts were obscene and hid practically nothing. He turned away, swallowed hard, and lifted his mug. Of course he swore when he burned his tongue, and Kip jumped up and got him an ice cube from the freezer, holding it to his lips. Jos sucked on it, the cold helping, and noticed that Kip didn't take his gaze from his lips.

"You know, you're really beautiful," Kip said. "Guys aren't usually pretty, but you are." Kip touched Jos's cheek with his thumb, stroking lightly. Jos closed his eyes and soaked in the gentle attention. For a few seconds, he tried to remember how long it had been since there had been someone in his life who was gentle and caring. His mother had been neither; well, at least with him. When it came to Isaac, she'd been less cold and had spent more time with him, but she would never, ever have won Mother of the Year.

"I'm not...," Jos countered, desperately wanting Kip to argue with him. He liked being told he was pretty. Hell, he liked being the center of someone's attention in a good way, rather than how Tyler had acted in the alley. The way Kip looked at him, with warmth and gentleness, made him want to sit still and stay like that forever. He could escape into Kip's deep jade eyes and never move. Then he wouldn't have to worry about apartments and jobs and what was going to come next. He could just be and let go of everything building up inside to the point that he wasn't sure how much longer he could hold it together.

"Yes, you are," Kip told him. "Just let yourself believe it and give up some of the worry for now. I think you've been doing it for so long that you aren't sure how to let it go." Kip moved back slightly but didn't stop touching him. His hand did a little dance away from his lips, but Kip teased it around the side of his neck and just held it there, like if Jos became too tired, Kip would support him and hold him up. "Drink your tea. It'll help you sleep."

"What if I don't want to go to sleep?" Jos asked, lifting his gaze to meet Kip's. He saw a well of heat ready to spring up and engulf him. That was what he needed—heat and passion to burn hot and rise up around him, to take him away and make him forget everything if only for a while.

Kip leaned close enough that hot breath, scented with tea, ghosted over his lips. Without thinking, Jos licked them in preparation for the kiss he hoped was coming. "You need to. Part of the reason you're on edge is because you haven't really rested in a long time." He didn't move back, and Jos wondered what Kip was thinking.

Just when he figured Kip wasn't going to make any sort of move, he leaned in farther and Kip's lips touched his. Jos wasn't sure what he'd been expecting. In books, the first kiss was always electric and eye-opening. This one was nice—soft and gentle. It didn't incite an all-encompassing passion, but Jos's heart beat faster, and he was warmer. Kip pulled back, and Jos opened his eyes. Their gazes held fast, neither of them moving.

"You should finish your tea and go on up to bed," Kip whispered.

"But…," Jos began and stopped. He was not going to ask Kip to take him to bed. Yeah, Kip had kissed him, but maybe he wasn't interested in him and that had been just some kind of pity kiss. Something to make him feel better, and nothing more. "Yeah, I should go upstairs."

His tea had cooled off some, and Jos drank from the mug, turning to sit at the table, which provided a barrier so Kip couldn't see how excited he was. It also gave him something to look at other than Kip's honey-gold skin. He still found himself sneaking looks every now and then, huffing to himself. Once he finished the mug, Jos took it to the sink and rinsed it out before saying good night to Kip and going upstairs.

Isaac didn't even stir when Jos got back into the bed, and he heard Kip come up the stairs a little while later, a few floorboards creaking as he passed the door. Jos rolled over, staring up at the white ceiling. He couldn't help wondering what that kiss had meant, if it actually had meaning or was just something Kip had done to comfort him. Kip had said he was beautiful, and he was pretty sure Kip didn't go around saying that to a lot of people. He decided to be happy about the kiss and try to let it go at that.

"You're turning into a teenage girl," he whispered to himself. Isaac snuffled in his sleep and rolled over without waking. At least he was able to sleep. Sometimes being an adult stank. If he were a kid, he'd be able to take the kiss at face value and be happy about it. Instead, he was lying there, wondering and worrying instead of being happy that Kip had kissed him at all. Eventually the wheels in Jos's head settled down and exhaustion took over.

THE FOLLOWING morning Jos was at loose ends. He heard Isaac laughing with Kip, but he was tired and pulled the covers up to his neck and closed his eyes once more. A scream had him up and on his feet within seconds, but as soon as he reached the stairs, he realized it was laughter and glee. Whatever Kip was doing to Isaac, it was something he hadn't been able to do, because laughter had definitely been missing from his brother's life.

Jos went back to the room where they had put their bags and rummaged until he found something he could wear. Once he was dressed, he grabbed the bags and carried them downstairs.

"Everything you need is in the basement. Help yourself," Kip called happily. Jos thanked him and did his best to smile as Isaac waved from on top of Kip's shoulders. Jos started a load of laundry and ended up sitting on the rug in front of the washer, listening to the machine do its work.

"There you are," Kip said.

Jos hadn't even bothered to move when he heard him on the stairs.

"Jos, I'm flying," Isaac said, and Kip zoomed him around on his arms.

"That's great," Jos said as he forced himself to his feet. He had no energy and wanted to go back to bed and sleep for the rest of the day. "You and Kip are having fun, huh?"

"You can play too," Isaac said. He looked up at Kip when he set Isaac down.

"I think Jos is too big to fly like an airplane," Kip said. He placed his hand on Jos's forehead. "You're warm. Why don't we get you back up to bed. I'll make you some toast and get some juice."

"I'm okay. I have things to do." His feet felt like lead, but he forced them to move and made it up the stairs.

"Donald is going to be here about noon, and when he called he asked me to ask if you've ever waited tables."

"Yeah. I did that when I was in high school, and afterward I worked near full-time. Bookies closed a year ago, and that was when I was able to get into the warehouse. Why?"

"That's excellent. Donald said if you had experience then he might have a line on a job for you. One of the restaurants in town is looking for a server, and Donald told them about you. They said they needed someone with experience, apparently. Donald will tell you about it when he gets here."

Jos pulled out one of the kitchen chairs and collapsed into it. He barely had the energy to move at all. Kip poured him some orange juice, and he drank it slowly. After a few minutes, he felt a little better and drank the rest of the glass. Kip refilled the glass, this time with grape juice, and brought a piece of cinnamon toast. Isaac knelt on the chair next to him and ate his own piece of toast with a grin on his face.

As soon as he was done, Kip took his plate. "Isaac, why don't you take Jos and put him back to bed for me?"

Isaac got down from his chair and took Jos's hand. Climbing the stairs nearly wiped Jos out again. When he got to the bedroom, Jos climbed back into bed and pulled the covers up to his neck. He heard Isaac leave and then felt the covers lift behind him.

"Thanks," Jos said. He knew he should feel guilty for leaving Kip with babysitting duty, but he didn't have the energy to do anything. When he rolled over, he found Weeble in bed next to him.

"So you won't be lonely," Isaac said and then left the room.

Jos rolled back over and closed his eyes.

His dreams were disturbing and kept going in circles, like he was on a never-ending treadmill. At one point he woke as Kip helped him sit up and then lifted him into a chair and covered him with a blanket.

"You need to drink," Kip said, and Jos did as he was told, the cool, sweet juice sliding down his parched throat. "I'll be right back," Kip said when he took the glass away, and Jos closed his eyes. He must have dozed off, because when he woke Kip was stripping him of his clothes.

"If you want sex, just ask." Jos wasn't even sure what he was saying.

"You're soaked, and I want to get some dry clothes on you so you'll be more comfortable." Kip helped him into fresh clothes and then back into bed. "I'll bring you some more to drink, and then you can go back to sleep."

"Is Donald here?"

"He's come and gone. You've been asleep for hours. Don't worry, he said to call when you're feeling better and he'll take you down to Café Belgie to meet and talk to the owners. So just sleep and get better." Kip stroked his cheek and then left the room. He returned with more juice, which Jos drank. He also took the pills Kip offered and then handed the glass back, closed his eyes, and fell asleep. This time he was able to settle and his dreams were less frantic. He was also much more comfortable.

The windows were dark when he woke again and got out of the bed. The house was quiet, and Jos wondered if he was alone. He used the bathroom and went downstairs to find Isaac and Kip on the sofa in the living room, watching cartoons.

"Are you hungry?" Kip asked.

Jos nodded.

"Then sit down. I'll get something for you and a snack for Isaac here." Kip ruffled Isaac's hair and then left. He returned with a couple of plates. One had a piece of chocolate cake that made Isaac's eyes light up, and the other some scrambled eggs and toast that tasted better than anything Jos could remember.

"Are you feeling any better?" Kip asked.

Jos nodded, sitting back in the chair. "I guess. I don't know why I'm so tired and feel so bad. My stomach isn't pukey or anything. I just don't have any energy, and I ache all over." Kip brought him a blanket, and Jos wound it over his shoulders as a chill ran through him.

"Okay. The thing is, you need to rest as best you can." Kip sounded concerned as he gathered the dishes. "Why don't you go back up to bed? I'll bring you some more juice, and you'll be warmer under the covers."

"But I can't be sick. I have to take care of Isaac, and I need to be able to get a job." Jos wiped his brow as he began to sweat. He pushed the blanket away because he was getting too warm. "I'm going to lose my chance, and then I'll be back where I was." His heart raced and he began to breathe rapidly.

Kip hurried over and lifted him out of the chair. "You're not going to lose anything. Just calm down."

Kip carried Jos through the house and up the stairs. He heard Isaac talking behind them, whimpering, then Kip telling him everything was all right. Kip rested him back on the bed, and Isaac took his hand. When Kip returned, he helped Jos sit up and gave him some pills and something else to drink. Jos took what he was given and then lay back down. His head spun a little, and after a while—it was hard to gauge the time—the room settled and he started to feel better.

"I'm okay, Isaac," Jos said, realizing his brother was still standing by the side of the bed, peering at him.

"Here's some more to drink," Kip told him and helped him sit up again. His mouth tasted terrible, but the juice felt good, and once he'd had a few sips, Kip set the glass on the table and took his temperature in his ear. "You're still running a fever. I'll check it again in a little while." Kip stroked his cheek and then did something Jos didn't expect: he kissed him on the cheek. It was gentle and so very tender. Then he felt Isaac do the same thing, and when he looked up, Kip was holding Isaac in his arms. "I'll put him to bed in the other room. Isaac will be fine with Pistachio, won't you, buddy?" Isaac nodded, and Jos closed his eyes. He was too tired to argue even if he'd wanted to.

Jos slept reasonably well, with some weird dreams. At one point he pushed off the covers because he was hot and ended up pulling them back up a little while later. When he did, he finally felt comfortable and was actually able to sleep deeply.

When he woke, light streamed through the windows. He felt better and his head was clear. He blinked a few times to make sure and then slowly got out of bed. He wondered what time it was as he got some fresh clothes and headed to the bathroom. His mouth tasted like something had died in it, and his clothes clung to him in places. He brushed his teeth, then took a very fast shower, dressed, and finally felt human.

"Jos," Isaac said as he opened the bathroom door. "Are you all better?"

"I hope so," Jos said.

"Come on. Kip's gone. Uncle Terry is here." Isaac took his hand, and Jos wondered what the hell was going on. He let Isaac lead him down the stairs as he searched his memory for anyone they knew as Uncle Terry. When they reached the bottom of the stairs, they followed the sound of the television, and Isaac led him into a room with a stranger.

"You must be Jos," the stunning man said with a huge smile. "I'm Terry."

"Where's Kip?"

"He had to go in for his shift. But he called Red, the big guy who helped you get your stuff, and Red called me to see if I could come by and make sure this little guy"—Terry tickled Isaac, who laughed full volume. Clearly they were good friends—"wasn't alone. Kip said you needed to sleep, so I've been keeping him here and we've been watching cartoons. Kip left a number for you to call when you got up. He said to let you sleep as long as you wanted."

"What time is it?"

Terry hit a button on the television. "A little after three. Kip said that he managed to get a split shift, so he went in earlier than normal, but should be back about seven." Isaac climbed up on the sofa and began watching the television. "Sorry if I worried you."

"I didn't even know you were here," Jos said, realizing Kip had taken care of everything while he'd been out.

"Fever gone?" Terry asked.

Jos nodded. "I think so."

"Are you hungry?"

"I am," Isaac said, raising his hand. "Cake, please."

"You had cake an hour ago, remember? I think Kip said there were grapes. Do you want some of those?" Terry asked Isaac, who nodded vigorously. "How about you? Kip made up a plate that I can heat up, and there's juice and other drinks. You'll feel better now that the fever's gone. Red and I both had the crud a few weeks ago. You'll be wiped out for a day or so more, but then you'll feel normal again."

"Okay," Jos said, more than a little confused.

"You stay here while I help Jos, okay?" Terry asked Isaac, who nodded and held Pistachio as he watched the program. Terry led Jos back toward the kitchen. "You have a great kid for a brother."

"Thanks. I think he's pretty special."

"You should bring him by the Y when you're feeling better. I can get you a guest pass, and he could come swimming. I work there as a lifeguard and train there. I had just finished for the morning when Red called."

"You're the swimmer, the one Kip said was going to the Olympics." Jos smiled.

"That's me. I made the team, and now I have to keep up with the training. I have a coach, and after Kip gets back, I'll go to the pool for some timed runs. In the morning I swim for stamina and fluidity. In the afternoons it's for speed."

"How can you do that? Doesn't it wear you out?"

"Yeah. I eat a lot of the right foods. I don't have to worry about gaining weight, but I have to keep from losing it. That can happen pretty quickly, and of course I need to keep my strength up." Terry pulled a plate from the refrigerator and put it in the microwave. After a minute or so, he took it out and placed it on the table. Jos noticed that Terry didn't ask a lot of questions about where he'd come from or what he was doing there. He was simply this happy guy with more energy than Jos could ever remember having.

Jos ate as Terry brought him juice and then got a bowl of grapes and set them at the table. He called for Isaac, who raced in and sat at his place, tucking into the grapes as though he had them every day.

"Is the television still on?" Terry asked him.

Isaac nodded.

"I'll go turn it off. You eat grapes with your brother."

After Terry left, Isaac grinned up at him. "I like it here."

"Did you and Terry have fun?" Jos asked.

"Yeah. He played horsies with me, and cars too," Isaac told him. "He's more fun than just about anyone." Isaac waved his hands in the air, sending a grape flying. It landed on the floor, and he climbed down to retrieve it.

Jos dropped his fork on the plate and held his hands over his face.

"Hey, it's all right," Terry said from behind him. "Nothing is that bad, you know."

Jos shook his head. It was. Everyone seemed to be able to make his brother happy but him. All he'd done was bring Isaac misery, homelessness, and hunger.

"Eat and you'll feel better. I promise. You've been sick, and though things look bad, they'll get better."

"How do you know?" Jos challenged. "You can't."

"Sure I do. I've been in a bad place before. Then I met Red and he saved me. I like to think I helped him too, but he's the real hero in our story. Because of him

I'm going to the Olympics and I have a good life, but I felt much the same as you do. I was in trouble too."

"But you had a home."

"Not really. Not one I could stay in, because I was afraid to." Terry hugged Jos around the shoulders. "Things will be all right if you let them."

Jos wasn't sure of that, but he didn't know Terry well enough to argue with him, so he nodded and pretended to go along. He finished eating only because it gave him something to do. When he was done, he took the plate to the sink, and since Isaac had finished his grapes, he carried his bowl over and handed it to Jos.

"Can we watch cartoons now?" Isaac asked, turning to Terry.

"Sure," Terry said, and Isaac ran over and took his hand, then led him out of the room. Jos stood there alone as the television started and high-pitched cartoon music drifted through the house. He decided to join them. When he went in, he found Isaac lying on his belly on the rug, feet in the air, hands propped up under his chin, enthralled with SpongeBob. Terry was sitting on the sofa with an iPad.

"Don't care for the Sponge?" Jos asked.

Terry nodded. "He's happy, and I have a few things I have to do, so he can watch and stay occupied." Terry motioned to the chair, and Jos sat down. "I know this must seem weird for you."

Jos rolled his eyes and nodded. "I don't know what to think about all this most of the time." Actually, he felt like a complete failure, but Jos kept that to himself. Isaac was happy and entertained, and it had nothing to do with him.

"Donald called a little while ago." Terry pulled out a slip of paper. "He said when you get up to call him."

"Thanks." Jos stared at the number for a few minutes before getting up and going into the kitchen to use the phone.

"How are you feeling?" Donald asked when Jos explained who it was.

"Tired, but feeling better. I got those papers you needed."

"Kip gave them to me, and things are looking good. I got a colleague to help file them, and he may have a line on a place to live. Café Belgie is looking for a server. It's both lunch and dinner shifts, but I understand the tips are quite good there. Darryl is the chef-owner, and his partner, Billy, runs the restaurant portion. They'd like to see you tomorrow. Do you have a nice shirt and pants?"

"I don't know."

"I can bring some by. The important thing is to dress for the job and to be prepared to demonstrate your skills."

"What time do they want me there?" Jos asked, excitement filling him for the first time in quite a while.

"Be there at ten. I'll stop by with clothes. You can bring Isaac. They understand about kids and taking care of them. At one point they turned the back room into a sort of day care for Billy's twin brothers. Just be on time. I'm sure they'll talk to you, and don't be surprised if they ask you to go right to work to check your skill level. They need someone right away that they can easily train."

"I'll do my best."

"Great. See you in the morning." Donald disconnected, and Jos figured he finally had something to be happy about. This time when he joined the others, he sat on the floor next to Isaac and watched cartoons with him. Terry seemed content to read, and as the afternoon wore on, he got ready to go.

"Call if you need anything," Terry said as he walked to the front door.

Jos got up from the floor, his legs a little stiff. "Say good-bye to Terry," he told Isaac, who jumped up and raced to his new friend, giving him a hug.

"Can we really go swimming?" Isaac asked Terry, jumping up and down until Terry lifted him up.

"Sure. You and Jos let me know when you want to come, and I'll arrange it." They shared a hug, and then Terry put Isaac down and he raced back in front of the television. Isaac was happy, as witnessed by the fact that he didn't walk or shuffle anywhere, but zoomed, and his eyes held the same sparkle they'd always had before their mother passed away. Jos had begun to think he'd never see that again. It made him happy, even if it was directed at someone else.

Jos walked Terry out and stood on the porch as he descended the stairs with a little lift in his step. "Thanks for everything."

"No problem," Terry said, stopping to turn around at the bottom. "Get some more rest and don't try to do too much. Kip was really worried about you when he left. He said if you weren't feeling better that he was going to take you to the hospital when he got home, and I was to watch you carefully. His words. I don't think I've ever seen him like that."

"I don't understand," Jos said.

Terry rolled his eyes. "He and Red are a lot alike. They're both in-charge kind of guys, and they're cool under fire. They assess situations and act rationally even when the world is falling apart around them and bullets are flying. It's what makes them good cops. But

Kip was really worried. Before he left, he went in your room and stayed a few minutes, just watching you and biting his nails. The guy cares about you. Red and I were beginning to think that he was going to get serious about that twit Jeffrey." Terry shuddered slightly.

"But I don't understand what he can possibly see in me," Jos admitted, looking down at himself.

"Maybe you should ask him," Terry suggested. "I know what it feels like to have all your confidence ripped away. You feel like you can't do anything right and you just want to hide. But then if we're lucky, we meet someone like Red—or Kip—who can see past all that. It doesn't happen very often, but when it does it's pretty special."

"But I've only known him a few days. How could he know that much about me?"

Terry chuckled and took a few steps back up the stairs. "They're police officers. They're trained to know who to trust and assess lies and truth within seconds. They have a sense for people, and I can tell you that if Kip didn't see something in you and didn't care about you in some way, you wouldn't be here. These guys don't let people come into their lives easily. There has to be something special."

"Isaac," Jos said, but Terry shook his head.

"If that's what you think, then you're way off. Kip could have called child services and had him put into protective custody if all he was concerned about was Isaac." Terry bounced down the stairs once again. "Think about it and see if you don't come to a different conclusion." He walked to his car, and Jos went back inside, joining Isaac in the living room in front of the television.

After a few minutes, Isaac got up from the floor and sat next to him on the sofa, leaning against him as he watched the show. "Why did Mama have to go away?" Isaac asked.

"I don't know," Jos said and thought about what he could say to try to help. "There are a lot of things I don't know the answer to, and that's one of them. Sometimes people die and go to live with the angels. Someday, a long time from now, you'll go live with the angels too, and then you'll see Mama again."

"Will she know me when I'm big?" Isaac asked, his eyes filled with disbelief.

"Your mama will always know you." Jos felt tears welling and hugged Isaac to try to cover them. The last thing his brother needed was for him to go to pieces. He was so close at the moment, every emotion built up over weeks right at the surface, and Jos knew if he let them come, there was no way he could stop them again. "Mamas always know their children, especially angel mamas. And I think that sometimes, late at night, if you're really quiet, they come down and watch over you when you're sleeping to keep the monsters away."

"So it's good to have an angel mama," Isaac said.

"It's good to have a mama who loved you and cared for you, angel or not. And you'll always have me to care for you too."

"Like an angel brother," Isaac said, and Jos nodded, thankful when Isaac turned back to the television so he didn't see the tears as they ran down his cheeks.

WHEN KIP came through the door a few hours later, neither of them had moved much. Isaac bounded off the sofa and ran right up to Kip, laughing as Kip lifted him into his arms.

"How are you feeling?" Kip asked Jos as he carried Isaac into the room. Kip set Isaac down almost immediately. "Where's Pistachio?" Isaac looked around. "Why don't you go find him so he isn't lonely?"

Isaac nodded and hurried away while Kip sat next to Jos on the sofa, gently wiping Jos's cheeks with his fingers.

Jos sniffed and took a deep breath. "I'm okay."

"Are you sure?" Kip stood and pulled the blanket from the back of the sofa, spreading it over Jos's legs before sitting back down on the edge of the cushion.

"Yeah." He sat quietly and then leaned against Kip to share his warmth. God, he smelled good. Jos inhaled again just to take in another dose of his musk. "I talked to Donald, and I have an interview tomorrow. He said he'd help me so I have some clothes to wear." Jos shook his head. "I still can't figure out why everyone is being so kind."

"Sometimes people are nice," Kip said. "Not always, but there are times in our lives when we have to accept that not everyone is a pile of crap."

Jos stiffened. "Sounds like you know firsthand."

Kip nodded. "I didn't have stellar parents either, and I spent a lot of my time on the streets with my friends. See, my mom and dad loved something more than my sister and me."

"You have a sister?"

"Had," Kip corrected. Isaac bounded back into the room with Pistachio under his arm and flopped down onto the floor to watch more cartoons. "I had a sister," Kip clarified and then grew quiet.

"What happened to her?"

"She died," Kip said.

"Okay," Jos said, growing more and more curious by the second. "What happened?" He figured that since Kip had brought it up, it would be okay to ask, but as soon as he did, he regretted it. The look of sheer pain that filled Kip's eyes left him cold, and Jos pulled the blanket more tightly around him.

"Like I said, Mom and Dad loved something more than they loved us: alcohol. They were both really big drinkers, so Adrienne and I didn't have very much. Mom and Dad went out to bars a lot. I was six years older than Adrienne, and one Saturday when she was eight, Mom took us to the beach. She seemed sober and was in a really good mood. So we packed a picnic and went off for the day. Of course Mom included a flask in the things she packed, and while we were swimming, she was filling her lemonade glass with something more than summer fun."

"How did you get home?" Jos asked.

Kip shook his head. "It was always my job to look out for Adrienne. I knew what my mom was like, but I let my guard down that day. We were at the state park at a lake, and they had one of those floating rafts that the kids love to play on. Everyone was having a great time, and Adrienne wanted to show me how she could swim. Somehow Mom had paid for swimming lessons for her."

Jos held Kip's arm a little tighter. "Oh my God." He could see where this story was going, and it was already scaring him. He glanced at Isaac, who was engrossed in what he was watching and didn't seem to be paying them any attention.

Kip shook his head. "She and I swam out together, and she did really well. She climbed out of the water and jumped up on the floating dock with her hands in the air like Rocky." Kip smiled and then it faded. "I was still in the water when some of the bigger boys started getting rough. They were pushing kids off, and I saw Adrienne get pushed off. I jumped up on the raft and muscled the kid off the side, sending him flying into the water. I was so mad. I remember yelling at the kid to leave my sister alone, and when I went to the side to find her, I couldn't."

"What?"

"I dove in and tried to find her, but the water was cloudy and I couldn't see much. Others dove in and so did the lifeguards, and they got her pretty quickly and brought her to shore. My mother was hysterical when she saw Adrienne on the sand. She wasn't moving, and they did mouth-to-mouth, but she never came around."

"It was an accident," Jos said.

"I know that. The kid hadn't meant to hurt her—he was playing. But my mother never saw it that way."

"She blamed him?"

Kip shook his head. "She blamed me. I should have been watching out for her and taking care of her. My mother was too drunk to do it, so it was my job, and Mom never let me forget it."

"She blamed you... when she was drunk?"

"It was easier than blaming herself. I was fourteen, and my childhood effectively ended that day. Adrienne was gone, and for the most part so was my mother. She drank even more trying to forget, and my dad could barely talk to me for a long time. At one point he told me that it wasn't my fault. Dad eventually got sober. He blamed my mother for what happened. Home was not a very happy place after that."

"What happened?"

"My mom went downhill from there. My dad tried to help her, but I think after that, she was beyond help. Eventually she just drank herself to death."

"At least your dad didn't blame you."

"No. But by then I blamed myself. Dad said I should let it go, but I couldn't. Adrienne's death haunted me. There had to be something pretty badly wrong with me."

"My God. Jesus. My mother was no real prize…." Jos sighed. "Believe it or not, I can see my mother reacting the same way." Jos had stayed at home longer than he'd wanted—even though he'd needed to get out of that house pretty badly—for Isaac's sake.

"It took me a lot of soul searching before I could let myself believe that I wasn't to blame for Adrienne. Not that I really believed it. I never realized how powerful guilt was until I tried to deal with it."

"How did you?" Jos asked. He wasn't sure he could handle it if anything happened to Isaac.

"I had this friend. I used to mow her grass and take care of her yard. After Mom died and I got older, she took me in. Joanie was more like a grandmother than a friend, and she had this mother-in-law's house in the back of her property. She said I needed some time away from my family to think about what happened. She also said it was time I was on my own. Her son, Parker, was a police officer. He came around a lot, and he used to talk to me about what it was like."

"What about your dad? Did you work things out with him?"

"Yeah. As I let go of some of the guilt and really started to heal, I learned just how much my dad was hurting too. He'd lost Mom and his daughter. We were each other's only real family by that point, and we got to know each other as adults. Of course he died a few years ago, and I ended up moving back into the house I grew up in. Joanie died last year, and I saw Parker when he came back for the funeral. He and his partner live in Frederick, Maryland, and they have two children through a surrogate."

"So you don't feel guilty now?" Jos asked, wondering about this widely circular story.

"I think I always will. I keep wondering if I'd have paid more attention to Adrienne, if things might have been different. But I've learned to live with it. I don't feel guilty about it as much as I regret what happened. Joanie told me once that Adrienne would be really angry with me if I hung on to what happened for the rest of my life."

"What was she like?"

"What was who like?" Isaac asked. He got up off the floor, climbing on the sofa to sit next to him. Jos put an arm around Isaac's shoulders.

"Kip was telling me about his little sister. She died when she was young."

Isaac blinked and looked up at both of them. "So she's with the angels, like Mama."

"Yes," Kip agreed. "Adrienne is definitely with the angels." Kip stood up and turned away. Jos saw him wiping his eyes. He and Isaac hadn't had the best mother in the world, but she hadn't turned her back on them. Not that it mattered now. His focus had to be on raising Isaac and trying to make sure he was happy.

"Who's ready for dinner?" Kip asked.

Isaac jumped to his feet. "Me!"

"How about you?" Kip asked Jos as he scooped Isaac into his arms.

"I'm a little hungry. I ate what you left a few hours ago." Jos followed them out of the room, his heart feeling a little lighter. He really wasn't sure why. Maybe it was the fact that in some ways he had been lucky, or at least things hadn't been as bad as they could have been.

KIP MADE pasta for dinner, which Isaac seemed to wear more of than he ate. After they were done, Kip sent them upstairs so Jos could give Isaac a bath and then put his brother to bed. Jos wasn't particularly tired when he was done, so he helped Kip down in the kitchen and then joined him in the living room.

The two of them sat together on the sofa and watched television. Jos had slept all day, so as the evening went on, his body and mind came awake. The sickly sleepiness and haze that he'd been in for the last day vanished, and Jos was hyperaware of Kip. He'd been carrying the blanket around with him, but he folded it up and leaned against Kip, letting his warmth surround him. He wasn't sure if Kip would be welcoming or not, but he went with the memory of his kiss the night before. Kip put his arm around his shoulders, and Jos sighed and closed his eyes.

"How long has it been since you were cared for? Really cared for?" Kip asked.

"I don't know. Maybe before Mom got pregnant with Isaac. I'm not sure."

"What about your boyfriend?" Kip asked.

"That didn't last long, with Mama's anger. Back in high school I had a girlfriend. Well, she was more a special friend than a real girlfriend. She knew I was gay, and we were close friends, so she helped me keep up appearances so no one would bully me and stuff. When we graduated, she went to Cal Tech on a scholarship. I lost track of her when she went on to her new life. Since then I've just been trying to survive." It felt like his life had been one long struggle, and right now, at this moment, he could breathe, because of Kip.

"I can understand that. But surviving isn't living," Kip told him. "And you need to let yourself live."

Jos chuckled. "I have no idea what that means. Survival sometimes took all the energy I had. Maybe that's why I got sick. I didn't have anything left."

Kip lightly touched his chin, and Jos lifted his gaze until it met Kip's. "You don't have to do everything alone. Not anymore. You have friends who can help you."

Jos wanted to believe that more than anything. He was so tired of worrying about their next meal or if Isaac was going to be safe or if they were going to be put out in the cold. Jos nodded, and Kip leaned a little closer. Jos's eyes slid closed and he waited.

When Kip's lips touched his, it was like a shock went through him. He had been contemplating getting the blanket because he'd been feeling a little cold, but within seconds he was warm. A moan reached his ears, and Jos realized it came from him. He sounded so needy to his own ears, but Kip must have liked it, because he held him tighter, deepening the kiss. Jos wound his arms around Kip's solid midsection.

"You taste good," Kip murmured.

"Must be the chocolate cake you made," Jos said, opening his eyes.

"No. I think it's you," Kip whispered. "But I'll need to run a test to know for sure." He smiled and leaned closer.

"Test away," Jos agreed, and Kip kissed him once more, shifting until he pressed Jos back on the cushions. Kip's weight combined with the intense kisses and then his hands under Jos's T-shirt roaming over his chest had him shaking harder than he had at the height of his fever.

"Damn," Kip gasped when he broke the kiss, burning his gaze into Jos's. "You're something else. You have goose bumps wherever I touch you."

"Well...," Jos began. "I've fantasized about being touched like that."

"No one has ever touched you like this before?"

Jos shook his head. "Sex has always been... rushed."

Kip backed away and climbed off the sofa. Jos was surprised and blinked, wondering what he'd done wrong. Kip helped him up and took him by the hand, leading him out of the room. "We aren't going to do this here." Kip turned off the television and the lights as they went, closing up the house as he led him up the stairs.

Kip stepped into the room and peeked at Isaac, who was sound asleep with Weeble and Pistachio next to him. He closed the door most of the way and then led Jos to his bedroom. He stopped at the door, turned toward him, and drew Jos into his arms. It felt so good to be held and to let someone else take the lead.

When Kip lifted him off his feet, Jos wound his legs around his waist, and Kip's groan rumbled deep. Jos joined him, returning the kiss as Kip supported his ass with his big, strong hands. He walked him to the bed and stood there, kissing him so deeply Jos felt it in his heart. "I haven't been able to take my eyes off you since I first brought you home."

"But...."

Kip stroked the hair out of Jos's eyes, smoothing it back and then stroking down his cheek. "I'll never forget as long as I live the moment you moved that blanket away and I first saw your eyes. They touched me, and I know it sounds stupid, but if I never saw you again, I know I'd remember your eyes forever." Kip leaned in to kiss him once again.

"I'm sorry I worried you last night," Jos said.

"You really did. I sat in the chair beside the bed for hours."

Jos stilled completely. "I didn't even know you were there."

"I know. But I was worried and didn't want to leave you alone. I put Isaac in my bed, and I spent the night either on the sofa or in the chair. You had a fever, and I was worried you might need to go to the hospital. Then you finally settled down and began to sleep deeply. Every few hours I checked your temperature and then fell asleep myself."

"But why?"

Kip smiled. "You fascinate me. Getting you to smile is the highlight of my day because when you do, you light up and you flash me your dimples."

"I do not," Jos countered, trying not to smile.

"See?" Kip said when he failed and pressed lightly on his cheeks. "Dimples." Kip turned and set him on the edge of the bed. Then he pushed him back, leaning over, with heat swirling in his eyes. "Damn, I said you were beautiful, but you've never looked better to me than right here, right now, in my bed."

"I do?"

"Oh, yeah. You look amazing in my bed." Kip tugged Jos's shirt up over his head.

Jos had always thought he was skinny and plain. He never let anyone see him with his shirt off if he could help it. Jos had already seen Kip, with his strong,

manly chest, flat belly, and narrow hips. He longed to
see him again and feel Kip's skin on his own, but he
kept wondering what Kip would think of him. From the
smile and then the lick up his chest followed by a swirl
of his tongue around one of his nipples, Kip seemed
happy with what he saw and felt.

"I knew you'd be beautiful."

"Not like you," Jos said as he worked the buttons
of Kip's shirt until they parted and he was able to push
it over his rounded shoulders and down his thick arms.

"Hey, we're all different. If I wanted a guy that
looked like me, I'd go to the gym and try to meet someone. Instead, I kept my eyes to home, and look what the
fairies brought to my doorstep."

Jos giggled. "The fairies? Are you saying something about my manhood?"

"No," Kip chuckled. "When I was a kid, I asked
my grandmother how she found Grandpa and knew
he was the one she wanted to marry. She said it was
fairies. She had never looked at Grandpa, and then one
day he was outside when she walked by. It was like
she'd been hit by a spell, so she always said that fairies
opened her eyes to the man Grandpa was."

"So you figured the fairies delivered me to you?
Don't you think they'd pick someone better?"

"Grandma said never to question the fairies. They
get angry and vengeful. Just take what they give and be
grateful and happy. She always said that she was." Kip
grinned and kissed away his protest.

Jos figured if Kip believed in fairies and thought
he was a gift from them, who was he to pop his bubble?
After all, the way he plucked at Jos's nipples had him
groaning and pulling Kip tighter. They kissed harder,
because all Jos wanted to do was scream, and if they

woke up Isaac, that would put a damper on their amorous activities in a hurry.

Kip lifted Jos and positioned him higher on the bed. Jos gasped when Kip licked down to his belt, pulling it open and then teasing the line of skin just above his pants. Jos's belly fluttered with anticipation and he pulled in his stomach, loosening his pants around the waist in the hope that Kip would get the message and accept his silent invitation. But Kip seemed in no hurry, stroking his hands up to Jos's chest and then down his belly again and again until Jos was sure he was going to go out of his mind.

His cock throbbed. Jos couldn't remember the last time he'd been this close to coming in his pants. Sex hadn't really been a part of his life since Isaac had come to live with him, and frankly, Jos hadn't thought much about it before meeting Kip. In fact, for weeks he'd done his best to hide who he was and to protect himself and Isaac by staying under the radar. That was the exact opposite of what he wanted now.

Jos moaned softly when Kip ran his fingers along the top of his pants. "Are you going to do something or just drive me crazy?" Jos asked as his frustration got the better of him.

"Oh, I'll do something," Kip teased, licking a small circle and then dipping his tongue into Jos's belly button. "How about I follow this trail…." His words fell off, and Jos held completely still as Kip began to open his pants. He didn't dare move in case Kip changed his mind. "You're okay with this?" Kip asked.

"God, yes…," Jos breathed, and Kip undid his pants, tugging the fabric apart and then pulling them away.

"Jesus," Kip whispered as he pulled Jos's pants past his hips and ran his lips over Jos's briefs-enclosed cock.

Jos swallowed. "Is something wrong?" Jos asked, hoping like hell Kip was as turned on as he was.

"Wrong?" Kip lifted his gaze. "Sweetheart…. Let's just say I like your proportions." Kip lifted the waistband of Jos's underwear, then sucked on the head of his cock, which was already peeking out. "Damn."

"Oh," Jos breathed. "I guess I'm okay."

Kip pulled his lips away, much to Jos's disappointment, and kissed him once again, hard, possessively and yet sweetly, and with enough intensity to send ripples down his spine and legs. "You're amazing from head to toe, and don't doubt that." Kip kissed him again and then worked his way back down Jos's body, the licks and kisses becoming more and more intense until Kip sucked the head of Jos's cock between his lips and kept going, taking more and more of him until Jos gasped for air.

"Kip," Jos squeaked.

Kip hummed around him. "Fuck, you're big," he said with a groan, backing away.

"You don't have to if—" Jos began, but Kip took him again, deep and long, until Jos shook with the energy from him. His body was on fire, and he hoped like hell it wasn't his fever returning. Then he realized it was—a fever, a need, for Kip. The way Kip touched him sent fire running to his brain, and there was nothing Jos could do to stop it. "Kip, I'm not…." Jos gasped and closed his eyes, trying to prolong what could not be put off. His cock had already been sensitive from all Kip's teasing and the fact that Jos had ignored it for weeks. He balanced on the edge and ran his hands through Kip's soft hair, trying to warn him.

Kip backed away and stroked hard and fast. "Open your eyes. I want you to see me when you come." Jos did, and the passion in Kip's eyes was the last straw. He came in a mind-numbing rush, thrusting into Kip's fist.

Jos lay on the bed, unable to move, half floating, with Kip stroking his cheek. He felt Kip shift on the bed, and then he kissed him. Light kisses deepened quickly, and Jos tugged at Kip's jeans, desperate to have them off.

Kip helped and soon he was naked, lying on top of him. Jos stilled his movements and motioned for him to roll over. Kip lay on his back and Jos sat next to him. "It's my turn to look," he groaned and swallowed hard. Kip was male perfection. "They should make statues of you."

"Yeah, I can just see that," Kip said.

Jos ran his fingers over Kip's chest and then down his belly, tracing the lines on his stomach.

Kip laughed and actually tried to move away.

"Ticklish?" Jos asked and grinned. "I'll remember that for later." He continued his explorations, which ended with cupping Kip's heavy balls in one hand and wrapping the other around his thick cock. "Imagine you as a statue, standing in a square. There'd be so many accidents."

"I wouldn't be naked."

"You make your imaginary statue, and I'll make mine." Jos licked up Kip's length and then took his cock in his mouth, sliding it over his tongue. Salty bitterness burst on his palate, and Jos slid his lips down farther, stretching to accommodate his girth. The man was a mouthful, and Jos loved all of it. He swirled his tongue around the head and slid his lips along the shaft to a chorus of groans and muttered curses.

"God, just suck me," Kip moaned.

Jos had always been good at taking instruction.

Kip's reaction was heady, adding excitement, and Jos sucked harder, loving the way Kip's fat cock filled his mouth. He wondered more than once how he'd feel inside him, and his butt throbbed with excited anticipation combined with nerves that he pushed away, determined not to let what had happened a few days earlier intrude on his happiness with Kip.

"Yes!" Kip hissed and thrust upward, pushing off the bed. Jos relaxed his mouth and let Kip move, taking in his half-lidded eyes and open mouth as he filled the room with sounds that were as melodic as any song he'd ever heard. "Gonna…." Kip groaned and pulled away. Jos dove onto him, taking him deep and swallowing hard as Kip tumbled into his release.

Jos let Kip slip from between his lips as Kip panted and tried to catch his breath. Jos loved that he'd stolen it away. Jos lay down next to him. The window across from the bed was open slightly, and a cool breeze blew over his now hot skin. It felt amazing, and after a few minutes, once they had a chance catch their breath, Kip rolled onto his side and engulfed Jos in his arms.

"I should go back to Isaac," Jos said.

"Stay. We'll hear Isaac if he wakes up, but that isn't likely now." Kip tightened his hold slightly, his warmth encircling Jos.

"Are you sure?" Jos asked. "I can just go back to my bed, and we can forget this happened, if you want. I mean…."

Kip released him. "You need to explain."

Jos sighed. "This was wonderful, but you don't need to saddle yourself with a guy like me. You deserve better, that's all." Jos didn't move, but he also didn't reach out to touch Kip. "I'm not good enough for you. Every time I make a decision, it's the wrong one."

"So you're saying that you know more about what I want than I do?"

"No," Jos said and rolled over. "I'm saying I don't know anything, and you deserve someone better than a guy who can't hold a job or manage to keep a roof over his and his brother's head. You're a wonderful guy. Not many people would take in Isaac and me. They'd call child services, and he'd disappear into the foster care system, and I'd spend all my time trying to jump through whatever hoops they set up in order to get him back."

"Hey, I know what I want and what will make me happy," Kip snapped. "I don't sleep with guys just because they're convenient." Kip pulled away and rolled onto his back. "Did you think this was some sort of requirement? Was it your way of paying me back because I took you in?"

"That's not what it was for me," Jos said, knowing he was blowing everything. That wasn't what he'd meant. He wasn't a whore, and he didn't sell himself. "I just didn't want you to think…."

"How about we worry less about what the other is thinking or might think and just say what we want? Okay? If you don't want to stay with me, then you don't have to. I won't force you to do anything." The hurt in Kip's voice went straight to Jos's heart. He hadn't meant to hurt him. He'd only wanted to give Kip a way out.

"You didn't force me, and I know you never would. You don't ask for anything."

"I didn't think I had the right. You need to be able to make your own decisions about what you want." Kip stared up at the ceiling. "You keep saying that you don't think you're good enough, but what if I'm the one who isn't good enough?"

Jos giggled a little. "How is that possible? You're one of the best people I've ever met." Jos rolled over and slid his hands across Kip's chest and around to his side. Then he moved in closer and rested his head on his shoulder. "You're my hero."

"I'm just a guy, the same as you. People can hurt me the same as they can you. Hell, my mother wanted to drink and blame me for what happened to my sister more than she ever loved me."

"She was selfish," Jos said. "My mom was too. She made sure she got what she wanted and needed. I had to fend for myself, and I know that if she'd have lived, eventually she would have treated Isaac the same way." Jos grew quiet for a few minutes, thinking. "Maybe that's the whole issue. We're used to the people in our lives being selfish, so when we encounter someone who isn't, we don't know how to handle it."

"Maybe. You met Jeffrey."

"Was he your usual kind of boyfriend?" Jos asked. Kip deserved so much better than anyone like Jeffrey.

"I guess so. He was nice enough to start out with, and then he got demanding and bossy." Kip smiled. "Yeah, selfish. Maybe I have this ability to pick people who aren't good for me. I have this instinct at work. I know when people are lying and when I can trust them. But in my personal life, I tend to pick losers."

"Well…," Jos began quietly. "Maybe that's why I should go back to my own bed."

"Now, don't start that again. You aren't a loser."

"How do you know? I ended up on the street trying to find a shelter for Isaac and me. That doesn't sound like someone with a successful future ahead of them."

"The guys I dated were all successful. They had these great jobs. Jeffrey is a lawyer, and I swear Shakespeare had guys like him in mind when he said to kill all of them. But they were still selfish. You aren't. I know that because you always put Isaac first, the way you should. So how about you stay where you are and stop putting yourself down." Kip wrapped him in his arms. He was so strong and yet so gentle, at least with him.

"Okay," Jos answered and got comfortable. "You know, you make a good pillow. I really like it." Jos patted Kip's chest a few times. "It doesn't fluff very well, though." He felt Kip tense his muscles.

"I'll show you fluff." The happy gruffness in Kip's voice made Jos smile, and he closed his eyes, yawning before he could stop it. "Okay, well, maybe I'll show you tomorrow." Kip pulled up the blankets, and they both got comfortable. "Night, sweetheart," Kip said and kissed him. Jos wasn't sure what made him warmer, the kiss, the blankets, Kip next to him, or the endearment. Maybe for now it didn't matter.

CHAPTER 5

KIP FINISHED his shift and breathed a sigh of relief. The last few days he'd been running nonstop. He would have thought it was still summer with the number of calls he was answering about pranks and mischief from the kids in the high school. Apparently one of the clubs at school had devised a new initiation. The Chevy dealership in town had a tall fence around their back lot, and the initiation involved breaking into one of the cars from the front lot and driving it through the gate into the back lot.

"Good job apprehending that kid. That should put a stop to that," Red told him as he left the station. The kids had so far ruined five cars.

"Yeah. He thought he was really tough until I took him through the jail. He cracked fast when the whistling and catcalls began. Gave up all his buddies, and now we have all the kids responsible." Kip was pretty proud of himself. "Say, I was going to dinner...."

Red checked his watch. "Terry is at the pool already."

"Then why don't you join me? I'm heading to pick up Isaac at day care, and then I thought I'd surprise Jos by stopping at Café Belgie. He started there three days ago, and by all accounts is doing great." The smile burst onto his face with no effort at all. "I can meet you there in half an hour if that works?"

"Great," Red said, and they left the station and got into their cars. Kip drove right to the day care. Because of Jos's work hours, it cost more to keep Isaac there until later in the day. Kip hadn't told Jos that part and had simply paid them the extra for the first month so Jos wouldn't have to worry. When he pulled up in front, Isaac raced out and into his arms.

"Uncle Kip, look what I drawed," Isaac said, jumping up and down. Kip took the page and stared at the various blotches of color. He knew better than to try to guess what they were. Instead he knelt down and let Isaac tell him. "That's Spistachio, and he's in his own stable with his horsey friends, Vanilla and Chocolate."

"He seems fixated on food," Carrie, one of the caregivers, said as she came out to meet him. She always did that, and he thought she might have eyes for him. "Today he insisted the colors weren't colors, but flavors of ice cream. Red was raspberry and blue was blueberry, brown was chocolate and yellow was lemon. Thankfully, orange was orange, and he got that one right." She smiled with concern behind her eyes.

Kip had noticed that as well. He tended to associate other things with food. "He and his brother have had a tough time of it. But things are getting better. Just humor him and make corrections gently. We're hoping it will dissipate on its own. It isn't just ice cream. When

I got out a saucepan yesterday, he asked if we were having wacamoni and scheese," he said with a grin. "That was the pan I had made macaroni and cheese in the last time." Kip hoped having enough food on a regular basis would make that go away. "Say good-bye to Miss Carrie," he told Isaac, and Isaac waved and took Kip's hand, leading him to the car.

Once Isaac was strapped in, Kip drove right home and hurried inside. He settled Isaac in front of the television and raced upstairs to get out of his uniform and into clothes for dinner. When he came back down, Isaac met him at the bottom of the stairs.

"I'm hungry," he said quietly, sticking out his belly and rubbing. "It keeps talking."

Kip got Isaac a cheese stick from the refrigerator and handed it to him. Isaac tore open the package and ate it quickly. "We're going to get some more to eat where Jos works. So can you turn off the television, and we'll go feed your talking tummy."

Isaac raced away, and Kip disposed of the wrapping. He caught up with Isaac as he came out of the living room and led him out to the car.

The drive to the restaurant took less than five minutes. He got lucky and found a place to park nearby. Red was already at a table inside, so they joined him. "Jos already took my drink order, but he's really nervous because you're coming."

"Hi, Jos," Isaac called, waving and grinning when he saw his brother. Jos brought Red's beer, and Kip ordered one and asked him to get whatever Isaac would like.

"I love this place. Terry wants to go to Europe, and I said we would after the Olympics."

"Sounds like fun. I never really thought about traveling much." It had never been on his radar. Maybe he would someday, though.

"What about you?" Kip asked Jos when he brought the drinks. "Have you ever wanted to travel?"

"I used to dream about going all sorts of places. Now my hopes are a lot smaller and closer to home." He said hello to Isaac and gave him a raspberry kiss on the cheek. "Have you decided?"

"What would Isaac like?" Kip asked Jos.

"Chicken bingers," Isaac pronounced, like he was king of the booster seat. Jos nodded, and both Kip and Red ordered the steak frites. Kip figured he could share his fries with Isaac. Jos went to put in their orders, and Kip watched him go.

"You got it bad," Red told him with a slight snicker.

"Got what?" Isaac asked. "Is he sick?" Isaac reached toward Kip's head, and he thought the little guy was trying to take his temperature the way Kip had when Jos was sick.

"No, little man," Red answered. "I was just teasing him." Red made one of those faces like he had to keep an eye on everything he said. Kip nodded.

"He's really smart and picks up on everything," Kip said with a hint of pride. He knew he shouldn't become too attached to Isaac, but he was finding it hard to keep his distance. The longer Jos and Isaac stayed in his house, the more he liked it and the less he wanted them to leave. But he wasn't Jos's family, and once Jos was on his feet, Kip figured he'd find his own place and get on with his life.

"Don't know what that frown's for," Red commented as he followed Kip's gaze. "You need to talk about how you feel toward him."

"That's the problem. I can tell Jos what I want, but he isn't going to believe me. He's had too much hardship for him to believe anything. You know the situation. He still thinks he's some sort of charity case. We just talked about it again last night, and I swear whenever I ask to talk to him, I can see the fear well up that I'm about to tell him and Isaac to leave."

Yesterday he'd wanted to talk about getting Isaac more comfortable in the room he was using and having Jos stay with him. Jos had seemed scared to death, and then he'd only nodded toward the end of the conversation. Kip had told him he could sleep in the bed with Isaac or with him, wherever he wanted. "No pressure," he said over and over again. By the end of the night, he'd been more confused than ever. In the end, Jos came to him, and Kip held him all night. Having Jos in his arms was amazing, and they hadn't done anything more than sleep. He didn't want Jos to think he had to have sex with him or even that he had to sleep with him. That wasn't a requirement, but the more he tried to tell Jos that, the more confused Jos seemed to get.

"You have to give him time. Have you wondered if maybe you're rushing things? You've known Jos a week. Let him decide what he wants to do and set the pace." Red smiled. Kip had never really seen Red's scars. Sure, they'd always been there, especially the one on his cheek. They made him look tough, but when he smiled, the scars completely receded and the man inside shone through clearly. Terry truly was a lucky man. Both he and Red were.

"I suppose you're right. Instead of pushing for answers…." He trailed off when Isaac pulled on his sleeve.

"My belly's talking again," he said, pulling up his shirt. "It says it's hungry."

Jos returned to the table with some bread, and Kip buttered part of a roll for Isaac and handed it to him. "How was work?" Jos asked as he filled the water glasses.

"It was a busy day, but it's much better now." Kip flashed Jos a smile and got one in return.

"Kip here busted that ring of kids who kept messing with the car lot. It was pretty awesome," Red said.

"And Isaac had a great day at school. He drew a great picture that's at home. How is it going here?"

Jos's serious expression gave way to a grin. "I had a large party that left just before you came in, and they gave me a hundred-dollar tip. They were celebrating something, and I think they wanted me to join in. Billy said they're from a law firm here in town, and whenever they win a big case, they come in. He helped me with the table but said the tip was all mine." Jos excused himself and practically floated to the next table to check in with them. Then he went back to the kitchen.

"Like I said, you got it bad," Red said.

"I like that he's happy," Kip said absently as he watched Jos. The spring in his step was incredible to see.

Jos returned with their orders. "The plate and chicken fingers are hot, so be sure to blow on them, okay?" he told Isaac, and Kip helped Isaac by cutting them up. He also put a few french fries on his plate, and Isaac dug right in, checking that each bite was cool enough before shoving it into his mouth.

Kip kept an eye on Isaac as he began eating his own meal. He was doing well. Sure, there was some spillage, but Isaac didn't let much of his food get away.

"He has a good appetite," the older lady at the next table said. "I have a grandson about his age, and he's so picky about everything he eats."

"Isaac is an eater, there's no way around that," Kip told her. "He's a great little boy."

"Is he your son?" she asked.

"No," Kip said with a stab of regret that surprised him. "He's Jos's brother." Kip looked to the drink station where Jos was filling glasses. "I'm watching him while he's working."

"Where's your mother?" the lady asked Isaac. Kip was about to answer, but Isaac turned to her.

"She's with the angels. We had a fun-ral and everything. I cried, but it's okay. I have an angel mama now." He turned back to his plate and took another bite.

Kip didn't know what to say to that, and apparently the woman didn't either. She nodded and turned back to her companions while Kip began eating.

"Is everything okay?" Billy asked as he approached the table.

"The food is great," Kip said. He wanted to ask how Jos was doing, though that seemed a little like going behind his back. "Like it always is."

"That's good to hear," Billy said. "I understand you and Donald are responsible for our new waiter." Billy looked to where Jos was helping a couple at another table. "He's doing great. When you see Donald, be sure to thank him for us." He smiled and hurried off to another table.

While Isaac continued eating, Kip took the chance to enjoy his meal. He had found that once Isaac was done, he tended to want to be entertained.

A crash sounded from across the dining room. All conversation stopped in the dining room, and a few people clapped like idiots. Kip tensed as he saw Jos bend down, picking up pieces of broken glass. Billy hurried over to him, and the two of them talked briefly. Jos stood, staring, and Kip followed his gaze to a woman who had just walked through the restaurant door.

"Who is that?" Kip asked. Red turned to look and shrugged. She looked to be in her late forties, maybe early fifties. Her lips drew up in a severe expression, and when Billy approached her she motioned and said something to him and then Billy looked back to Jos.

"She's interested in Jos, that's for sure," Red said, and Kip's blood ran cold. Not that there was anything hostile about her, though she looked grumpy and most definitely unhappy, but Jos didn't need anything else heaped on him right now. He was just starting a new job and doing well. He smiled more now and had energy in his step. Kip caught Jos's attention as he cleaned up the last of the broken glasses.

He nodded and came over when he was done. Isaac's plate was nearly empty, and Kip added a few more french fries, which Isaac scooped up with a smile. Other than being startled by the crash, the tension that filled the dining room didn't seem to affect him.

"Do you know her?" Kip asked.

"Yeah. She's my mother's sister. Aunt Kathy. I haven't seen her in years, and I…." He shook a little. "What could she want?"

"I don't know. We're almost done. Why don't you talk to her and try to find out. You can ask her to meet you at the house once you're done here, if you like. Maybe she wants to try to help you somehow." Her disapproving expression left him doubting his words, but Jos nodded slightly. Kip patted Jos's hand softly. Jos moved away from the table and approached the woman. They talked briefly, and then she looked over at them and stood a little straighter, without so much as a smile or a nod.

Jos didn't move for a few seconds, and Billy hurried over, lightly touching his shoulder and guiding him into the back room.

"It'll be okay," Red said, most likely sensing Kip's agitation. "Dude, you really do have it bad. Not that it's bad, but Billy has him, and he'll take care of things. After all, he is working." Red took his last bite and put down his fork. "If you weren't here, Billy would take care of things," Red added after he swallowed.

"I guess I want to be the one to take care of him," Kip said before he realized exactly what had crossed his lips.

"You can't. Not always." Red picked up his water and made funny faces at Isaac, who giggled and then reached for more french fries. Kip put what was left on his plate, and Isaac continued eating.

"He must have a hollow leg," Red said, and Kip took a second to realize he was talking about Isaac. His mind was definitely elsewhere. "Take a deep breath."

Kip did and turned his attention to the woman who stood near the door, looking around. She seemed to be debating about something, and then to Kip's surprise she walked over to their table. Kip stood and met her before she could reach Isaac.

"Can I help you?"

"I saw you speaking to Josten, and since he disappeared…. Is this Isaac? My nephew." She put a weird emphasis on the word *my*.

"Jos said you were his aunt, and yes, this is Isaac." Because of Jos's reaction, he wasn't sure how to behave, but he figured friendly but cautious was best.

"Can you say hello to your aunt?" Kip asked. Isaac looked up and smiled, then he said hello and ate the last of his food. "I'm Kip, a friend of Jos's."

She looked around and then back at him. "Interesting place for a homeless person to be eating."

"Excuse me?" Kip said.

"I know my nephew is homeless and was kicked out of his apartment a few weeks ago. The detective I hired found them a week ago and reported that Jos and Isaac were living on the streets. I assumed that he was doing that because he didn't have friends who would put him up, so I assumed that as a friend, you were homeless as well."

"No. As I said, I'm a friend, and Jos is living with me at the moment. He has a good job here and is working to get his life back together." He wasn't sure why he felt compelled to explain and then decided that none of this was her business and sat back down. "Did Jos invite you back to the house?" Kip asked as he picked up his water glass. As snooty and full of herself as she seemed, he didn't intend to invite her to sit down.

"He did ask me, but I'm afraid of the kind of hovel I might find." He half expected her to pull out hand sanitizer. "If it's all the same, I'm staying at the Carlisle House Bed and Breakfast. Since you're a friend...." Her tone was enough, but Kip was surprised she didn't make air quotes. "He said he could meet me at nine, so if you would be good enough to ask him to come there, I'd appreciate it."

"I'll be sure to tell him," Kip said, and she turned and left the restaurant without another word.

"She's a piece of work," Red said.

"I wonder what she wants and what she said to upset Jos so much." He turned toward the kitchen and saw

Jos come out. He tended to his tables, but the spring in his step was gone. He still had a smile, but it was plastered on and held none of the warmth or excitement from a few minutes earlier.

"Your aunt left a message for you," Kip said when Jos came to their table. "She said to meet her at the Carlisle House." He left out the part about not wanting to visit a hovel.

"Okay," Jos said. "Is there anything else I can get for you?" Jos set the check on the table when Kip shook his head. "I really need to meet her. Would you put Isaac to bed for me?"

"No," Kip said. "But I will meet you at the Carlisle House at nine." He wasn't going to let Jos face that viper alone. "Did she say what she wanted?"

Jos shook his head. "Only that she wanted to talk to me about some of my mother's ridiculous decisions." Jos's hand shook a little as he refilled the glasses. "I have a pretty good idea what that means."

Kip pulled out a credit card and placed it on the bill. "Just relax and take a deep breath. I'll go with you, and you can hear her out, and then if you don't like what she has to say, tell her to take a hike. When was the last time you saw her?"

"Maybe ten years ago. She and Mom didn't get along, so I don't know her well."

"She reminds me of Cruella De Vil," Red said, and Jos smiled genuinely for the first time since she'd made an appearance.

"That's how Mom referred to her. She said that Glenn Close must have met her at some point, because the portrayal in the movie was spot-on."

"Like I said, we'll meet her, and then we can see where to go from there. Don't jump to any conclusions."

Jos nodded and took the check folder. Red opened his wallet and put some bills on the table as a tip, and Kip signed the slip when Jos brought it back. Then he cleaned up Isaac and got him out of his seat. "I'll see you there," Jos said. "And Kip... thanks."

He smiled and wanted to kiss Jos hard to let him know there was nothing to thank him for. Kip touched Jos's arm instead and then left the restaurant with Isaac in his arms.

"Terry should be about done with his training, and I should get home, but call if you need anything," Red said. "You know everyone on the force will help if you need it."

"I do." Kip didn't think it would come to that, but he appreciated his friend's support.

"Call Donald if she starts giving Jos trouble about Isaac. He has a lot of say in what happens, and his support could mean a lot if things start to get nasty."

"You know that's what Jos is afraid of," Kip said.

"Of course he is. People think that homelessness means that you're a failure and a criminal. Neither of which is true. Jos did the best he could and is now getting the help he and Isaac need. That says a lot, and having a job means a great deal too."

"We're getting ahead of things. She might want to help Jos," Kip suggested, even though he didn't believe it. "You need to go, and I promise to call." Kip shook hands with Red and got Isaac to the car. "You up for ice cream?"

Isaac shook his head. "I'm full."

"Then how about we stop at the store and get some ice cream to take home. That way we can have some for when Jos comes home. You'll be hungry again by then."

"Yay," Isaac said. Once he was buckled into his seat, Kip gave him Pistachio, and they went to the store for ice cream and the other things Kip needed. Then he drove home and let Isaac play until it was almost nine.

The Carlisle House was only a few blocks from home. Isaac asked to walk, so Kip got him ready, and with Pistachio under Isaac's arm, they left the house and walked. It was indeed a glorious night. A little cool, but dry. Isaac had a coat on, and he was excited to stop and pick up some of the pretty leaves that were just starting to turn and fall to the ground. It was dark, but the streets were well lit, and Isaac seemed more than happy to look around and watch the cars as they went by.

As they approached the B&B, Isaac started to tire, so Kip picked him up, and Isaac settled right against him, head on his shoulder. This, the closeness to Isaac, as well as the amazing intimacy he felt with Jos, were going to be hard to give up once Jos eventually moved out.

He pulled open the front door and was met by Fred and Mary Braithwaite.

"Kip, we weren't expecting you," Fred said.

"A friend was meeting with one of your guests, and…."

Mary pulled a face and rolled her eyes. "They're in the morning room." She motioned to the door. "Go right on in. If your friend is the young man who arrived a few minutes ago, I think he'll need the support. She's a barracuda." Mary was one of those ladies who never had an unkind word to say about anyone, so that was like a damnation to hell from her.

"Thanks for the warning," Kip said and opened the door. He put Isaac down, and Isaac ran over to Jos and jumped at him, still holding Pistachio.

"You bringed me a good dinner," Isaac said and rubbed his little belly. "Spistachio is hungry, though. He wants ice cream."

Kip smiled. "We have some at home," he reminded him.

"This is a private meeting with my nephew," Jos's Aunt Kathy said.

"I asked him to be here," Jos said.

"I am not going to sit in a room with some homeless stranger—" She turned away from Kip and glared at Jos. "—who you consider an appropriate babysitter for *my* nephew."

"He's my brother," Jos said. "And Mom left instructions for me to care for him in her will."

Kip sat down on the sofa next to Jos in time to hear his aunt scoff lightly under her breath. "Your mother couldn't make a rational decision if her life depended upon it, and as it turned out, it did." To his surprise, she turned her cat eyes at him. "My sister was an alcoholic. Actually, she was a drunk. Alcoholics go to meetings. So whatever she put in that will of hers will be easy enough to contest." She opened her purse and pulled out a tissue. She dabbed the corners of her eyes and then put the tissue back. "And it will be easy enough to convince the authorities that I could give Isaac a better home."

"I don't think so," Kip broke in. "Jos has a job and is providing a good home for Isaac."

"Where? Some hovel he's sharing with you?" she said as she looked down her nose.

"Kip is—" Jos began but stopped when Kip shook his head.

"Do you know either of your nephews at all?" Kip asked.

"My sister and I hadn't spoken much in the last few years, so I didn't have the chance to get to know Isaac or Josten. But I'm hoping to change that."

"By contesting their mother's wishes and fighting to break them apart?" Kip argued. "Sounds to me like you're the one who's a little off."

"And you are? I mean, really?"

"Kip Rogers," he said extending his hand. "I'm an officer with the Carlisle Police Department. Jos and Isaac have been staying with me. He's been working with someone from child services already. Jos has gotten a job and is getting his life put back together for himself and for Isaac. He has plenty of people who are helping him." Kip saw her expression soften for just a few seconds.

"So you aren't homeless?" she asked.

"No. I'm a police officer," Kip said firmly. "So if you wish to cause trouble, I suggest you think twice about it. A good percentage of the police force knows Jos and Isaac. The man we were having dinner with tonight is also a police officer, so more than one of us has seen you do your ice-queen routine…."

"Josten, are you going to allow this… this… person to speak to me that way?"

Jos stared at her. "I barely know you," he said gently to his aunt. "Kip has done a lot for Isaac and me. I had a run of bad luck, and Kip was there for both of us." The defeat in his voice rang through loud and clear.

Jos's aunt stood. "I appreciate you getting my nephews off the street. I can't do much for Josten— he's grown and old enough to make his own decisions and his own way. But I can help Isaac, and I intend to."

"I'd appreciate your help," Jos said.

"I can help by ensuring that Isaac has a proper home and is taken care of in the best way possible. I will be hiring a lawyer to explore what my options are in this situation."

Jos lifted Isaac onto his lap, and Kip could see him retreating into himself. If their aunt understood anything or had the ability to see past her own immediate wants and needs, she'd see how badly she was hurting Jos. Kip saw it instantly and put his arm around Jos's shoulders. He had to let him know that he was there for him.

"Let's go," Kip said gently.

"I'd like to be able to spend some time with Isaac," she said as they reached the door.

Kip turned to Jos, who seemed confused, and his eyes a little glazed over. Most likely in fear. "You don't owe her anything," Kip said.

"I know. But she is my mother's sister," Jos told him and then turned to her. "I'll think about it." Jos took a step out of the room, holding Isaac's hand.

Isaac stopped in the doorway and turned back to his aunt, waving once, then took Jos's hand once again. Kip thanked Mary, who let them out, and then he lifted Isaac into his arms and took Jos's hand.

"Did you eat at work?" Kip asked as they started the walk home.

"Yeah. Darryl tried out some new recipes on us before we started our shifts. It was pretty good but a little weird. Sometimes he gets these ideas for things like brains—offal and stuff. At least that's what Billy told me." Jos stuck out his tongue. Kip figured Jos didn't want to talk about his aunt and what had just happened, and he decided not to force it. "He tried out a liver dish, and it wasn't bad, but it stank up the entire restaurant.

Billy and I ran around trying to get the smell out before we opened. Darryl agreed that he wasn't going to put that on the menu." Jos grew quiet as they walked.

Kip waited for him to say something, but they just continued walking. With each step they took, they seemed to descend further and further into the night, silence pressing tighter around them. When they reached the house, Jos still hadn't said anything more, and when they went inside, Jos took Isaac right upstairs to put him in bed.

Isaac had been asleep most of the way, and Jos must have had an easy time putting him down, because he joined Kip in the living room a little while later.

"I was going to make some tea," Kip said.

Jos shook his head. "All I want is for the crap that keeps getting piled on me to stop."

"Isaac is yours to care for. Your mother said so in her will. There's very little your aunt can do."

Jos nodded. "But what if she really can take better care of Isaac than I can? From the looks of her and what my mother said, she could give Isaac things I could never afford. And she is our aunt, my mother's sister. I suppose if she wants to spend time with Isaac, I can't say no."

Kip sighed. "I told you about my mom." Jos nodded. "After she died, my dad and I went to counseling. He said we were both pretty messed up because of her drinking. I thought we were messed up because of what happened to Adrienne. Dad said no. That was an accident and wasn't my fault. It was my mother's drinking that caused it. Anyway, Dad enrolled both of us in counseling, and it helped. I think he realized he was an enabler. One of the things I learned about myself was that children of alcoholic parents are often nurturers. I took care of Adrienne because my mom couldn't, just like you take care of Isaac."

"Is that bad?" Jos asked.

"No, it's not. But the other thing is that we always try to make everyone happy. I used to think that if my mom was happy, she wouldn't need to drink. I was wrong, but it's what I thought. Is that what you're doing?"

Jos shrugged.

"Did you ever join a group for the families of alcoholics?"

Jos shook his head but didn't answer otherwise.

"I did for a while. I didn't get a lot out of it at first. But once I opened up, I realized a lot of things, including how much mom's drinking had affected me and turned me into the person I am. I also saw how I kept trying to make everyone else happy."

"Yeah. I guess I do that." Jos looked up from where he'd been studying his feet. "If people are happy, then maybe they aren't drinking or they'll like me." Jos met his gaze. "So you're saying I shouldn't worry about what Aunt Kathy wants?"

"I'm saying the only people you need to worry about when it comes to you and Isaac is you and Isaac. If you don't want her visiting, then you can say no."

"But what about if she tries to take Isaac away?" Jos shook as he said the words. Kip saw, and he hated the idea of Jos hurting. He'd been through enough already, and just when things were starting to go his way, this happened.

"We'll call Donald in the morning. He should be able to help us. The thing is, she can't just sue for custody. Well, she can, but it isn't like a regular lawsuit. Family courts are different. With children and custody, there are all kinds of things that have to be done, and she would need to prove a lot to get Isaac."

"I need to get a place of my own. A home for Isaac, so I can demonstrate that he has a safe place."

"I don't know." Kip was about to say that Jos and Isaac had a home right where they were. But he wasn't sure if that would only push Jos away. Also, Kip wanted Jos to choose to be with him, not move in because he thought he had to in order to keep his brother. If Jos felt he had to get a place of his own, then Kip would help him, no matter how happy he was with the two of them staying with him. "We can ask Donald all your questions in the morning."

"Okay." Jos stood and leaned down, kissing Kip on the lips. Then he left the room, and Kip heard him on the stairs. He sighed and then began turning off the lights and locking up the house. By the time he got upstairs, the door to Isaac's room was mostly closed. Kip went to his own room and found an empty bed.

He stared at it and groaned softly. Jos had been staying with him, happily sharing his bed, for the past week. Now it felt to Kip as though something precious and special had been ripped away from him. However, it was Jos's choice, and Kip wasn't going to ask or intrude. If Jos needed to be away, then that was his choice and Kip would respect it.

Kip cleaned up and undressed, getting into bed and turning out the lights. He ended up tossing and turning for a while, then stared up at the ceiling. A soft squeak came from the hallway. Kip figured it was Jos getting up to go to the bathroom. He heard water run and then stop. Finally the door opened and closed. Kip heard the squeak again and rolled away from the door. He had to go to sleep or he'd never make it through his shift.

"Kip," Jos said.

Kip rolled back over and saw Jos standing just inside the door. Kip lifted the blankets, and Jos came over and slid into bed.

Jos felt good in his arms, and all Kip thought about was how he was going to show Jos how much he wanted him in his bed and in his life. Words fell short, so Kip pushed up the shirt Jos was wearing, tugging until it slipped over his head and off his arms. Then he worked Jos's shorts off, stroking his warm, smooth chest and belly. He couldn't seem to get enough, running his hands over Jos's arms, becoming more and more frantic the more he touched and felt.

"You're like an octopus."

"I can't get enough of you, and I could feel you pulling away from me," Kip said as he continued his explorations. He'd never know what Jos would have said next, because he kissed the words away, and Jos wound his legs around Kip's waist. Kip licked down Jos's neck and over his shoulder, sucking lightly on his salty skin, loving when he found one of those spots that made Jos shiver.

"How come I'm naked and you're not?" Jos asked. Kip paused in his amorous adventure to tug off his shirt. Jos pressed his hands to his chest, and Kip's skin pebbled with energy. He'd never experienced anything like it with anyone else. It didn't seem to matter where Jos touched him—he could raise goose bumps in seconds. Kip managed to clear his mind enough to shimmy out of his briefs and toss them out of the bed. Then he tugged Jos closer, chest to chest, hips to hips, Jos's cock sliding alongside his. God, he loved that, and he shivered his own excitement when Jos gyrated his hips.

Jos pressed upward and Kip went with him, letting Jos push him onto his back. Kip liked the way he felt on top of him, and when Jos sucked at his nipple, Kip closed his eyes. Jos lightly scraped his skin with his teeth, and Kip hissed softly as the zing shot straight to his brain and to his dick, which throbbed where it pressed to Jos's belly.

He expected Jos to kiss down his belly, but instead he licked across his chest, lifting Kip's arm over his head. Then he licked down Kip's side, worrying the spots that sent Kip into orbit. Who knew he had a spot just above his hip that felt so damn good? He hadn't, but Jos found it and seemed fascinated.

"Jos," Kip whined. He actually fucking whined.

"You have fun spots all over, and I want to find them all," Jos told him.

Kip wasn't sure how many more of those fun spots he could take him finding before the top of his head blasted off. Jos kissed lower, just above his hip. Kip's leg twitched when Jos licked a spot on the inside of his hip. His cock did a little happy jump, and he wished to hell Jos would shift his attentions. He wasn't sure how to take all this. It felt strange and wonderful, sort of tingly, all at once. "Dammit," Kip groaned.

"What do you want me to do? Suck you?" Jos lifted his face away from Kip's skin and slowly climbed back up him, making small circles with his hands on Kip's belly and chest as he went. "Do you want me inside you?" he asked, and Kip felt him shake in his arms.

"Does that excite you?" Kip asked. "Is that what you want?"

"Yeah," Jos breathed. "I want to see you when I fill you up and watch you when you come just from me being inside you."

Kip shook for a second and then stilled when what Jos had said kicked in. The way he'd said the words, low and deep, had carried him away, though the words themselves didn't sink in right away. "You want to...."

"Yeah," Jos said. "You're really sexy, and I want to watch you when I...." Jos paused and started. "Haven't you ever... bottomed?"

"A long time ago, and I didn't like it very much," Kip admitted. He really didn't want to think about things like that. "I guess I thought that since...." It was his turn to trail off.

"You thought since I'm a little smaller than you that I would be the one to bottom and you'd top? I like both." Jos snuggled closer. "I can make you feel so dang good."

Kip chuckled, letting go of his fear. This was Jos. "You can, huh?"

"Oh, yeah. I'll fill you up and touch that place down deep that will drive you crazy and have you begging me to never stop." Jos slid down his body, and Kip didn't stop him. He wasn't so sure about being the one to get fucked, but he also wasn't selfish and wanted to make Jos happy.

Jos rolled him onto his belly and straddled his legs. Kip felt Jos's long cock slide along his ass, and then Jos stroked his back, massaging deep, from his shoulders to just above his ass, then back again. Over and over he stroked, and for a second, Kip wondered what had happened. He was the one who was supposed to be comforting Jos and making him feel better.

He groaned when Jos massaged his ass, working his fingers into his cheeks and then spreading them apart. He moaned shamelessly as Jos came closer and closer to his opening, teasing him with gentle, magic fingers before finally ghosting them over his opening. Kip quivered and reached for the nightstand. He got out some supplies, fumbling, but managed to keep them from tumbling onto the floor.

Jos got the slick and teased him some more, sliding his fingers around his opening before slowly pressing inside. "What kind of person were you with before?" Jos asked.

"I was young." Kip's answer turned to a groan when Jos curled his finger and rubbed over a spot that sent lightning running to his mind. Kip was well aware of the love button; he'd found it on other guys and had had an amazing time searching for it on occasion, but he'd never had anyone look for his. "So was he," he managed to add.

Jos whispered something about new tricks, and Kip would have growled—in fact, he might have; he couldn't remember, because Jos added a second finger and then pulled away. Kip knew he was getting ready, and soon Jos was right there, cock sheathed, pressing to his entrance. Kip did his best to relax and trust that Jos would make this good for him.

"I want to see you," Kip said. He slowly rolled over. Lying on his belly made him feel too far away from Jos. He needed that connection.

Jos settled between his legs and leaned over him, their lips close together. "You have no idea what this means to me. That you trust me enough to—" Jos swallowed.

"Of course I trust you," Kip said, cupping Jos's cheeks and tugging him into a kiss. As he did, Jos pressed forward and Kip's body opened to him. He hissed against Jos's lips, breaking the kiss as the stretch overwhelmed him. Pain brought tears to his eyes for about two seconds, and then Jos slid inside him and it was all Kip could do to catch his breath.

"Am I hurting you?" Jos asked and stopped.

"Yes… no…. Don't you dare stop," Kip told him as he went through a gamut of sensation in a few seconds. Jos nodded and slid deeper. By the time Jos pressed his hips to Kip's ass, Kip had never felt so full in his life. Jos held still for a few seconds and then withdrew. "Oh God."

"Yeah. In is good, out is amazing," Jos whispered and stroked up his chest. "I know you want to scream. Hell, I do too, but if we do, we're going to have a visitor we don't want at the moment. So you have to be quiet." Jos actually snickered at him.

"I'm not the loud one."

"You will be by the time I'm done with you."

Jos began to move faster. Kip spread his legs farther apart, and Jos shifted a little lower and proved he was right. It took all Kip's restraint not to scream at the top of his lungs. Jos's fingers in him had been one thing, but when he scraped over that spot with his cock, it sent Kip into orbit. And he managed to do it again and again.

Within minutes Kip was gasping for air and riding the edge of control. He felt like a teenager again, and it was all because of Jos. Kip stroked himself a few times and then released his dick because if he didn't, it would all be over in seconds, and he wanted this to last.

Jos seemed to have other ideas. In addition to the fucking driving him crazy, Jos's hands were busy finding more and more ways to touch him to blow his mind.

"Are you trying to tickle me?" Kip growled and stilled Jos's hands.

"No. That's one of your spots, right above your belly button." Jos stroked him there, making little circles, and Kip wasn't sure if he should laugh, groan, or come. He'd have to ask Jos how he knew all this, but for right now he was too far gone to think about it.

"Jos," Kip moaned. He tried to remain in control of his own body, but it wasn't working. Jos was taking care of him and sending him over the moon. Kip bit the inside of his lip as he tried not to scream. He was so close, right there. If Jos gave him just a little bit more, he'd tumble into the abyss, but Jos held him on the knife-edge until his thrusts became ragged, then he picked up the pace, and Kip lost it. He closed his eyes and did everything to keep from flying apart. Kip swore he was flying when his climax slammed into him, and he held on for dear, delicious life. He felt Jos coming as well, but he was so far gone it was on the edge of his awareness.

When Jos lay on top of him, Kip squeezed him close. "You're amazing," Kip breathed once he was able to speak.

"So are you, honey," Jos told him, breathing deeply and settling against him. It was wonderful, the two of them in the darkness, no sound other than their breathing, and nothing at all between them. "I think we need to clean up or we'll be stuck together."

"No one I'd rather be stuck to," Kip breathed, not wanting to move at all. Once their bodies separated, Jos slowly got off the bed and tugged Kip to his feet. They ended up in the shower in the near dark, groping and holding each other up as the warm water coursed over them. Kip didn't want to open his eyes and simply held Jos until the water went cold. The nightlight he kept in the bathroom was enough light for them to dry each other and hang up the towels. Then, to be safe, they both pulled on shorts and got back into bed.

Jos snuggled close, his butt and back pressed to Kip. "Thank you," Jos whispered.

"For what?"

"Giving me what I needed." Jos rolled over. "I know you're strong and big and sexy. You're used to being in control, but tonight I needed that more than you can possibly know, and you gave me that."

Kip swallowed hard and pulled Jos close, holding him without saying anything. He didn't want to burst his bubble, but all he had wanted was to make Jos happy. Sometimes things just worked out. "Go to sleep," Kip whispered, and Jos rolled back over. Kip spooned against him and closed his eyes. Within minutes he was asleep.

A clap of thunder woke him in the middle of the night. Kip snuggled deeper under the covers and closed his eyes once again. He loved storms and listening to the rain. After a few minutes, however, the door opened. "Jos, Spistachio is scared."

He didn't even answer before Isaac ran around to the other side of the bed and climbed in next to Jos, who shifted away from Kip slightly.

"It's okay. Just a little thunder and lightning. It won't last too long," Jos said, and Kip heard Isaac whisper something about God being mad. Jos soothed him, and eventually Isaac settled back to sleep.

For a while, as Kip dozed off once again, he was able to imagine that he was part of a family once again. Of course, just like the one he'd had and lost piece by piece, he knew he needed to make the most of what he had before something happened and he lost Jos and Isaac as well. That seemed to be the way of things for him: people left, and he tended to end up alone, like it or not.

CHAPTER 6

THE FOLLOWING day Jos's Aunt Kathy contacted him, and Jos brought Isaac over to the bed-and-breakfast before his shift at work. She was his only living relative, and Jos thought Isaac should get to know her a little. Jos was very wary around her, and when she asked questions about how he'd been living and if he needed any help, he gave vague answers. When she asked if she could help, Jos told her that he had a lot of support and that he was currently looking for a place of his own. What he felt he really needed was some money to help him until he got paid and so he could contribute at Kip's, but he'd be damned if he would ask her for anything. So he kept quiet and let Isaac be Isaac.

"What's your bear's name?" Aunt Kathy asked.

"This is Weeble," Isaac said, holding up the worn animal. "And this is Spistachio. Uncle Kip got him for me. I said I wanted a real horse, and he got me one." Isaac hugged him tight. "I know this isn't a *real* real

horse. But it's better than a Lego horse." That seemed
to settle things for Isaac, and he ran Pistachio around
the room, making galloping and neighing noises.

"Do you like where you live?" his aunt asked
Isaac, and Jos stiffened slightly.

"Yes. It's really nice, and I have a big room with
a big-boy bed all my own." Isaac returned to playing,
and Jos breathed with relief that Isaac didn't add information about where Jos had been sleeping. He wasn't
ashamed that he was gay or that he was sleeping with
Kip. That was the best thing to come out of this whole
mess that he'd made of their lives. But he didn't want
to give his aunt any additional ammunition if she truly
decided to try to make trouble.

"Do you have other toys?" she asked.

"They got splatted," Isaac said and went back to
playing.

"I found a place I could afford, but the landlord
was a crook," Jos said. "I lost my job and he kicked us
out. It's a long story, but I wasn't able to take anything,
and he tore the building down with most of our stuff
still in it. Kip and his friend Red made it so we could
get some of our important things. The landlord said we
were just being given notice, but he really kicked us
out. The guy's slime. But a lot of our things were lost.
Kip dug through the rubble when Isaac told him where
Weeble was." Jos smiled. "You should have seen him.
He pushed aside bricks and pieces of drywall. He and
Red even lifted a piece of wall and shoved it aside until they found what was left of Isaac's bed. He'd put
Weeble under it when the men had come, to try to keep
him safe."

For a second Jos thought he might have seen a flash
of emotion in his aunt's eyes, but then she looked as

detached as usual. His aunt sat in her chair and watched Isaac play. After a few minutes, Jos called him over. It was clearly evident that his aunt wasn't going to join him or spend much time interacting directly with him. It was almost like she wasn't sure quite what to do.

"Where does Isaac go during the day?"

"When I'm working, he goes to a day care school. They aren't just babysitters. They're very highly rated and work with Isaac on his numbers and letters. Everything is very constructive and fun. Isaac loves it. Donald, the partner of another of the officers Kip works with, helped me find it and get Isaac in. He's with child services and has been very helpful." Jos lifted Isaac onto his lap.

"Can we go now?" Isaac asked.

"Yes. I have to take you home to get ready for school. Pistachio and Weeble can keep each other company while you're gone. Uncle Kip will pick you up like he did yesterday."

"Can we eat with you like yesterday?"

"I don't think so. But Uncle Kip said he'd make you macaroni for dinner." That was always a hit.

"And chicken nuggets?" Isaac asked.

"I swear you're going to turn into a chicken nugget," Jos said, tickling Isaac, who giggled and squirmed.

"Hi, Uncle Kip," Isaac said and slid off Jos's lap, running over to Kip when he came into the bed-and-breakfast's morning room. Jos hadn't been expecting him, but he did a double take when he saw him in his uniform. Kip looked extra strong and imposing in it.

"Are you ready to go?" Kip asked Isaac, sharing a nod with Jos's aunt but nothing more. Jos figured his unexpected appearance was meant to intimidate. Jos wasn't sure how much of an effect it would have on his aunt, but dang, he was enjoying the view. "Your shift starts in an hour, and I figured I could help get Isaac to school to give you time to get ready. I need to be at the station in half an hour."

Jos looked at his aunt. "It was good to see you."

"We'll talk soon, I'm sure," she said formally and a little ominously before shaking Jos's hand.

"Say good-bye to your aunt," Jos told Isaac, who pulled away from Kip and ran over to her, barreling into her legs. Isaac hugged her and said good-bye. Aunt Kathy lightly touched the top of Isaac's head.

"Bye," she said with the first hint of a smile reaching her lips. Isaac pulled away and then raced back to Kip, who scooped him up into his arms.

"Let's go, little man. We have places to be, and you have friends to meet." Kip shared another nod with their aunt and left the room. It was surprising. He could be so stern with others and on the job, but with Isaac and him, Kip was nothing but warmth and care.

Once they stepped out of the room, Kip leaned closer and lightly kissed him.

"Ooooh, kissing," Isaac crooned and made a yucky face. "Carly tried to kiss me." He shook his head violently, still making a face. "I told Carly to keep her girly lips to herself."

"You don't want girls to kiss you?" Jos asked.

"I don't want nobody to kiss me. That's yucky." He nodded as though he'd said the final word on the subject. Jos helped Isaac into his jacket and then put on his own. Kip's car was parked right out front, and as soon as Isaac was buckled in, Kip drove them home to get ready for the rest of their day.

THE NEXT week was quiet. He and Kip worked, and Jos took care of Isaac. On his break one day, he talked with Donald on the phone. Donald had been having a difficult time finding an apartment Jos could afford at the moment.

"I might have something coming up. A friend who owns the building next to Café Belgie told me a tenant just gave them notice. It's a small place, but it has an extra room that could be a bedroom for Isaac," Donald told him. "Do you think you can wait?"

"I hope so," Jos said, hesitating. "We're all getting along at Kip's, but I don't want to overstay my welcome. He's been so good to us, but I'm sure he wants to get his life back to normal." A jab of cold shot through him, and he shivered.

Donald didn't answer right away. "Okay. I'll get your name in for the apartment. I got word that you should be hearing from Social Security soon. It may take a little while to get payments flowing, but I'm hopeful the approval will come through."

"What about my aunt and what she said?" Jos asked.

"Have you heard from her in the past week?" Donald asked.

"No. She left and hasn't called or anything," Jos said. "I'm hoping that means she's changed her mind. I don't know my aunt very well, but she doesn't look like the type to not get what she wants."

"It won't be easy for her, especially the more you put your life together and build a stable home for Isaac. Every day her chances get slimmer and slimmer."

Jos breathed a sigh of relief. "That's good to hear." He looked at the clock and realized his break was almost over. "I have to go, but I'll talk to you later. Please tell your friend that I can stop over to see the apartment whenever they have time."

"I will. And let me know if you hear anything from your aunt." They disconnected, and Jos put his phone back in his locker before returning to work. When he entered the dining room, he was surprised to see Kip at one of his tables, looking amazing in his uniform.

"This isn't the donut shop," Jos teased. "You must be in the wrong place." His nerves kicked up just like they had when Kip brought Red and Isaac in for dinner. His belly fluttered and he took a deep breath. "What would you like?"

"Just a cup of coffee," Kip said. He motioned for Jos to sit down when he returned. "There was a message on the answering machine at home from a friend. It seems your aunt has filed for custody of Isaac. There weren't any details in the message, and I don't want you to get upset. She can do whatever she wants, but she isn't going to be able to take your brother away."

"How do you know?"

"I think your aunt is so used to getting her own way that she doesn't see that she has no standing here. Not really. I debated about telling you later, but I didn't want it to be a surprise if a process server were to find you or something."

"But what do I do?" Jos could feel the world he'd just started to build for him and Isaac starting to crumble around him.

"At the moment, nothing. You still need to work and do your job. That's the biggest thing in your favor. You have a job and a place to live. You can demonstrate that you can take care of both you and Isaac, and you've fulfilled your mother's wishes. All of that is going to be hard to fight."

"But I can't afford a lawyer," Jos whispered. "I don't have any money, and I won't allow you to pay for that like you did the extra day care charges." Kip's expression turned sheepish. "Yes, I know what you did, and I'm grateful, but this is something I have to figure out for myself."

"There are plenty of ways you can get help. We'll call Legal Aid."

Jos nodded. He figured that was true. But he'd been helped enough by Kip, Donald, Red—everyone he'd met recently. Jos was starting to feel like he and Isaac were everyone's charity case, and that had to end. This whole thing had to end. "Let me think about what I have to do," Jos said and stood up. "I need to go back to work."

"I'll let you know if I hear anything else, and you do the same," Kip said. Jos nodded as his mind began throwing out options, none of them very attractive. "Try not to dwell on it. There isn't anything she can do right away."

Kip could say that, but Jos was scared and angry. He wasn't going to let his ice-queen aunt take his brother away from him. "I'll try," he said, but he knew it was a lie. How could he think about anything else?

"We can talk over dinner and decide what to do," Kip said, finishing his coffee. "I promise we'll figure this out."

Jos nodded. Kip handed him some money for the coffee and then left. Jos crumpled the bill in his hand without thinking about it. He cleared the table, automatically going about the tasks he had to do. He knew what had to happen. Without a doubt, he had to make sure Isaac remained safe.

"Is everything okay?" Billy asked.

He nodded and asked if he could make a phone call. Billy told him it was all right, and Jos hurried to the back and called the day care center, making sure they knew that only he or Kip were approved to pick up Isaac, and if anyone else tried, to call the police. They agreed and explained that was their policy. Feeling a little better that Isaac was safe at the moment, he began to plan what he was going to do to ensure that continued.

"WHAT ARE you doing?" Kip asked that evening when he came upstairs. "I stopped to pick up Isaac, and they said you already had." He came into the bedroom as Jos put clothes for him and Isaac into a bag.

"We have to go. I can take him away, and she can go to hell." Jos slammed the drawer on the dresser and looked around the room.

"Running isn't the answer," Kip told him, but Jos wasn't up to listening. All his energy was focused on Isaac and keeping his family together.

"She called me today, and… this is what I have to do," Jos said. "You saw her. My aunt has money and she can buy what she wants."

"Did she actually say that?" Kip asked.

"Not in so many words." Jos shrugged. "I don't have money to hire fancy lawyers like she can. Whatever I do, she'll make me look like a homeless person who couldn't take care of Isaac, even though I did everything I could for him. When we had food, I made sure he ate first. Once there was only one bed in the shelter, so I slept on the floor next to him so he could have the bed." Jos picked up the bag and began carrying it down the stairs. "He's the only family I have, and I'm not going to let some stranger take it away."

"She's your aunt, your mother's sister," Kip said.

"I thought you would be on my side," Jos said, severing Kip's last threads of hope. "You don't think I'm good enough either. You think I should let her take Isaac away." Jos dropped the bag near the front door and whirled around. "How could you?" He shook with fury and ached deep in his heart, but he couldn't stop.

"I am on your side," Kip said, but it sounded hollow to Jos's ears. Kip held Jos's shoulders, staring into his eyes. "You can't do this."

"I have to." His desperation was taking over, and he had to get out of there.

"If you run and the courts can't find you or Isaac, they'll issue a warrant for your arrest, and guess who'll have to try to find you? Red, Carter, me…. All of the people who care about you. Do you think everyone has been helping you just to help you? All of us have grown to care for you and Isaac. If you leave, all of that will vanish."

Jos stood still, blinking as Kip's words and tone got past the need to flee.

"You have a job, and you and Isaac have a safe place to live. You're rebuilding your life, and you have to stop thinking that all of it is going to be yanked away from you at any second."

"Then what do I do?" Jos asked. The air around him seemed thin, and he felt as light-headed as he had after he'd been attacked. Hell, he was being attacked again, only this time it was his aunt, and she was going to use lawyers to fuck him over rather than… the way Tyler had tried.

"You fight. If you want to raise Isaac, then you have to stand up to her and let her know that you aren't going to back down."

"Uncle Kip," Isaac called as he came down the stairs, Pistachio and Weeble each under an arm. "Are you mad at Jos?" Isaac shuffled over, and Jos's resolve crumbled like a house of cards. He couldn't put his brother back out on the streets again.

"No," Kip said. "He and I are discussing things, and I was talking too loud." Kip tightened his grip and then pulled Jos against him. "You can't go, because I don't want you to," Kip whispered. "You have to fight so you and Isaac can have a home together."

"But what if I lose?" Jos asked, his voice muffled.

"Then we'll fight some more, but if you run, you'll definitely lose, because all the good things you've made happen will be gone. No job, no home…. That means that the courts will step in. But you're building a better life for Isaac, and anyone can see that—well, except your aunt. Maybe if you invite her to visit, she'll be able to see the life that you're trying to build, and maybe she'll support you too, rather than try to fight you."

Jos shook and Kip held him tighter. "I don't want to see her again either, but it can't hurt to try." Kip's phone went off like a siren. "I need to get that. It's Carter. He was doing a favor for me." Kip stepped away, and Jos leaned against the wall and then slumped down it. Isaac climbed on his lap and handed him Weeble.

"It's okay. Don't be sad."

Kip whipped around, the phone still pressed to his ear. "Hold on," he said into the phone and nearly dropped the phone in his haste to set it on the table. Then Kip helped Jos to his feet and got him and Isaac to the sofa. "Breathe, sweetheart. Carter is looking into something for me, and I have to talk to him, but I need to make sure you're okay."

"I'm okay." He clutched Weeble to his chest. "Really. I just need to catch my breath." Jos breathed deeply, and Kip went to get his phone. Isaac sat next to Jos and then climbed into his lap, and Jos set Weeble next to him and held Isaac. Jos knew his brother could feel his agitation, and he needed to get it under control.

When Kip came back in the room, he sat with them. "I'll go make some dinner."

"What was the call about?" Jos asked and then realized he really didn't have a right to ask.

"I asked Carter to take a look into a few things for me, and he had a few questions." Kip picked up Isaac. "Come on, little man. Let's make dinner and give Jos a few minutes. Okay?"

Kip lifted Isaac's shirt and blew on his belly. Isaac giggled and squirmed as Kip then zoomed him out of the room and down toward the kitchen. Jos breathed steadily and tried to rationalize what Kip had told him. He did have a job, and he was going to get a place to live. Isaac was happy and making friends in school. Things were a lot better than they had been a few weeks ago, and they would continue to get better. He just kept wondering if it was going to be good enough.

"Jos," Isaac said, running in. "Kip is making pancakes!"

"For dinner?" Jos asked, and Isaac nodded vigorously, licking his lips.

"I asked him what he wanted, and he said pancakes, so that's what we're having," Kip said from the doorway with a mixing bowl in his hand. "Do you want to come help us?"

Jos nodded and got up. Isaac raced to the sofa and grabbed Weeble, carrying him into the kitchen. Pistachio sat on one of the kitchen chairs, and Isaac put

Weeble on another before hurrying over and climbing back up the stool that Kip had brought over for him.

"What should I do?"

"Make bacon," Kip said, rolling his eyes with a smile. "If we're going to have breakfast for dinner, then let's go the whole way." Kip set down the bowl and put an arm around him. "I know this is hard for you, and your aunt isn't making it easier."

"Family is supposed to treat you better than that," Jos said. "Isaac and I deserved better and never got it."

"I didn't either. At least not very often. But sometimes we make our own family and to hell with the rest of them."

"Uncle Kip said a naughty word," Isaac crooned.

"It's okay. Uncle Kip was being naughty, and he's sorry." Jos understood what Kip was saying. At least he thought he did. Was Kip speaking rhetorically, or specifically about them? Jos turned so he could see Kip's eyes because he wanted to be sure. But Kip released him and turned to the griddle on the stove.

"Can you make a pancake shaped like Weeble?" Isaac asked, watching from his stool as Kip poured the batter. Kip made a teddy bear shape, and Isaac clapped, watching as Kip waited for it to cook and then flipped it over.

When the pancake was done, Kip put it on a plate and added some butter and syrup. Then he settled Isaac in his chair with a glass of juice and a fork. "Be sure to blow on the bites so they aren't hot."

Isaac grinned and then began to eat like he was starving. "Good," he said with a syrupy smile.

"How is that bacon coming?" Kip asked him. Of course Jos had been too busy watching everything else to actually do much. Kip lit the burner farthest from him, and Jos began cooking the bacon.

"Slow down," Jos said gently to Isaac. "There's plenty more, and no one is going to take it from you. Kip will definitely make you more."

Isaac barely slowed down. He finished his pancake and brought his plate back to Kip, dripping syrup on the floor as he went. Jos was about to yell at him, but he paused when Kip took the plate. "Let me clean up your drips, little man, and then I'll make you another one."

"Can you do Spistachio this time?" Isaac asked.

"I'll try. Now go sit down and wait a little bit, okay?" Kip wiped up the floor and got Isaac settled while Jos took off the first strips of bacon and added more to the pan. "Every Sunday night after my mom died, Dad and I had breakfast for dinner. He loved waffles and pancakes, so this was our thing once a week. He and I cooked together, and then we sat and talked. It was always our time as a family."

Jos nodded and finished the bacon. His heart raced as he wondered again exactly what Kip was saying. "I never had a lot of family time. Mom wasn't interested in much other than where her next drink was coming from, so I don't know how a family should behave. I want to give Isaac a better family than the one I had, but I don't know how to do it."

"Hey." Kip gripped his shoulders. "If it wasn't for my dad and the fact that after Mom died he got us both help so we could learn just how much Mom's drinking had affected us, things would have been very different for me. Your mom's drinking affected you, and I know you're trying not to let it affect Isaac. But it will."

"I know. Sometimes I fall back on the things I learned from her. How do I know how to be part of a real family if I never have been?" Jos turned off the burner and transferred the bacon to a plate. Kip took the stack of pancakes to the table, including one that looked like Pistachio—or at least it was a vaguely horse-shaped blob. He placed it on Isaac's plate and fixed the pancake for him.

"It's all right. I'm no expert, but we'll figure it out together." Kip looked him straight in the eye, and Jos nodded without thinking. "We have good friends and people who care. That helps a lot." Kip set the plates on the table, and they sat down. Isaac reached for the bacon, but thankfully it was out of his reach. Jos gave him a piece, and Isaac dug right in.

"Do you ever think he'll get used to having enough food and won't stuff himself?" Jos asked.

"It'll happen. Everything takes time. The memories of being hungry need to fade." Kip took some pancakes and passed the plate to Jos.

When Isaac was too stuffed to eat any more, he played in the corner of the kitchen with Weeble and Pistachio.

"So I was thinking that I could try to invite my aunt for dinner or something," Jos said. "I think I want to try to take your advice and let her see where Isaac and I are living. I was wondering if she'd actually come, but then she can't not come. Otherwise she's giving up a chance to get to know the nephew she's supposedly so interested in taking care of."

Kip grinned. "Now you're thinking. Go ahead and invite her, but say nothing about the lawsuit. At this point, pretend you don't know and just act like you're being nice. That will throw her off. When she agrees, we'll plan what we hope to get from her that evening."

"What do you mean?" Jos asked. "I was hoping to convince her to drop the whole thing."

"Maybe. But she has information we need. You don't know much about her, so we need to find out what we can. Oh, and when you get a chance, do an internet search. Everything we can find out will help." Kip seemed way too happy. Jos didn't know why, but was less nervous now that he had a plan to start dealing with his aunt. His appetite, which had been lacking, returned with a vengeance. He reached for some of the bacon and actually began to feel better about everything. Kip seemed to have that effect on him.

"After dinner I'll search and see what I can find," Jos said.

"Good decision. Everything seems better when you have a plan of attack. And you don't feel as out of control, which is settling in and of itself."

JOS PUT Isaac to bed, and then, while Kip cleaned up the kitchen and did the dishes, he sat at the kitchen table using the laptop, with a notebook nearby. He whistled a few times, and Kip looked over in time to see Jos jotting down notes.

"She runs a wedding business, it looks like. Dresses, events, flowers, catering, the whole works. It looks like she does everything for the bride but get the groom to propose. The prices are—" He whistled again. "I was able to find out her address. It's hard to see from Google Earth, but it looks like a nice enough house."

"Does it look like she's ever been married?" Kip asked.

"Only if she was and changed her name back. I found her under Katherine Applewhite, so I'm going to guess that she never was."

Kip humphed. "Didn't she say that she had someone find you?"

"A private detective or something. Yeah," Jos said.

Kip nodded. "Why? She's never met Isaac before, and you haven't seen her in years. Why would she care? If you weren't part of her life, then why wouldn't she just leave you alone?"

"She's family?" Jos answered, but his tone clearly registered that he didn't believe his own answer. "I don't know. I mean, if she really cared, she'd try to help both of us instead of just taking Isaac. My mother hated her, and I've met her twice and I can say I don't much like her either. She wouldn't play with Isaac, and when he offered her Weeble, she looked as though she was going to get germs and carefully set him aside. I don't get it." Jos sighed and closed the computer. "I got some information, but…."

"It confused me too. So I asked Carter to look into her when he had a minute. I want to believe that she's doing this because she thinks she can provide a better life for Isaac than you can. At least that would mean that she has a heart." But he wasn't so sure. If that were the case, then she'd have been warmer and would seem genuinely interested in Isaac. He also thought she'd be interested in helping them both. "Something doesn't feel right, and he can dig things out of computer systems that other people can't. There are limits to what he can do since this isn't an investigation, but he said he'd try."

"I have her address and telephone number, so I'm going to try calling to leave a message."

"Okay. Do you want me with you?" Kip asked as Jos stood and began pacing the floor. Jos dialed, and Kip stayed where he was, close enough to be there, but if this was something Jos felt he had to do on his own, he'd let him. The call seemed to go to voicemail, and Kip heard Jos leave a message inviting her to come to dinner. He did just as they discussed and didn't let on that he knew what she was planning.

"All right. Now we'll see if she calls back," Jos said and set his phone down, staring at it as if he expected it to ring at any moment.

"Come on," Kip said. "Let's go up to bed. It's been a rough day, and we need some rest. We'll figure out something."

Jos picked up his phone, and Kip put an arm around his shoulder. "I'm really starting to believe that," Jos said.

"Good." Kip stopped and drew him into a kiss. "You really need to." They went upstairs, turning out the lights as they went. At the top of the stairs, Kip released Jos and let him choose where he wanted to sleep. He hoped Jos would stay with him, but he didn't want to put pressure on him. Jos took his hand, and Kip slowly went to his bedroom.

They took turns getting ready for bed. Jos used the bathroom first, so when Kip took his turn and came out, turning off the light, he joined Jos in bed. They curled together and Jos held him. Kip made no move for sex. With everything that had happened, being close was enough. Jos needed to know he was there; that was what was important. Kip was beginning to see the delight to be found in just holding Jos in the dark.

CHAPTER 7

JOS WAS on pins and needles. He'd called his aunt and was still wondering if she was going to call back. She did, finally, after a whole day and said she would come to dinner. Neither of them had said a word about the nebulous custody battle. Jos still hadn't heard anything official, and he hoped he could head this off.

"Should we serve wine?" Jos asked.

"Let's have some in case your aunt likes it." Kip smiled. "Maybe a few belts will loosen her up."

Kip chuckled, and Jos did as well. Over the past week, Jos had begun to feel comfortable in his own skin. It was a new feeling for him, but it was good. Work was going well, and Social Security had approved survivor benefits for Isaac. It seemed when enough people pushed for something and knew how to work the system, things happened. He'd been told it would be a few months before he began getting the money, but it was coming. His life—their life—was coming together.

A knock cracked on the front door. Jos jumped slightly, and Kip stroked his shoulder. "Remember the plan and don't let her get to you. We have a purpose." He smiled as Isaac raced through the house and opened the front door.

"Aunt Kathy," Isaac said happily.

Jos cringed slightly, but he'd kept everything that was happening from Isaac, so a visit from their aunt was just another person Isaac knew coming to visit. When Jos and Kip entered the hall, Isaac had his arms wrapped around her legs, and she patted his head uncomfortably. Something about this picture did not make sense at all to him. "Come and see my pony." Isaac took her by the hand and began pulling her toward the living room.

"Pony?" Aunt Kathy said. "Oh, your toy," she said from the other room.

Jos hurried to the kitchen and got the plate of meat, cheese, and crackers that Kip had made and set it on the coffee table.

"Is this where you live?" Aunt Kathy asked.

"It's Kip's house, yes, but I just got an apartment, and Isaac and I will be moving there in a few days." He had a place to live, a job, and Isaac was cared for while he was at work. "Kip was good enough to take us in and help us." Jos sat down. "Would you like something to drink? I have some wine, or there is also water and soda."

"Me too?" Isaac said.

"I have juice for you," Jos told Isaac and excused himself. He got the cup from the refrigerator and brought it to Isaac. By then Kip had left to get some wine, and he returned with three glasses and handed each of them one.

"What do you do?" Jos asked, sitting down. He wasn't going to let on that he'd investigated her.

"I plan weddings," she answered. "How is the job going?"

"I really like it. They pay me pretty well, and I'm good at my job, so I make pretty good tips. Darryl and Billy own Café Belgie and two other restaurants in town. One is Greek and the other Italian. Darryl really knows his business, and this past week they needed help at Napoli so I got an extra shift there."

"Who watches Isaac? You certainly don't leave him alone, and he must work interesting hours," she said, gesturing toward Kip.

"He goes to a day care that doubles as a preschool. I get vouchers for day care, and that helps a lot. A friend helped me find an apartment I can afford. As I become more established, I'll become more self-sufficient." Jos sipped from his glass, and he could almost see his aunt calculating behind her eyes. "Isaac and I were having a difficult time of it, but I think we're on the right track now."

"So you don't plan on living here?" she asked, looking around. "With him."

"Kip offered," Jos answered warmly. He liked that Kip had made him the offer. "But in the end he and I decided to take things slow. I'll get my own apartment, and we'll date."

She nodded. "It sounds as though you have everything thought out."

"I have to. Isaac deserves the best home I can get for him." Jos glanced to where Isaac was playing on the floor. "It's so good to see him happy." He lifted his gaze back to Kip and saw him tilt his head toward his aunt. "What sorts of weddings do you plan?"

"Whoever can afford me," she added and cleared her throat. "I started the business ten years ago. I needed something to occupy my time, and I was always good at throwing parties."

Jos glanced over at Kip and then back to his aunt. "What did you do before you started the business?"

"This and that," his aunt answered evasively. "I don't know what your mother ever told you about how we grew up, but she and I each had a trust fund from our parents. When your mother got hers, she spent most of it very quickly." Aunt Kathy seemed to have eaten something distasteful. Jos knew his mother was no saint, but his aunt's disdain was perfectly clear, and it hurt. "I was careful. I got an education, lived simply, and worked hard. If you must know, I taught school for a few years and worked in a library for a while. I was put in charge of the library fundraisers and found I could throw a great party. Eventually I used the money from the trust to start the business."

"That sounds really nice," Jos said. "I'm working hard too. You probably know Mom didn't leave much, so I'm building my own life and one for Isaac without the help you had." Jos kept his head high. He'd come a long way in a short time.

"I think it's only fair to tell you—"

"What?" Jos interrupted. "That you think you can give Isaac a better life than I can?" Isaac whined softly at the tone and hurried over, standing between Jos's knees. "Children need a lot more than money and things. They need love and care, and you can't give him that." Jos put an arm around Isaac's chest, holding him to him. "You saw how he greeted you. Isaac was happy to see you. He'd only met you once, but he greeted you like an old friend, and you treated him like he was a leper."

"I've never had children."

"Is that why you want to try to take him?" Jos asked, veering off the script they had prepared. "Because you have to know that it won't happen. I have a job, a place to live, Isaac has friends at day care, and we're building a life."

"Kathy," Kip interrupted. "Your lawyer has to have warned you how difficult what you're trying to do is going to be. The courts aren't going to give you custody of Isaac over his mother's express wishes."

"Is that why you asked me here? To try to convince me to drop my bid for custody?" she asked, setting down her glass.

"No," Jos said. "I asked you here because you're our only relative. Neither of us knows you very well." Jos tried to get the conversation back on plan. "You're our aunt, and we have no other relatives. What I don't understand is why you want to take Isaac away instead of trying to help us. You could be part of both our lives instead of trying to tear our family apart." Jos held Isaac a little tighter. "We need you, but not like this."

Aunt Kathy looked at all of them and then stood up. "I think I need to be going now."

"No. I think you need to sit down and hear what Jos has to say," Kip said in the same tone he'd used that first night when he told Tyler to get on the ground. It was a tone that was hard not to obey, and Jos watched Aunt Kathy slowly lower herself back into the chair. "I don't know what's going on yet, but you do realize I will get to the bottom of whatever it is you're trying to hide." Kip's gaze was hard as stone, and Jos felt a chill for a second. He hoped that look was never leveled at him.

"I have no idea what you're talking about," Aunt Kathy said, holding her shiny black purse on her knees as though it was a shield.

"I think you do. The economy has taken quite a toll on your business in the last few years. Brides who used to pay a fortune for your services have cut back. Some are doing it themselves and others are making do with less. In a business like yours, built on excess, that has to hurt."

"I don't need to stay here and—"

"I think you do," Kip countered, and Jos watched, wondering where Kip was going with this. It was obvious that Kip had hit on something. His aunt had paled slightly, and her knuckles were whiter than they had been, especially where the leather of her bag was now creased from where she gripped it.

"I'll dig as deep as I have to, and so will some of my friends. They're experts at finding nuggets of information, including details about your business."

"Those records are not public. How could you possibly know how my business is doing?" Aunt Kathy snapped.

"I didn't," Kip said. "You just told me." He turned to Jos and smiled. "So I bet a costly legal battle isn't going to do you any good. And it will be very costly—we will see to that. A month ago, when you first found Jos and Isaac and did nothing, you might have been able to help them. Instead you had a detective report back to you. You didn't lift a finger to help them. Why?"

Aunt Kathy shook.

"Whatever you're hiding, I will find it, and then I'll use it to our best advantage and your worst. If it's even remotely illegal, or just smells bad, I'll make sure you face charges, and then what will happen to your business? Your business will turn around if you can hang on long enough, but if your reputation is damaged, you'll never recover." Kip stepped back. "I think you should go now and think about what you truly want."

Jos's aunt got to her feet. She was visibly shaken and said she thought staying for dinner wasn't appropriate. Kip seemed dang pleased with himself. Isaac looked at each of them in turn, clearly confused.

"Say good-bye," Jos whispered.

Isaac nodded. "Bye, Aunt Kathy." He didn't move for a few seconds until Jos prodded him. Isaac pulled Weeble off the sofa and tucked him under his arm before approaching his aunt. This time Aunt Kathy knelt down and hugged Isaac gently. She was clearly still uncomfortable, but she was making an effort. "Bye-bye."

Jos walked his aunt to the door. Neither of them said a word, and his aunt fumbled slightly as she stepped outside. "Are you staying at the bed-and-breakfast again?" Jos asked as he followed his aunt out onto the porch.

"Yes. I'll be leaving in the morning," she told him. She descended the stairs and shuffled down the walk. Jos stood under the porch light, watching as she got into her Lexus and then drove away down the street.

"What was all that about?" Jos asked when Kip came up behind him. "Did Carter call you about something?"

"Nothing other than the last time he and I talked, but he mentioned that her business must be tough right now, and that got me thinking. There was something about the way she sat and how nervous she was. She didn't want to talk about herself or the business that she should be so proud of, so I took a shot and hit pay dirt." Kip chuckled. "I didn't think it would be that easy."

"Do you think she'll give up now?"

"She looked pretty defeated, and she has to see that you and Isaac have a home and a life now. There is nothing for her to gain, but.... I'm still wondering what's behind it. She had a reason and something she wanted."

"How will we find out?"

"Carter. He'll dig into it." Kip took his hand. "We should go back inside and see what Isaac is up to, and get some dinner. We spent enough time making it—we might as well enjoy it."

Jos nodded and let go of a sigh of relief. "I hope this is over."

"I do too. But my instincts are telling me that we're missing something. I'll talk to Carter tomorrow and see if he has any ideas. For now, though, we aren't going to worry about it." He smiled and pulled Jos close to him.

"We're outside and don't want to scare the neighbors," Jos whispered, and Kip moved in for a kiss.

"They can call the police, then," Kip told him and then cut off his amused chuckle with a kiss that curled Jos's toes. If anyone was watching, they got an eyeful, especially when Kip slid his hands down his back and grabbed his buttcheeks, pressing them tighter together.

"Ewww, kissing," Isaac called from the doorway.

Kip pulled his lips away, chuckled, and then kissed him again. Jos closed his eyes, reveling in the salty richness of Kip's lips. He was safe, and he realized he'd felt that way for a while. Kip made him feel as though nothing could touch him and that no matter what happened he'd be there for him— for both of them.

"Yucky," Isaac said, and Kip released Jos. They shared a warm smile, and then Kip raced to Isaac, scooping him up to giggles that echoed through the house and out into the night. Jos shivered from the fall chill and went back inside, closing the door, shutting out the cold.

The house looked, felt, and sounded warm. Jos couldn't help thinking that a few weeks ago he'd been on the other side of that door, out in the cold with no one. Now he was on the inside with Kip, where everything seemed right. When he and Kip had talked a few days ago, he'd thought he needed to be on his own, to make it himself independently. But now he wasn't so sure that was what he wanted. All the good things that had happened to him had been because of Kip. What if he couldn't take care of himself and Isaac? What if he moved in with Kip and things didn't work out? Jos knew he had to be able to survive on his own. Jos cared about Kip a lot, and in a way he loved him for everything he'd done for them. But was what he felt based on relief or something more? All these questions raced through his head like cars on a superhighway of angst and uncertainty. The truth was that he didn't trust himself at the moment to make the right decisions. Kip and his friends had guided him in the right direction so far, and he'd allowed them to. He trusted Kip, but what if he couldn't make the hard decisions when he needed to? What kind of partner would he be for Kip? Hell, that raised the question of whether Kip even thought of him as a partner. Maybe Kip only liked him because Jos needed him.

"Jos, it's time to eat," Isaac said and grabbed his hand. "Come on," he coaxed, and he dragged Jos out of his thoughts and toward the dining room. He and Kip hadn't expected things to go as they had with his aunt, so everything was set for a classy dinner. Kip grabbed the dishes and plates and carried them into the kitchen.

Isaac climbed up into his usual place, and as soon as everything was in, Kip began dishing up. As soon as food hit Isaac's plate, he began to eat. More than anything else, that was a reminder of what Jos had put his brother through.

"Hey," Kip said softly, and Jos pulled himself back to the present. "You okay?"

"Yeah. Just thinking too much," Jos answered.

"Don't worry. Whatever your aunt decides to do, we'll be ready for it." Kip pulled out the chair, and Jos sat down. He remembered that he was always safe with Kip and did his best to put the questions and worries aside, at least for the moment.

ONCE THEY were done eating, Jos helped Kip clean up, and then he took Isaac upstairs for a bath. He splashed and played in the tub, nearly soaking Jos in the process. They both ended up laughing until they were hoarse, and once Jos got Isaac dry and into his nightclothes, he put him to bed with his stuffed friends.

"I like it here with Uncle Kip," Isaac said. "He's nice… even if you kiss him." Isaac made his yucky face and then giggled. "Why do you and Uncle Kip kiss?" he asked once Jos was about to turn out the light.

"Because we like each other."

"I like him, but I don't kiss him," Isaac said logically.

"See, I like you and I kiss you," Jos said and leaned over Isaac, planting a big smacking kiss on his forehead. "Don't worry—you'll understand about grownups when you're older. I promise. Now try to go to sleep." Isaac sat up and wound his small arms around Jos's neck. This show of affection and trust from his brother always left a lump in his throat. Isaac was the best part of his life, and just the thought that he might not always be there was enough to rip at Jos's heart.

Isaac lay back down, and Jos pulled up the covers and kissed his brother on the forehead again, lightly this time. "Good night."

Jos stood and left the room, closing the door partway and turning off the hall light. He thought about going downstairs to look for Kip, but instead he went into the bedroom himself. He was really tired. His job was very physical, and on his day off he usually tried to rest, but he had been on edge all day because of his aunt's impending visit and hadn't been able to lie down. So instead of going back downstairs, Jos lay on the bed with one of the books Kip had loaned him to read.

He must have fallen asleep. When he slid his eyes open, he found the book resting on his chest and Kip gazing down at him.

"Everything is locked up." Kip removed the book and set it on the nightstand. Then he leaned closer. The kiss began gently, but deepened quickly, turning heavy and deep within seconds.

Jos forgot about his questions and doubts when Kip held him and slowly divested him of his clothes. Jos was too busy soaking in the attention from Kip to reciprocate, but Kip took care of that quickly enough and joined him in bed.

"Everything is going to be okay. I'm here and I'm not going anywhere," Kip said.

"How can you say that?" Jos asked. "You've only known me for a few weeks. How do you know that you're going to want me around all the time? What if you get tired of me?"

Kip took Jos's hand and placed it on his chest. "Can you feel that? It's my heart racing like I just ran a marathon. You make it do that just by looking at me. Whenever I see you sitting in the living room with your head in a book, I have to remember that Isaac is in the house or otherwise I'd strip you naked right there and take you on the floor. It's what I always want to do." Kip released his hand and nuzzled the base of Jos's neck. Jos stretched to give him better access, and Kip took advantage, sucking at the base just hard enough that Jos quivered on the bed. "See. You're not the only one who can go looking for those kind of spots." Kip chuckled and then licked the spot again. "You're going to have a mark there."

"Kip. If Billy sees it, he'll know how I got it and…."

"I know he will, and everyone will know you're mine and that I care enough and want you enough to mark you like that."

"Is it a macho thing?" Jos asked, remembering how Kip had given himself to him. Kip was a guy who definitely liked to be in control.

"No. It's a Josten thing. I can't get enough of you." Kip wiped his cheek. Jos had no idea why he was tearing up. "I'm not going to ask you to stay here with me—I understand that you need to be on your own for a while."

"But I'll know you're here," Jos said and pulled Kip into a kiss. "And that doesn't mean we can't visit."

"And have sleepovers?" Kip asked, wriggling his hips, sliding his cock against Jos's, sending a shot of ecstasy through him.

"Definitely sleepovers," Jos agreed, and Kip got down to the sleepover part of the evening and very quickly had Jos forgetting about aunts, worries, questions, and everything else except the way Kip touched him, sending tingles through him. Kip rolled him over and found a spot just above his butt that if he rubbed a certain way had Jos humping the mattress like a mad-man and whining into the pillow. When Kip rolled him back over and slid two fingers into him, Jos gasped, and when those fingers were replaced by Kip slowly sliding into him, filling him up to the point he could hardly gasp for breath, Jos knew he was in heaven.

The way Kip looked at him, remaining connected with his eyes as well as his cock, sent Jos into instant orbit. All he wanted was more of what Kip had to give, and he got it.

"Jesus," Jos whispered when Kip changed the an-gle and made his head spin.

"I know I'll never get tired of you because I... I just know it." Kip was mumbling and driving into him. Jos didn't bother to correct his circular logic. All he did was hold on for the ride of his life.

CHAPTER 8

MOVING DAY for Jos and Isaac came much faster than Kip wanted, but he kept quiet and helped Jos carry the few things he and Isaac had out of his house and pack them into his car. After carrying out the last bag of clothes, he went back inside to check that all the lights and fans were off.

The house seemed so quiet and lifeless. He'd gotten so that when he came inside, he looked forward to Isaac's footfalls as he ran toward him, and Jos's smile when he first came into the room. Now the house seemed gloomier. Yes, he understood Jos's reasons for moving into his own apartment. Jos had been dependent on others for enough of his life that he needed to know he could be independent. Kip understood that; he really did. But that didn't soothe the part of him that was instantly lonely at the thought of coming back to the house once they were gone.

"Isaac is all set in his seat," Jos said from behind him.

"Okay." He turned and left the house, locking the door behind him, closing off the impending loneliness as he shut the door.

Then he drove them downtown. It was only half a mile at the most, but it felt like so much farther, like he was driving them away from him. Kip knew he was being stupid and that it was most likely his own fault. He should have simply told Jos that he wanted him and Isaac to stay and then gone on to tell Jos how much he meant to him and how he felt. But he hadn't been able to say the words. He'd done it in a roundabout way, but he hadn't wanted to scare Jos off, or rush into anything. All he'd ended up doing was denying himself what he truly wanted, and now it was too late. Jos was moving out, and telling him now would only muddy the waters and complicate things.

He and his friends had helped Jos get off the streets and get his life back on track. Jos was happy, and little Isaac had bloomed like a flower. Kip would do nothing to put that in jeopardy, and if Jos needed to be on his own in order to test his legs, then he'd be there for him. And he'd try to be patient, even though he had the feeling he'd spend a lot of time looking forward to Jos's visits and those sleepovers they'd promised each other.

Kip pulled up in front of the building and began helping Jos unload. With his arms full, he followed Jos and Isaac through the door and up the stairs to the second-floor apartment. It ran across one side of the building, with two windows that faced the street in the front and then a hallway down the center of the building, with the kitchen, bedrooms and bath off of it. The living room was nicely sized. The rest of the rooms were small, but judging by the grin on Jos's face, it seemed like a castle to him.

"Some furniture was here, and Donald helped me get some of the basic things," he said as he opened the bedroom doors. Each room had a twin bed with a dresser, but from Jos's excitement you'd have thought they were the living end, and maybe they were to Jos. Kip tried to be as happy for Jos as he could, but to him, this meant the end of something he hadn't realized he'd come to count on.

"It looks great," he said with a smile that he hoped like hell didn't seem too forced. He wanted Jos to be happy—more than anything—but he also wanted to be happy himself. Hell, he deserved it, and Jos and Isaac moving out made him sad, but that was beside the point. Kip set what he was carrying on Jos's bedroom floor where he told him to and then wandered back out to the living room and looked out the window. Sometimes people journeyed together through life, and then there were times when their journeys had to part. The counselor he and his dad had seen told him that. At the time he'd applied it to the loss of his mother, but it applied to his situation as well. Maybe his and Jos's journeys needed to be separate for a while. He blinked a few times as the wind shook the tree that nearly reached window height, sending orange-brown leaves swirling up into the air and then falling toward the street.

"I think Isaac and I can be happy here, and we can learn to live."

"You have been," Kip said, swallowing the rest of what he really wanted to say. For a moment he told himself it wasn't too late, that if he told Jos how he felt he'd change his mind about all this, but as soon as Kip turned around, the excitement on Jos's face killed that urge instantly. This wasn't about him. It was about Jos and what he needed. "I'll go get the rest of the stuff."

He hurried down and out to the car, then brought in another load of things. When he reached the top of the stairs, a loud, piercing giggle filled the room. Kip put down the bags and followed the sound to the back room, where Isaac stood barefoot, dancing in circles, Weeble held tight in his arms, crooning at the top of his lungs that they were home now.

"Uncle Kip," Isaac called as he raced over. "Jos says this is my room. My very own. I like it, and Weeble likes it too." He set his bear on the bed and picked up Pistachio, handing the horse to Kip. "Will you take him home with you?"

"Why?"

"Spistachio is sad and doesn't want you to be lonely. He likes the room at your house."

Kip resisted the urge to take the horse. "Why don't you put him next to Weeble so they can help each other get used to their new home?" He wasn't going to take Isaac's horsey. He knelt down in front of Isaac. "You and Jos are going to be happy here, and I think Pistachio will come to like his new room as much as he did the one at my house. Don't forget that you and Pistachio and Weeble can come over to visit whenever you want." Kip pulled Isaac into a hug and stood, carrying Isaac along with him. Isaac wrapped his arms around Kip's neck and held him tight.

"I love you, Uncle Kip," Isaac whispered, and Kip clamped his eyes closed.

"I love you too," Kip said, miraculously without his voice breaking. "You and Pistachio will be happy, and you're going to have your own room with your own bed."

"I won't have to sleep with Jos?" Isaac leaned back. "He snores." Then he did a pretty good imitation of his brother.

"I do not," Jos said as he came in the room. "You take that back." He ticked Isaac's belly, and Isaac giggled and squirmed in Kip's arms. "I don't snore."

"Yes, you do," Kip said.

"See?" Isaac said in triumph.

Kip put him down, and Isaac grabbed Pistachio and Weeble so he could show them all around their new home.

"I have one more load in the car, and then I need to go and get changed for work," Kip said. He knew he should go and get the rest of their things, but his feet felt plastered in place.

Jos stepped closer, hugging him around the waist. "I'm so excited about this, but you know I'm going to miss you." He buried his face in Kip's shirt. In that instant Kip knew how hard this was for him. Yes, this might've been something Jos thought he needed to do for himself, but that didn't mean it was easy for him either.

"You know I'll be there if you need me, but you aren't going to. You're going to build a good life for you and Isaac. This is a nice apartment."

"And with the rent subsidy, my job, and Isaac's benefits, we should be good as far as money goes. But I keep going over it in my mind and wondering just how I'm going to make it, and it scares me so much. I keep wondering what I'm going to do if I fail again the way I did the last time."

"You won't. You have a job and people there who care about you, just like you have friends who care and will be there if you need them. But I don't think you will. You're going to be able to stand on your own two feet. The only reason you didn't before was because of some bad luck and people who took advantage of you."

"But what if I can't do it?" he whispered. "What if I fail again?"

"Then we'll figure it out. But I know you can do it. We've gone over your budget again and again. You know it by heart. Sure, you and Isaac aren't going to have the top-of-the-line cable or a really fancy phone with all the bells and whistles, but you'll be able to take care of each other, and there's money for having fun. Just keep working hard like you are." Kip hugged him, and they stood still for a few minutes. He didn't want to let Jos go. "I'd better get your things," he finally said and then went to bring in the last of load of things.

"HOW IS Jos doing?" Carter asked when Kip found him at his desk, behind his computers, a few hours into his shift.

"Good. He moved into his apartment today."

"You don't have to sound so happy about it," Carter teased. "C'mon, it isn't the end of the world."

"Sometimes it feels like it," Kip admitted. "I know he's just downtown and I could walk there. We haven't broken up or anything, but…."

"Have you told him how you feel?" Carter asked.

"In a way," Kip answered, leaning over the desk.

Carter groaned. "What the hell does that mean? Morse code? Did you tap it on the wall or something? I know, you told him you love him in your own made-up language."

"You've been watching way too much television," Kip said.

"Really." Carter stopped typing and glared at him. "If you want Jos to know how you feel, then you need to tell him, and not in some beating around the bush way that's designed so you don't have to put yourself out there."

"That's easy for you to say—you have Donald."

"Yeah. And do you think it was easy telling Donald 'Ice' Ickle that I loved him? You remember what he was like. Thank God he's thawed a lot, because I love the guy with everything I have, but it was dang near pants-crapping scary… and the best decision I ever made." Carter turned back to his computer. "I bet you didn't come in here for relationship advice, and I should mind my own business, so what did you need?"

Kip was so grateful Carter had changed the subject he wanted to hug him. "I was wondering if you'd found out anything more on Jos's aunt."

"There's only so far I can look, but I found something strange. Sometimes searching when you don't know what you're looking for requires a lot of luck, and I think I may have had some. But I'll confess I don't know what it means. I do know that Josten's family comes from close to where his aunt lives, and there are some probate court records that Jos's mother and aunt were named in. It could be nothing, but I requested copies. The records are open, so I did it as a citizen's request. It could be just an old will, but within a year, Aunt Kathy bought her house and opened her business, so something changed in her life."

"Interesting," Kip said. "It could be nothing."

"That's true," Carter said, turning to look at him. "But there was suddenly quite a bit of money that was available to her. We're police officers, and we don't believe in coincidences. You told me the story she told Jos, and it seems too American-dreamy for me. Too perfect. You told me she seems like a really driven person, and parts of that story just don't fit."

"She did say that she got an inheritance, and that her sister spent all of hers," Kip said.

"All right. But something doesn't feel right to me. I don't know what it is." Carter turned back to the computer. "Like I said, sometimes you get lucky and sometimes there are lots of blind alleys. Only additional information will tell us what this is. You could be right and it's nothing, or it might help us follow a trail someplace else."

"We'll have to wait and see," Kip said and checked the clock. "I'll see you later, and thanks for everything."

"No problem. These things are what I love." Carter flashed him a smile and then went back to his work. Kip quickly ate his lunch, then checked in for any information he needed before returning to his car. He'd been assigned to what was becoming his usual area of town, the northeast quadrant, although that could change as calls came in. During the afternoon he dealt with kids skateboarding on the sidewalks and pointed them to the park where boarding was allowed. He didn't give them a ticket, because they seemed genuinely surprised, and the kids were polite and hurried off in the direction indicated when he told them where they could go. His mission was to help where he could.

It got dark early. Kip drove south on Hanover, watching people as they walked the sidewalks. A rough-looking man shuffling down the sidewalk caught his eye. Since encountering Jos, Kip found he paid more attention to the people who spent their time on the streets. He'd gotten to recognize a number of them and knew some of their routines. People who had once been faceless had come into higher relief for him. There were more people like Jos out there than he'd ever imagined. He stopped at the light on Louther and watched a tall, poorly dressed man cross the street, coat pulled closed, bracing against the cold. The signal changed and Kip glided through, glancing over at him again, but he was already out of sight.

Kip had some time, so he pulled over and got out of the car, getting a pretty good idea what had happened. Sure enough, Kip found the man hunkering down in the same deep doorway where he'd first met Jos. "Can I help you?" Kip asked, staying at the ready and not getting too close.

The man turned around.

Kip stepped back and stared into the face of Tyler Adamson, the man who'd attacked Jos. Kip's first instinct was to go off on someone who had hurt someone he cared for. But he was a police officer and his training kicked in. "What are you doing here?"

"Just looking around," Tyler answered and turned to leave.

"Stay where you are," Kip said and called in to the station. "Aren't you supposed to be in jail?"

"I got bailed out a few hours ago," Tyler answered.

"Just sit down on the ground and don't move." Kip called for backup through the radio.

"You can't hold me for no reason. Innocent until proven guilty and all that," Tyler argued.

"Either sit or I'll assume you're trying to threaten me," Kip said. He received the response that backup was on the way. A set of lights appeared behind him, and Carter joined him.

"What's going on?"

"This is the suspect I apprehended attacking Jos. He's saying he was bailed out, and I need to verify. He has a tendency to be violent."

"I'll watch him," Carter said, and Kip returned to his car, made some calls, and requested the appropriate information through his computer. The answer shocked him.

"How did you make bail?" Kip asked when he got back. As far as he could tell, Tyler didn't have anything.

"My brother," Tyler spat, and Kip wondered why this guy could hold such contempt for someone who was willing to put his money on the line for a loser like him.

"Your brother posted bail?" Kip asked.

Tyler nodded. "Can I go now?" he asked, hands in the air like he was a minister or religious figure giving a benediction. He should've won an Emmy for overacting. "The Salvation Army will open its doors in a few minutes."

"Where is your brother?"

"At home."

Kip backed off and Carter did the same. For now they had to let him go. Kip wished he had a reason to search him to find anything that could be used to return him to jail. If Kip had been later and Tyler had stayed hunkered in the doorway longer, he might have been able to make a loitering charge stick, especially based upon the new No Loitering sign that hung in the doorway.

He and Carter watched as Tyler walked down the sidewalk. Kip shivered as the wind picked up and the first drops of rain fell around him. "Jos can't seem to catch a break no matter what."

"Sometimes it's two steps forward, one step back," Carter said. "It sucks and we know it. The law we're supposed to uphold sometimes does things that drive us crazy. It's to protect everyone's rights, including mine, yours, Jos's, and even that guy's."

"Still sucks sometimes," Kip muttered.

"You won't get any argument from me." Carter got back into his car. Kip called in, letting Dispatch know he was free, and got into his car as well. Now he had to explain to Jos what had happened.

Kip spent the rest of his shift on edge. He'd never been so happy for rain and the chill in the air in his life. It meant the night was quiet. He got back to the station on time and pointed his car toward Café Belgie as soon as he could. He got a place to park just down the block and hurried inside. He didn't see Jos anywhere.

"Hi, Kip," Billy said a little breathlessly. "Jos left about ten minutes ago. He said he was going to get Isaac from day care."

"In this weather?" It was only a few blocks, but still….

"He had an umbrella and a good jacket, so he thought he'd be okay. It wasn't raining too hard when he left, but I see it's picked up since then. You can probably catch him without a problem."

"Thanks," Kip said and left, going right out to his car and following the route he hoped Jos would take. He reached the day care center and went inside.

Isaac hurried over, a large piece of paper waving as he ran. "I made this for you," Isaac said gleefully, and Kip took it. Of course he couldn't discern exactly what it was. "It's you and Jos holding hands under the table." Isaac giggled, and Kip saw the rough outlines of what Isaac was telling him.

"Are you going to be a famous artist?" Kip asked, keeping one eye on the door, his heart pounding. If it were pounding any harder, his shirt would vibrate.

"No. I'm going to be a policeman like you," Isaac told him definitively. "Then maybe I'll be an artist… and a cowboy, so I can ride Spistachio."

Kip suppressed a chuckle. He loved that Isaac had dreams now, and he liked to think he had a part in that. "That's wonderful. You can be anything you want."

"A cowboy policeman?" Isaac asked.

"You certainly can. They have them in lots of places," Kip turned to Miss Carrie. "Jos was on his way over to pick up Isaac."

"He hasn't been here yet," she said.

Kip nodded and kept looking at the door. He hoped like hell he'd only taken another route, and that Kip had just missed him. Seeing Tyler back out on the street had really messed with his head. But still, Jos wasn't here yet, and he wouldn't be late to pick up Isaac. Kip pulled out his phone and dialed, but the call went to voicemail.

"Let's get you dressed to go outside, and we'll find Jos. He's probably walking over." As more and more time passed, Kip's nerves grew and grew. He stared at the damn door, willing the thing to open and for Jos to walk in.

By the time Isaac was dressed and ready to go, Jos still hadn't shown up. Kip gathered Isaac's papers and drawings and tucked them carefully under his coat. He unlocked the car with his key fob and hurried Isaac out to it and got him in his booster seat.

Kip pulled away and traced the routes Jos could have gone. He didn't see him and stopped at Jos's building. His windows were dark, so Jos obviously wasn't there. As he and Isaac sat in the car, Kip called Miss Carrie, who confirmed that Jos still hadn't been there and that the center was about to close. Kip hung up and pulled out once again. He put on his lights and turned around, determined to follow Jos's possible routes as best he could. Something had happened, and all Kip could see was Tyler and Jos beside that house. He gripped the wheel, damn near paralyzed with fear that Tyler might have found Jos.

He went yet a different way, taking Bedford over to the day care. A block away he pulled to a stop and jumped out of the car. A figure lay in the street by the wheel of a parked car. Something fluttering in the wind caught his attention. It turned out to be the remnants of an umbrella. When he got close enough, he saw a familiar blue jacket and light head of hair.

Kip pulled out his phone and called 911. "This is officer Kip Rogers. I need an ambulance and police assistance on Bedford between Pomfret and South right away." He kept the panic out of his voice for the length of the call. As soon as he hung up, Kip knelt next to Jos, afraid to touch or move him in case he made things worse. He did manage to lightly touch Jos's neck and found a pulse. He raced to the car, and after reassuring Isaac that he had found Jos and was going to help him, he yanked an umbrella from the floor of the back seat, opened it, and used it to shelter Jos from the continued rain. He heard sirens within minutes. An ambulance arrived first, and the EMTs got to work covering Jos in blankets and transferring him onto a backboard. Kip's fellow officers arrived next and began taking pictures, trying to piece together what had happened.

Kip stayed with Isaac while Jos was loaded into the ambulance, then followed them to the hospital and carried Isaac inside the emergency entrance. Kip explained who he was and why he was there. Then he sat with Isaac and tried not to fly apart from nervousness.

He did manage to think clearly enough to call Donald and Carter, to let them know what was going on, as well as Billy at the restaurant.

"As soon as we close I'll be down there," Billy said. "We added Jos and Isaac to our insurance when he started, so I need to get you the information."

Isaac knew something was wrong and that Jos was hurt. Kip held him, letting Isaac rest his head on his shoulder as he clung to him. "Is Jos gonna be okay?"

"Yes," Kip answered each time Isaac asked, hoping like hell he wasn't lying.

He soothed Isaac and waited. Eventually they were able to see Jos. They didn't want to allow Isaac back, but Kip flashed his badge and explained that Isaac needed to see his brother. They relented, and Kip carried Isaac in.

Jos lay on a bed in a curtained-off area. They had him on oxygen.

"What's that for?" Isaac asked, pointing at the monitor.

"It tells them how Jos's heart is. All those numbers help them help Jos."

"Is he asleep?" Isaac asked.

"He hit his head," a doctor said from behind them. "Are you his family?"

"As close as he has here. This is his brother, Isaac. Jos and I have been dating." He knew there was very little the doctor could tell him without Jos's express permission, and he'd had no chance to give it. "Don't worry, I understand the rules." He sighed, dying to know what had happened. "I only brought Isaac back so he could see him."

The doctor nodded and went about his work. He checked Jos over carefully. "I'm ordering some tests."

Of course he couldn't say what they were, and that was frustrating as hell.

"I'm a police officer. I'm the one who found him."

"Are you here in an official capacity?"

"I can be," Kip said. He gently set Isaac down and kept him close before calling in. He explained where he was, and Dispatch confirmed that they needed information on Jos's condition.

"I'll relay to the officer in charge that you'll get that information and pass it on to him," Helen told him. "They'll be grateful. It's turned into a busy night."

"It's official," Kip said and pulled a small notebook from his shirt pocket. He'd been trained to always have one, so he carried it everywhere.

"He sustained a concussion, most likely from a collision with a car. It's possible he has at least one cracked rib, and there are multiple abrasions." Kip wrote it all down. "At this point, we don't know how severe his concussion is," the doctor explained. Kip saw Isaac stand closer to the bed, holding Jos's hand.

"Jos, wake up," Isaac said, and then he turned to look at Kip.

"It's okay," Kip said, trying to reassure him. He moved closer to Isaac and turned to the doctor.

"We'll know more after we're able to run some tests. We'll admit him and put him in a room once we're done. I honestly don't expect him to wake up tonight. Leave a number at the desk, and we'll call you when he wakes up."

That was like kicking Kip's legs out from under him. That meant it was bad—Jos might have slipped into a coma. "Thank you," he said and quickly called in the information he'd received. Then he lifted Isaac into his arms. Kip hated to leave Jos alone, but staying here wasn't going to be good for Isaac, and he had to be the first priority. Kip walked to the bed and took Jos's hand, rubbing the back of it lightly with his thumb. He stood silently at Jos's side, willing him to wake up and hoping like hell he hadn't lost him already.

"He's supposed to wake up when he's sleeping," Isaac said. He rested his head on Kip's shoulder, whimpering softly. Kip wanted to join him. He understood just how Isaac felt at that moment.

"Let's get you home," Kip said. "You can see Jos in the morning." He hoped that was a promise he'd be able to keep, for both their sakes.

Kip left and stopped at the desk, leaving a number for them to call if Jos woke during the night. Then he got Isaac in the car and drove through the wet and rainy roads to Jos's apartment. He let them in with the key Jos had given him because he sometimes picked up Isaac, and went upstairs, helping Isaac get ready for bed.

"Will I see Jos in the morning?" Isaac asked, eyes watery, looking up at him from around his covers, Weeble and Pistachio next to him.

"I hope so." Kip turned out the light.

"I don't want Jos to be dead like Mama," Isaac said, and Kip's throat constricted. He wasn't able to talk for a few seconds.

"I know. Me either." He stroked Isaac's head and did something he hadn't done in many years: he said a prayer. It was simple, but he said it for Isaac, who didn't deserve to lose another person who loved him, and he said one for Jos to stay strong and to get through this. Hell, he said one for himself because he didn't know what he was going to do about the hole in his heart that would be left if anything happened to Jos. "Good night. I'll be here, I promise."

Isaac nodded and turned over. He was obviously tired, and Kip was relieved when he went right to sleep. He wished that were possible for him. After watching Isaac for a long time, Kip left the simple room and returned to the living room. He sat in the chair that he had given Jos when he moved in, turned on the old television, and stared blankly at the screen. Eventually he found a blanket and tried to get some sleep, but of course every sound made him jump a little. More than once he reached for his phone because he thought it had vibrated, but it was just his nervous leg playing tricks on him.

He eventually fell asleep, but he jerked awake when his phone actually did vibrate. Turned out it was a Facebook message from someone trying to sell him Mary Kay. Kip wanted to fling the dang phone across the room, but he sighed and put it away, trying to still his restless mind long enough to go back to sleep.

As soon as light shone through the windows, Kip gave up even trying to sleep and stretched his aching neck and back before going to the kitchen to make some coffee.

Isaac wandered out in his horsey pajamas, carrying Weeble under his arm. "I'm thirsty."

Kip got some orange juice for him and made him a bowl of cereal. While Isaac ate, Kip called the hospital to see if he could get any information. He was able to find out that Jos was in a room and that visiting hours began at nine. Nothing else.

"Let's get you dressed, and then I'll take you to school."

"I want Jos," Isaac said, sucking his thumb. Kip hadn't seen him do that before, even at the height of the stress in their lives when they'd first come to stay with him. Maybe Isaac could deal with just about anything as long as he had Jos. Kip was beginning to understand how he felt.

"I know you do. But let's get your teeth brushed and then you can get dressed and go see your friends at school. I'm going to go see Jos and make sure he's okay."

"I wanna go with you," Isaac said, whimpering, and Kip's will collapsed like a house of cards. He'd take him with him and hope there was some good news.

"Okay. Eat your cereal and then go get dressed, and we'll go up to see Jos." What the hell else was he going to do? Jos was Isaac's only family—well, other than the ice-queen aunt, and Kip was putting off calling her because as soon as she got her hands on Isaac, she wouldn't let go.

Kip finished his coffee and called Donald to give him an update. "We're on our way up to the hospital now."

"Okay. I hope he gets better fast," Donald said. "You know things will get very complicated quickly if he doesn't." Kip knew that all too well. He wasn't a relative and had no real standing to make any decisions for Isaac.

"I'm done," Isaac said as Kip hung up with Donald.

"Then let's get ready to go."

Isaac hurried away, and Kip made a few phone calls and then went to check on him. Isaac was in his room. He had put on a shirt, but it was backward, and he was jumping around to get into his pants. Kip grinned and helped him into the pants and got his shirt on right. The kid was so adorable. Kip had never given much thought to having kids, but now, after having Isaac around, he could see him and Jos with a house full of kids, maybe a baby.

"Can you put your shoes on?" Kip asked, and Isaac ran and got a pair of shoes. Kip found some socks and watched as Isaac flopped down on the rug and pulled them on. Kip made sure the Velcro on Isaac's shoes was all set, got him a coat, and then took him to the living room and let him watch cartoons while he cleaned up as best he could. He was shocked at the mess a little boy could leave in his wake inside of five minutes.

Before they left, Kip called in to the department. He had some personal time, so he used one of the days. His captain had children and was pretty understanding when it came to family matters. Besides, Kip took shifts for guys who needed coverage all the time, so he didn't feel too guilty.

"Are you ready?" he asked Isaac when he was done.

Isaac jumped up and grabbed Pistachio, and Kip turned off the television. Then he took Isaac's hand and they left the apartment.

The rain had stopped sometime in the night. It was still cloudy, but the sun was desperately trying to peek through. Somehow Kip got Isaac in the car without him racing off to play in one of the nearby puddles. He saw him eyeing them, and on a different day he might have made a run for it, but instead Isaac sat quietly while Kip buckled him in, and then Kip drove as quickly as he dared to the hospital, his nerves ramping up by the second.

He was a police officer, trained to handle difficult situations, but he felt like he was seconds from falling apart. If for no other reason, he held it together because Isaac was in the car, and pulling off the side of the road so he could go to pieces with fright and worry wasn't an option. He parked the car and held Isaac's hand as they crossed the parking lot to the hospital. Isaac held Pistachio tightly under his arm. He was an amazing little boy, just like his brother was an incredible man.

"Josten Applewhite," Kip said.

"I'm sorry, but he's too young to go up with you," the lady said.

"Isaac is Josten's brother."

"I'm sorry," she said.

Kip was in no mood, and he wasn't going to let anything keep Isaac from seeing his brother. What if the worst happened? He didn't want to think about it. Kip pulled out his wallet and showed her his badge. "I'm not here in an official capacity, but this little boy is going to see his brother."

"Okay," she said. "He's in room 304."

"Thank you." Kip lifted Isaac into his arms and carried him to the elevator. They rode up, and Kip kept wondering what he was going to find when he got there. He walked down the hallway, past room after room, and then stopped outside 304. He pushed open the door and stepped inside.

Jos lay on the bed, looking much as he had the night before. The machines were still there, flashing their numbers.

"Jos," Isaac said, squirming to get down. He hurried to the bed and patted Jos's hand. "You need to wake up."

"Buddy, I don't...." Kip's voice caught in his throat when Jos's eyes slid open and that familiar blue, the warmest color he'd ever seen, shone in the dark room. Isaac burst into tears, and Jos lightly stroked his head. Kip wasn't even sure if Isaac knew why he was crying, but Jos stroked his hair as Isaac put his head and shoulders on the bed.

"I'm okay," Jos whispered. "I'm gonna be fine."

"I thought you were going to the angels like Mama," Isaac said, sniffling, and then he began crying once again.

"I'm not, and I'm going to be here for you for as long as you need me," Jos said, comforting his brother gently. Kip stayed back, watching the two of them with a smile on his face.

"I heard you come in," Jos said over Isaac's head. "I couldn't see you, but I knew you were here and that it was time to wake up."

"I wasn't…." He stepped closer, approaching the other side of the bed. Kip took Jos's hand. "You have no idea how bad you scared me. When I found you by the side of the road—" He gave up trying to talk.

"We looked for you," Isaac whispered. "You were in the street, all wet, and you didn't move, like Mama." Had Isaac seen his mother die? The thought hadn't occurred to Kip until that moment. He would have to ask, but he hoped Isaac was talking about when he saw his mother at her funeral.

"I was crossing the street, and I heard brakes. That's the last thing I remember," Jos said. "I'm okay now, and I have both of you with me. That's all that matters."

A nurse came in the room, and she smiled and left right away. She returned a few minutes later and began checking Jos out and fussing with his pillows. "Don't talk too much. You need to rest. I called the doctor and told him you were awake, and he said he'd be up to see you soon." She was smiling from ear to ear. "You had us all a little worried."

"He's my brother," Isaac said with the hint of a smile as he wiped away his tears.

"That's wonderful. Your brother is a very strong man, and I'm sure he knows how lucky he is." She gave Isaac a smile, and he leaned against the bed, putting his head on the mattress once again. Kip figured he'd crawl in with Jos if he could.

After checking everything, the nurse left, and Kip leaned over the bed. "I've never been so scared."

"I'm okay," Jos said.

"I know. I have to say I didn't remember that chair I gave you being so uncomfortable, but the dang thing gave me time to think about a lot of things. I wanted to do what was right for you, so I kept quiet. But I'm not going to be quiet anymore. I love you, Jos. Everything fell into place when I saw you last night. Life is way too short to wait for what you truly want."

"But...."

"I want you with me. I kept quiet before, and I let you move out, and worse, I nearly lost you. If you doubt you can make it on your own, just think of everything you've done. You've rebuilt your life almost from scratch, and you took care of Isaac, all while capturing my heart. I think you can do anything."

Kip leaned closer and felt tears come. He nuzzled Jos's cheek softly.

"Are you going to get mushy?" Isaac asked.

"Is it okay if I do?" Kip asked, and Isaac turned away. Kip took that as permission and kissed Jos lightly. "I do love you so much."

Jos sighed softly. "I love you too. It's been lonely without you. I guess I thought I needed to be on my own."

"You've spent a lot of time on your own, and so have I. So maybe the real challenge is learning how to be together, because that's what I want, and I hope it's what you want too."

"I do. I was happy being with you. Do you think Donald will be mad if I move back? He did help me find the apartment."

"I think he can find another family that will need it as badly as you did." He wanted to shout and dance for joy. "Now let's get you better, and we'll worry about the rest a little later."

Jos sighed and closed his eyes.

"Is he sleeping?" Isaac asked.

"Yes," Jos whispered and then smiled, which made Isaac grin and put a smile on Kip's face as well. He pulled up the chair and sat down. When Isaac came over to him, Kip lifted him onto his lap, and pretty quickly Isaac drifted off to sleep. He obviously hadn't slept much more than Kip had. When the doctor came in, he said that they were going to run some more tests now that Jos was awake, and that he had a cracked rib, but he was hopeful Jos would make a full recovery.

TWO DAYS later, Jos came home—not to his apartment, but to Kip's house. He was still sore and the rib was painful when he moved around, but Kip got him up into bed, and Isaac stayed with him for hours.

Jos was napping while Isaac played quietly in the living room when Kip got a phone call from Carter.

"I got the papers I requested today, and I think I've found something interesting. Jos and Isaac's grandfather set up trusts for them, and guess who the trustee is?"

"Aunt Kathy," Kip said.

"Exactly. They weren't huge, but large enough, and I bet good old Aunt Kathy figured if she had custody of Isaac, then she could 'invest' his money in her business. According to the terms of the will, Jos's money is already his, and it's just sitting there. She doesn't control it because he's over eighteen." Carter sounded so happy. This was the kind of thing he lived for—the answers to the puzzles that their job presented. It was his gift.

"She won't control any of it soon," Kip said. "Thanks. Send me what you have, and we'll get a lawyer to look into it. Heaven help her if she's done anything wrong." Kip hung up and paced the room. He was so angry his hands clenched into fists and then released again. After calming down, he went upstairs and found Jos slowly making his way from the bathroom.

"What happened?" Jos asked as Kip helped him back into bed.

"Carter called. He's been looking into your aunt for us."

"I remember," Jos said as he settled under the covers.

"Well, he found something. It appears your grandfather left a trust fund for you and any other of his grandchildren. You're old enough to claim your share of the trust. He named your Aunt Kathy as trustee. We think that if she got custody of Isaac, she planned to invest his portion of the trust in her business."

"Oh," Jos said quietly.

"She should have told you about the trust when you turned eighteen, but instead she kept quiet and the money away from you."

"So what do we do?" Jos said, as calmly as anything.

"We'll get a lawyer, and he'll take care of it. I also think we have enough to pressure your aunt to let someone else act as trustee for Isaac."

"Okay," Jos whispered.

"Aren't you mad? I mean, if you'd have had that money, you and Isaac might not have ended up on the streets. Heck, your aunt found you, and she still did nothing to help. That...." Kip stood and began pacing the floor as his anger grew fast. "How can you be so calm about this? She...."

"We knew she was up to something, and now we have our answer."

"But if you had known, you wouldn't have been on the street and...."

Jos sat up slowly and got back out of the bed. "I also wouldn't have met you. So how can I get angry about that?"

"Because you deserve to be. I wouldn't give up anything that happened. I swear I'd do all of it again, a million times over, if it meant I got to have you and Isaac in my life. You know that. But the fact that you went through all that you did—"

"I know, and I'll probably be angry about it later. But right now I'm too tired, and I don't want to think about her." Jos held on to his arm. "Would you help me get my robe? I want to go downstairs. I'm tired of being in the bed." Jos looked at him with heat in his eyes. "Unless...."

"You're not up for that," Kip said. "But if you promise to take it easy, I'll take good care of you later." Kip hugged Jos gently and wondered how on earth he had ever found a man like him on a rainy night in a doorway.

"You always have," Jos said, resting his head on Kip's shoulder. Kip didn't want to let go, but he reached for Jos's robe and helped him put it on. Then he slowly guided Jos to the stairs and down to the living room, where Isaac was sitting at the coffee table with paper and crayons, drawing away.

As soon as Isaac heard them, he looked up and grinned. "What are you drawing?" Jos asked as he sat on the sofa.

Isaac handed the page to Jos, and Kip leaned over the back so he could see it too. "That's me, that's you, and that's Uncle Kip. I drawed you holding hands but not yucky kissing."

Kip rolled his eyes, and then, just for fun, he lightly kissed Jos on the cheek. "How about we frame it, and then we can hang it on the wall?" He knew just the place for it—right next to the pictures of his mother and father. "It can be our first family picture," he whispered to Jos, who turned, smiled, and kissed him.

EPILOGUE

"I'LL BE right there," Jos called when the door-bell rang.

"It's probably Donald and Carter," Kip said from the kitchen. "They were going to come a little early to try to help out, and we figured Isaac and Alex could play for a while." A mild crash followed by muttering told Jos that something was giving Kip trouble. "It's all right."

"Okay." He opened the door, and a streak raced past him, Isaac squealing a little as Alex came in the house.

"I got lots of Legos," Isaac said. "Can we go to my room to play?"

"Yes. But remember you have to clean up any messes you make," Jos reminded him.

"We will," Isaac promised, and then the boys were off like streaks of lightning.

"Welcome to the funhouse," Jos said, closing the door against the cold before hugging Donald and then Carter. "Kip is in the kitchen doing battle with the turkey. I think it's winning." He hung up their coats.

"Red and Terry said they might be a little late. Red got a call at the end of his shift."

Jos nodded. "I planned for that." He was beginning to understand what it meant to be in a relationship with a police officer. Kip often got home late, and more than once Jos had sat on the sofa worrying when there was a report of an incident in town.

"It's part of having them in our lives," Donald said as he beamed at Carter. "Wouldn't change a thing... except the fact that he doesn't always call home." Donald bumped Carter's shoulder. "Where would you like me to put this?" Donald lifted the bowl he was carrying.

"In the kitchen," Jos said as he led the way. Kip was washing up some potatoes, and Jos figured the pan had been the crash he'd heard a few minutes earlier. Jos made room in the refrigerator and slid in the salad bowl.

Kip put the potatoes on the stove and sighed. "I think that's the last of it for now." The turkey was in the oven and scenting up the kitchen. The rest was on the stove ready to be started. "Anyone ready for a beer or wine? I know I am."

"Whatever you're having," Carter said, and Kip went to the basement and returned with wine. Jos got the glasses, and Kip uncorked the bottle and poured. After serving their guests, he handed Jos a glass and put an arm around his shoulders.

"You went quiet," Kip whispered.

He did that sometimes. The turns his life had taken still overwhelmed him sometimes. Mostly now they were good things, though, but he found that change of most sorts tended to make him nervous.

"I thought you might have to work today," Carter said.

"Darryl closes on Thanksgiving. It's a family time for them. They always spend the holiday with Billy's brothers, and it seems like kind of a big deal." He sipped from his glass and let the happiness in his life take over. The bad stuff was history. Sometimes it returned in his dreams, and more than once he'd woken in a panic thinking he was outside, especially during storms, but it was getting better.

"A woman and her daughter moved into your old apartment," Donald said. "They were so happy to get it, and the landlord was really understanding."

"He seemed nice when I talked to him." He and Isaac had officially moved out of the apartment and in with Kip just a few weeks ago. The things with his aunt were still up in the air, but the lawyer was handling it, and Jos was more than happy to let him. It didn't sound like Aunt Kathy had much fight in her, and it was only a matter of getting all the paperwork done. He had his money, and Kip had helped him get an account set up for it. He was determined to live on what he made and leave that money for emergencies and Isaac's future. There was no way he and Isaac were ever going to end up on the streets again. That alone gave him peace of mind.

The doorbell rang. "That must be Red and Terry," Kip said.

"I'll get it, I'm closest," Carter said and left the kitchen. Jos set down his glass to follow him. He heard Terry and Red laughing and then was hugged by both of them. He took their coats and the bottles of wine before leading them all into the kitchen, where they got glasses and conversations built.

"Jos," Red said as he came into the room. "Kip asked me to give this to you. We spoke to the judge, and he agreed to release it as long as you agree to return it if needed." Red dropped a gold coin pendant in his hand. "He said it was important to you."

Jos nodded and looked at it. His mother's necklace, the only thing he and Isaac had left of her. He honestly hadn't expected to see it again. He swallowed as he slipped the gold chain around his neck. "It is," he whispered.

Jos excused himself and went upstairs, saying he needed to check on the boys. While he did, he also needed a few seconds to himself. Even now, Kip's thoughtfulness and the kindness of his new friends sometimes took him by surprise.

The boys had been quiet, which was not necessarily a good thing. He found them in Isaac's room on the floor with every Lego in the house piled around them. Goodness knew what they were building, but they seemed to be having a ball. "We're going to put out snacks, so come down in a few minutes if you want some."

"Strawberries?" Isaac asked. He'd seen the packages earlier and had his eye on them.

"Yes," Jos answered, and Isaac looked at Alex, licking his lips.

"Uncle Kip got a chocolate cake, too," Isaac shared. They were still trying to figure out the whole thing around what to call Kip, and Jos figured he'd let Isaac choose. For now he was Uncle Kip, but who knew what Isaac would call him in the future.

"And Uncle Terry brought pumpkin pie," Jos said.

Isaac made a face. "I only like Halloween pumpkins, not eating pumpkins," he said, and Alex nodded. They were obviously chocolate cake guys.

"You can have whatever you want after dinner. So finish up here, and then you can join us." Jos smiled and went back downstairs. The television was on, the announcer already starting on the first game of the day. Kip was in the kitchen working on dinner, which was coming along amazingly well. Everything was cooking now. Jos got the appetizers set up and carried them into the living room before calling the boys to come down. They sounded like a herd of elephants on the stairs.

The guys helped them with the food, and Jos went back into the kitchen so Kip wouldn't be in there all day.

It took an hour, but dinner was finally on the table: carved turkey, potatoes regular and sweet, beans, cranberry sauce, salad, gravy, and stuffing—from a box, but he wasn't telling anyone else that. The candles were lit and the nice glasses held wine and water. Jos called everyone in, and he and Carter got the boys settled into their special places at the end of the table. Everyone took their places, and the food was passed around until they all had some of everything.

"Can you believe we pulled this off?" Kip said, and everyone at the table nodded. It had been a miracle that Carter and Kip had managed to get the holiday off and that they had been able to schedule dinner around Red's shift.

"Miracles do happen," Red said, looking straight at Terry.

Donald and Carter nodded at each other, and Carter leaned close to Alex, taking his little hand for a second.

Jos did the same thing to Isaac and swallowed hard. In a way, they had all gotten their own brand of miracle. Jos certainly counted himself lucky each and every day that he had Kip.

"Is Mama watching us from where the angels are?" Isaac asked.

"You bet she is," Kip answered, "and I think she's smiling." That seemed to be the answer Isaac wanted, and he grinned and went right back to eating. Kip shared a smile with Jos and took his hand under the table.

"You were our miracle," Jos said quietly.

"I was just about to say that you and Isaac were mine."

Jos swallowed hard and reached for his glass. Kip did the same and then stood. "I promise to make this short and sweet so we can all eat—won't that be a treat?" Everyone groaned, and Jos rolled his eyes. Sometimes Kip could be too cute for words. "All right, then, how about this…?" He raised his glass. "To family." Everyone stood, and six glasses met in the center of the table.

Carlisle Cops: Book Four

Fisher Moreland has been cast out of his family because they can no longer deal with his issues. Fisher is bipolar and living day to day, trying to manage his condition, but he hasn't always had much control over his life and has self-medicated with whatever he could find.

JD Burnside has been cut off from his family because of a scandal back home. He moved to Carlisle but brought his Southern charm and warmth along with him. When he sees Fisher on a park bench on a winter's night, he invites Fisher to join him and his friends for a late-night meal.

At first Fisher doesn't know what to make of JD, but he slowly comes out of his shell. And when Fisher's job is threatened because of a fire, JD's support and care is more than Fisher ever thought he could expect. But when people from Fisher's past turn up in town at the center of a resurgent drug epidemic, Fisher knows they could very well sabotage his budding relationship with JD.

www.dreamspinnerpress.com

CHAPTER 1

"HEADING OUT on patrol?" Red asked as JD Burnside stopped to grab his coat and hat before going outside. Red looked him over and shook his head. "Here. You're going to need these gloves, and put on an extra pair of socks."

"It's only November…," JD said, getting a little worried.

"Maybe, but the wind will go right through you, and they have you on foot patrol in the square. That cold concrete is going to leach the heat right out through your shoes unless you have something extra on."

JD sighed and sat back down in the locker room, going through his things until he came up with a second pair of socks. He slipped off his boots and pulled them on. Instantly his feet began to sweat, but he ignored it and pulled on his now-tight boots. "Is there anything else I should know?"

"Be sure to keep your citation book handy. Fallfest is just winding down, and everyone should be going home, but that also means the heavy-duty revelers will take it into the bars, so be on the lookout for people weaving and bobbing. We don't want them driving home."

"Is that why I'm supposed to be outside in god-awful weather like this instead of tucked in a nice warm patrol car like a regular person?" At least the patrol car would have heat. JD had not gotten used to the weather up in Central Pennsylvania, and he was beginning to realize that his first winter here was going to be hard as hell to get through.

"We always have someone visible to deter drunk driving. I did it two years ago, and Carter had the glorious honor last year. It's only for a day, and all you need to do is keep yourself warm and your eyes open. Everyone will empty out in three or four hours, and then you can come on back and grab a patrol car. These are always interesting evenings."

"Yeah?" JD inquired as he got to his feet.

Red grinned. "A few years ago, they had this cow parade thing where artists decorated fiberglass cows and they put them around the area. There were four of them in town, and one was on the square. That year we had someone decide it was a bull and that he was going to ride it... buck naked in the middle of town." Red began to laugh. "By the time we got to him, he'd turned half-blue and all his friends were getting ready to take their turn. We stopped them before the entire crowd turned into a streak-fest."

"What happened to the naked guy?"

"We hauled him away for indecent exposure, and he got a fine. The thing is, this may be a small town, but we have some crazies when they drink. So keep an eye out and call if you see anything. I'll be around and will stop by to check on you."

JD thanked Red for his help and the story, which had brightened his mood a little. He made sure he had everything and slammed his locker closed before leaving the station and heading out through town toward the square.

He was a block away from the square. When he arrived, he glanced up at the clock tower on the old courthouse to check the time.

"Assault in progress, courthouse common" came through his radio.

JD responded and raced forward, heart pounding. He rounded the courthouse and saw a group of three college students crowded around one of the benches.

"What the hell do you think you're doing, old man?" one of the boys was yelling, the sound carrying through the square. The others yelled as well.

"What's going on?" JD projected in his best police voice. The students backed away, hands exposed, which JD liked. At least they didn't seem to be a threat to him.

"This old guy was about to take a leak on the veterans' memorial," said the kid who'd been doing the yelling. "We sat him down and were trying to talk to him, but he tried to hit Hooper here." He took a further step back and gave JD room. A man in his late sixties, if JD had to guess, sat on the bench, shaking like a leaf. The front of his pants was wet, and he smelled. When JD touched him, the man felt cold, and he continued to shiver. JD tried more than once to get the man to look at him, and when he finally did, his eyes were vacant and half-lidded.

"I need an ambulance on High Street next to the old courthouse," JD called in. The man continued to shiver and shake. This wasn't just from the cold. The scent of alcohol permeated even the mess he'd made of himself. The man needed help.

"Is he going to be all right?" Hooper asked. "We didn't hurt him or anything. He was going to take a leak right there on the memorial, and we tried to stop him and help him sit down, but he swung at me and nearly fell." The kid seemed upset. His eyes were as big as saucers.

"Did he hit you?" JD asked.

"No. He was too slow. But David here, the big idiot, started yelling, and that must have been what you heard."

"How much have you had to drink?" JD asked David.

"Enough to know I won't be driving," David answered with blinky eyes.

"None of you had better," JD advised.

"I'm their ride," Hooper said. "I hate the taste of the stuff, so they buy me food and Cokes, and I drive the idiots home." One of Hooper's friends bumped him on the shoulder.

JD turned back to the old man, who was rocking slightly from side to side. JD tried to get his name, but he was becoming more and more unresponsive. JD got the students' information and sent them on their way. He could check with them if he needed to, but what they'd said rang true.

There must have been plenty of calls already, but an ambulance finally arrived and they got the man settled into it. He didn't have any identification on him. JD made sure to get the information he could, and then the EMTs took the man to the hospital.

At least during that excitement he hadn't had a chance to be cold. Once the ambulance pulled away, the square turned quiet. Dry leaves rustled in the trees, and wisps flashed in the lights that lit the side of the old courthouse. JD shivered when he realized those wisps were snow. God, he was going to freeze to death here.

JD pushed that thought aside and walked around the square, then along the side streets, watching for trouble. He passed a few people still huddled on the benches, but he figured they'd soon give up and head on home.

Now that the streets were no longer blocked off for the festival, traffic continued flowing through the main intersection, as it usually did. JD returned to the intersection, crossed High Street and then Hanover, then continued around to the narrow side street that ran next to one of the churches on the square. He hated that street. It wasn't well lit and there were plenty of shadows.

He peered down to check for movement and was preparing to move on when Red pulled up in a patrol car. JD opened the passenger door and got inside.

"I saw you heading this way and thought we could take a ride for a while," Red said.

JD was eternally grateful as he soaked up the heat inside the car. "I hate that street."

"We all do. The chief is going to demand a street-light. The church has been fighting it because they say it will mess up the light coming in from the stained-glass windows or something. But lately it's become a real hazard." Red put the car in gear and made the turn, slowly rolling down the street.

At the slight bend, two figures raced out of a corner and took off down the street toward the church's back parking lot. Red flipped on his lights while JD jumped out and took off on foot. Red raced past him to try to head the men off.

JD was fast. He had run track in high school and college, and no street punk was going to outrun him. He pounded the pavement, feet racing. One of the men dodged and got away once, but when he tried it again, JD was ready and grabbed the back of his coat, yanking the man to a stop.

He fell to the ground and rolled. JD stayed on his feet, and when the man stopped rolling, JD knelt and placed his knee on his back.

"I wasn't doing nothing," the man protested.

"Yeah, I'm sure," JD said as Red pulled up.

"The other one got away," Red said angrily.

"This one was throwing things out of his pocket as he ran," JD said, pointing back the way they'd come.

"Oh man. You going to try to pin shit on me now?" the man asked as he shifted on the ground.

JD cuffed him and made sure he was secure. "Nope. I'm going to make sure you get what you've got coming to you." JD watched as Red carefully photographed and tagged what had been thrown aside. The law had been the family profession for generations, so JD had decided to become a police officer. But once he'd started down the path, he'd discovered a love of fair play, protecting others, and enforcing the law. Maybe it was genetic? He wasn't sure.

Other sirens sounded, and soon two more cars joined them, bathing JD and the suspect in headlights.

"What have we here?" Aaron Cloud, one of the detectives, asked as he got out of his car.

"Cocaine, by the looks of it," Red answered. "Enough of it that he's going to be doing some long, hard time."

"That ain't mine," the suspect said.

JD shook his head. "I saw him throwing it out of his pockets, with his bare hands, as I chased him. It was his. His prints will be on the bags." The guy must be an idiot.

"Go ahead and read him his rights. We'll take him down to the station."

"There was another man with him," Red said. "JD here jumped out of the car when we saw him, took off like a shot, and got this guy. I followed the other man, but he ran between the houses over there and disappeared across High Street."

"We'll find out who he was," Aaron said, looking down at the suspect. "Won't we?" The menacing tone Aaron used had the guy shaking a little. JD knew it was an act. Detective Cloud was a "by the book" kind of guy, but if he hadn't been a police officer, he could have had a career in Hollywood.

Aaron took custody of the suspect, and JD helped Red confirm they had found everything that had been thrown by their suspect before driving to the station.

"I don't think I've ever been so grateful for a drug bust in my life," JD said as they rode, the wipers swishing back and forth to wipe the falling snow from the windshield.

They passed the square slowly. JD turned when he saw movement. A man stood up from one of the benches and slowly walked away. "Are there always people on those benches? They have to be freezing in this weather."

"Yeah. People sit there all day long. They have their favorite spots, and heaven help anyone who tries to take it. Mostly people just pass them by and don't really notice them." Red made the turn and continued to the station. JD pulled his mind away from the bench sitters back to the report he was going to have to help write.

At least the station was warm. JD went to his desk and got to work putting together his statement of events.

"You did good," Red told him as he passed. "Though I don't recommend jumping out of moving cars every day."

"Did we get any information out of him?" JD asked.

"Aaron is leaning on him pretty hard. He'll probably lawyer up pretty soon, but he says the other guy was just a customer," Red explained, which was what JD had figured. At least they got the dealer this time. Usually it was the other way around. "Did you send in your statement?"

JD nodded and stood up. It was time for him to go back out on patrol. At least this time of night he'd have a vehicle. "I'll head out with you." Red walked him to the parking lot, and they got in their respective cars. "Stay safe."

"You too." JD started the engine, then pulled out of the lot. He drove through town and turned into the same side street he and Red had gone down earlier. It was empty this time, and he continued on.

The snow was getting heavier, and he drove carefully as visibility got worse and the streets more slippery. Toward the end of his shift, he made one last tour of town. He passed the square and saw a single figure on one of the benches in the courthouse square. JD knew there was nothing wrong with sitting on the bench, but it was after eleven and cold as hell. He pulled to the side of the street and got out, then walked up to the man.

He was hunched and curled into his coat, arms wrapped around himself, chin to his chest.

"Sir, are you all right?"

The man looked up and then lowered his gaze once again, saying nothing.

"Sir, is something wrong? It's way too late and too cold to be out here. You should head on home."

"I'm fine. Doesn't matter, anyway. No one cares." He lowered his gaze once again and continued sitting where he was.

"You'll be a lot warmer and safer if you go home." JD was becoming concerned. "I can help if you like? Can you tell me where you live?"

"Of course I can. But it doesn't matter. Nothing matters." He got to his feet. He seemed steady enough. "People are crap, you know that? Everyone takes advantage of everyone else, and no one gives a crap about it." He took a few steps, weaving slightly, and then he straightened up and headed off toward the courthouse. "No one cares about anything or anyone."

"Do you need some help?" JD asked.

"No. There's nothing you can do." He walked off and JD watched him go. Something wasn't right, but he was cold and the guy seemed harmless enough. JD went back to his car and slowly drove down the road. He saw where the man turned, and then watched as he went inside one of the apartment buildings in the first block of Pomfret.

His phone rang, so JD pulled to a stop before answering it. "You heading back to the station?" Red asked.

"Yeah." He checked the time.

"Terry is going to meet me at Applebee's. They're still open, and we can get something to eat." Red had been nice enough to befriend him when he'd joined the force six months earlier.

"Sounds good. Let me get back and finish up. I'll meet you there."

JD drove back to the station, checked in, and then left. The snow barely covered the ground, but it was enough to make him itchier about driving. He knew people here didn't think too much about a little snow, but he'd rarely driven in it back home. As he clutched the wheel, he tried to remember the last time he'd actually driven in snow. It must have been four or five years ago.

JD approached Hanover Street and saw a hunched figure walking back toward the square. JD knew he was off duty, but he turned left instead of right anyway. He watched as the man went back to the same bench and sat down. There was something very wrong.

JD pulled off the road, then got out and jogged across the street to where the man sat. "I thought you'd gone home," JD said gently.

"This is my bench. I like it here."

"Dude, it's really cold, and you're going to get sick." JD helped him to his feet. "It's also really late. You need to get home where it's safe and warm." He hoped the guy wasn't sick, but he couldn't leave him out in this weather. "When was the last time you ate?"

The man shrugged. JD looked at his arm, checking for a medical bracelet. He'd had a friend who acted like this sometimes, a little loopy and strange. He'd been diabetic, and when his blood sugar got wacky, he'd act really out of it. "Why don't you come with me, and I'll see about getting you something to eat."

"Okay," the man agreed, and JD helped him walk across the street. He got him into the car, wondering what Red was going to think when he showed up with a stranger. The guy sat quietly, lightly fidgeting with his hands as JD drove to the edge of town and pulled into the restaurant parking lot.

"Let's get you something to eat, and then maybe you'll feel better." JD had committed himself now. He'd crossed a line between officer and public a long time ago—and if this turned out badly, he could be in a hell of a lot of trouble—but something told him the guy wasn't dangerous, just a little confused.

He parked and they got out, the man following docilely.

Red met him at the restaurant door, staring quizzically. "Who's this?"

"He's…." Shit, how was he going to explain this? "A guy who needs some help."

Red turned slightly, looking at JD like he'd truly lost his mind. "Is that some Southern thing?" Red asked.

"It's a human thing," JD answered.

Red rolled his eyes, pulling open the door to the restaurant. "Terry got us a booth already," he said, leading them toward the corner. Terry stood in all his toned swimmer glory, smiling brightly in his snug-fitting clothes. JD had met Red's partner only a few times before, but his shirts always seemed perfectly tight and his pants hugged his legs just so. JD did his best not to look too closely or ogle the man, but it was dang hard. "You remember JD," Red said.

"Of course. How are you, JD?" Terry said. "And this is…?"

"Fisher Moreland," the man answered in a clear voice.

"Glad you could join us," Terry added, shaking his hand and then sliding into the booth. Red sat next to him, and JD motioned for Fisher to take a seat before sliding in after him.

"How was your shift?" Terry asked.

"Interesting," Red said. "JD here tackled a dealer as he tried to run away." Red handed out menus. "It was something to see. He flew after the guy and brought him down with a grab. It was beautiful."

"I'm just glad it worked out," JD said, letting Red do most of the talking. The server approached and they ordered drinks. When Fisher didn't respond, JD ordered him a Coke, hoping the sugar was what he needed. She left and they went back to talking, but JD kept an eye on Fisher, who was once again huddling down into his coat. When the drinks arrived, Fisher shakily put a straw into the soda and drank. JD shared looks with the others, but he didn't say anything about it. He was starting to think he should have called an ambulance to help the guy, and that this was a huge mistake.

"Are you getting used to this cold?" Terry asked JD.

"God, no." A chill ran through him at the thought. "I had no idea it could get so cold, and it's only November."

"Yeah. You have some cold months ahead, but hopefully it won't be as bad as last year. It was frigid for most of January."

"Are you ready to order?" the server asked as she came up to the table, and JD turned to Fisher.

"Chicken wings, please," Fisher said softly. He'd drained the soda, and she took the glass to refill it. JD ordered a burger, and Terry got a salad with the dressing on the side. Red, on the other hand, ordered enough food to feed an army, and JD had no doubt he'd eat it all. Red was a man who loved his food.

"What do you do, Fisher?" Terry asked as the server brought back Fisher's refilled glass.

"I work as a dispatcher at one of the warehouses in that logistics complex out off I-81," Fisher answered. "I'm one of the guys who makes sure the trucks have a place to dock and then tells them where to unload or load up when we're shipping out." He seemed more lucid and his eyes less vacant.

"Do you have family in town?" JD asked.

"Yeah. My family has been here for a long time. But I don't see them very much." He drank some more and the server brought a basket of chicken wings in some goopy sauce along with a plate. Fisher picked up a wing, put it on the plate, and then began to cut it apart with a knife and fork. He ate carefully and slowly, taking apart each wing in the same exacting manner.

"Are they good?" JD asked. Fisher nodded, continuing to eat. As he did, he got more animated, and relief welled in JD that he'd been right and Fisher had needed something to eat.

"Are you all police officers?" Fisher asked once he'd eaten half the wings and the rest of their food had been delivered by the server.

"JD and Red are," Terry said. "I work as a lifeguard and swim instructor at the Y."

"Terry is going to the Olympics," Red said. "He's been training for a long time, and he's going to do well." Red was obviously proud of his partner.

"I saw an article about you in the paper a few months ago. I didn't recognize you. That's so cool." He seemed happy now as he returned to his wings. JD dug into his burger, noticing that Fisher's eyes were bright and clear now.

"Was there any other excitement?" Terry asked as he took a bite of his burger.

"Just an old man who needed some help at the square. He seemed to be having some sort of episode, and I got an ambulance for him. Other than that, it was an exercise in keeping warm. How about you, Red?"

"Nothing. The bars kept us busy, and I convinced some guys to call a cab rather than try to drive. It's what we do after things like this. People drink and then don't make the best decisions, and I'd rather guide them to good ones than arrive at an accident or make a drunk-driving arrest."

"Have you been a police officer long?" Fisher asked JD.

"A couple of years. I went to the academy in South Carolina and got my first job in my hometown there. But things didn't work out too well, and I started looking for a new job. Since I was willing to move, a recruiter got me in touch with the chief here. I never intended to move someplace cold, but the town is pretty nice." He left it at that. There was no reason to go into the whole story about why he'd had to leave his home. Things were different here, and he was grateful for it. "People here have been supportive." JD felt Fisher tense next to him. He turned slightly, but Fisher had returned to eating and the moment passed.

"What do you do for fun?" Red asked Fisher.

"I like researching antiques, and I like to cook," Fisher answered, setting down his knife and fork.

"What's your favorite dish to make?" Terry asked.

"I like to bake bread," Fisher said with energy. "Mixing the dough and then letting it rise, working and kneading it, then baking it, filling the apartment with the scent that means home and warmth. There's nothing better. I bake all my own from scratch, and when I don't have enough time, I have this recipe for a dutch-oven bread that you don't knead. It's really simple and rustic with a great texture. I love making it this time of year. It's a great winter bread."

"I love sourdough," JD said.

Fisher bounced on the seat. "I have a starter that I got years ago. I have to feed it every so often, and I love to use it to make rolls. They have this great crispy crust and that slightly sour flavor that mixes well with sweet melted butter."

JD still had food on his plate, but compared to what Fisher was describing, the burger and fries had lost some of their appeal. Fisher was grinning with excitement, and JD loved that look. He had a slight gap between his teeth, but it was perfect and added to Fisher's smile the same way the little lines that reached toward his eyes gave Fisher's face warmth and character.

"What about you, JD?" Terry inquired. "You have something you like to do for fun?"

"I used to go hunting with my dad. That was our thing. Each fall we'd go out in the woods, just him and me. Between the two of us, we'd get a deer. Bagging something was no big deal. It was spending time together that was the real fun. We'd pack up a tent and spend three or four days tramping through the woods, eating crap my mother would never let us eat at home and having a good time. My sister decided one year that she wanted to go along. My mother forced my dad to take her, and he agreed, just to keep peace in the family."

"How did that work?" Fisher asked.

"We had to take a second tent that my dad and I had to put up for her. Rachel was bored the entire time and kept wanting us to do things to entertain her. Either that or we'd go sit in the blind, and then she'd whine about how there was nothing to do."

"That doesn't sound like fun," Terry commented between bites.

"It wasn't. I was ready to kill her after a day, and I could tell my dad was at his wit's end. After two days, he said we were going to go home because he couldn't take any more. So that morning, we got up and went out for a few hours before packing up." JD looked all around the table. "We were sitting in our blinds. I could see Dad. He was strung tight, and he'd just said through the walkie-talkie that we'd give it another half hour and then go home. Then minutes later a shot rang through the woods, followed by a high-pitched bellow that sent chills through me. I honestly thought my sister had shot herself. Dad and I climbed down and raced toward the sound. We found Rachel standing over this huge buck. Had to be ten points. He was massive, and she was grinning like an idiot." JD paused. "All she said was 'Now I get hunting.' The look in her eyes was feral."

"Does she still go?"

"Every year, and she's always the one who gets the big one. It's like she's deer-nip. They come right to her." JD motioned with his hands, and the others all laughed. "Dad just shakes his head whenever anyone brings it up."

"So is Rachel an outdoor kind of girl?" Fisher asked.

JD laughed. "Hell no. She's this prim and proper Southern belle who loves dresses, looking perfect, and twisting the boys around her little finger, but once a year she and my dad head to the woods in jeans, boots, and flannel. Whoever she marries had better be able to look amazing in a tuxedo and be willing to keep up with her when hunting season comes around." They all laughed. "Oh, and he'll have to be the one to drag whatever she bags out of the woods, because she'll shoot it, but she isn't about to dress or drag it. She'd mess up her nails."

"What did your dad say to that?" Red asked.

"He was so shocked when she shot the buck, he found himself agreeing to anything. Especially after she looked him square in the eye and said that she shot it, and her job was done. She went back to camp and waited while we brought the deer. The thing was, she didn't even make lunch, which I suppose was a small blessing because Rachel can't cook worth a damn. It's a good thing she's pretty and determined."

"Dang. My sisters are cheerleaders," Fisher said. "At least they were the last time I talked to them. And my younger brother is pretty much perfect." Fisher finished eating the wings, and when the server returned he asked for a glass of ice water. He seemed like a very different person from the guy JD had met at the square. JD was still trying to figure Fisher out.

Red's plate was empty, and he sat back with a yawn.

"I know. We need to get you home soon," Terry said softly.

"I hate second shift. First is great, even third is okay, but second is always so hard. The days seem so out of whack. Thankfully I'm up for promotion, and with the job comes permanent first shift, so I'm really looking forward to that."

"So am I," Terry said, leaning close to Red and gently patting his stomach. "It'll be nice to have you working close to the same hours I do."

"Do you have plans after the Olympics?" Fisher asked Terry. "Will you still compete?"

"No. Win or lose, after the competition, I'm done. I love to swim, but we've talked about it, and after we get back from Rio, I'm going to finish school and get a degree in physiology so I can train other athletes. I'd like to be able to train the next generation of swimmers. But all that hinges on the games. If I win, I'll have a lot of credibility and might be able to work that into something lucrative while the publicity holds. Who knows? I'm happy to be going and competing. That alone is a dream come true."

Terry yawned as JD finished up his burger. It was past midnight, and the restaurant was closing. The server brought their checks, and JD paid for his and Fisher's meals. Then they all got up and began pulling on coats.

"I'll see you tomorrow afternoon," Red said as he hugged JD. Terry did the same to him and then to Fisher, who seemed ill at ease at first and then broke into a smile. Maybe he wasn't used to being hugged.

They left the restaurant and went to their cars. The snow had stopped, but the cars and grass were covered in a dusting of white. The pavement was wet and felt a little slippery. JD walked carefully and unlocked the car, letting Fisher get inside.

"Thank you for the food and the company," Fisher said as JD backed out of the space. "It isn't often that a stranger is kind to someone else." The tone of his voice told JD there was a lot more being said than was there in the words. He suspected quite strongly that Fisher was a lonely man, and he was glad he'd been able to help him. "It was what I think I needed. Your friends are very nice."

"They are. Moving to a strange town and a completely different area of the country has taken a lot of adjustment." Not that he had a great deal of choice in the matter.

"I've lived here all my life, and you have more friends than I do." Fisher shifted from watching out the windows as JD turned onto Pomfret. He pulled up at the curb, and Fisher got out of the car. "Thank you again. I really appreciate it." He closed the car door and hurried to the door of the building, then disappeared inside.

JD pulled away and drove the few blocks to his small rented house on South Street. He hadn't meant to get a house, but after looking around at tiny apartments, he'd found the house. It needed some love, but the rent was right. The landlord, who was older and had owned the house for decades, had agreed that any work JD did could be taken off the rent, and he liked the idea of a police officer living there, so JD had moved in and had already done a lot of work on the place.

He unlocked the front door and stepped into the house, which felt more and more like home every day. His furniture had been carefully gathered from consignment and secondhand stores. He'd worked on each piece to make it his. His one splurge was the flat-screen television that sat on the entertainment cabinet in the living room. Other than that, he'd stayed very close to budget. It wasn't as though he had anyone to back him up, not anymore.

JD put his keys on the table by the door and lugged his bag of gear toward the back of the house. He locked up his weapon and threw a load of laundry into the washer before flopping down into his favorite chair in the living room and turning on the television. He didn't bother turning on any lights. He leaned back to get comfortable and managed to fall asleep in the chair before he could really get interested in whatever had been on television.

He woke hours later with Fisher's face and smile on his mind. Something about him got to JD. Maybe it was the loneliness that seemed ever present in his eyes, a feeling JD tried to cover up but knew quite well. He had people he knew from work—friends, even, like Terry and Red—but there was no one here, not like back home, where there were people he'd known since he was a kid running through the sprinklers on a hot day, yelling and carrying on. Carlisle held none of that kind of history for him. Not that it had counted for much in the end.

With a sigh, JD pushed himself out of the chair, turned off the television, and went upstairs to bed. Tomorrow was going to be a long day; he felt it deep down.

BEING A cop often meant hard work and days that didn't seem to end, but his phone rang at eight in the morning, way too early. He snatched it off the dresser, expecting it to be work calling him in. "Hello," he said, trying to sound groggy and pitiful.

"Jefferson Davis, it's your mother." She always managed to sound as though she were snapping orders. "Your aunt died this morning. I thought I should call and let you know. Though we don't expect you to come back for the funeral, you might send flowers."

JD was at a loss for words. His Aunt Lillibeth had been the one person in the family who hadn't turned her back on him. This was just another reminder that he was truly alone, and whatever life he thought he'd once had was gone.

The sound his mother made was something no lady should ever make; at least his aunt would have said so. "Jefferson Davis, the family is just beginning to put this whole… disgraceful… display behind us." Each word seemed to be painful for her. He was her son, and his mother should have been standing behind him, as the rest of the people he'd been close to should have, but no. "It's best if you send flowers to show your respect and that you remember her, but stay away. Some distance and time will help everyone heal and move on."

"Meaning it would be best for you," JD pressed. "Don't lie to me, Mother. You don't want me to come to my aunt's funeral because you're afraid of what those bitches around town will be saying about me. Just admit the truth. You're a coward." He'd had more than enough of his mother's hypocrisy.

"Fine. Think of me what you will. Lord knows I gave up a lot for my children, and heaven forbid I should have some peace of mind and friends in my old age. I went through a great deal to take care of you and your sister while your father worked all those hours at the office and did God knows what with his secretaries."

"I see your ability to reach the heights of drama isn't affected by Aunt Lillibeth's death."

"Don't be flip with me. I've had about all I can take right now with your aunt's death and your father deciding he's going to retire. Lord, what am I going to do with him around the house every day?"

"Stop screwing your tennis instructor?" JD asked.

"Don't be crass," she snapped. "How dare you insinuate that I'm having an affair?" The indignation in her voice told him that his joke had probably come closer to the truth than he'd thought.

"All right, Mother. You're as pure as the driven snow and as gentle and kind as a lamb." He was getting fed up with this conversation.

"There's no need for sarcasm."

"Just send me the info about when the funeral will be, and I'll decide what I want to do," JD insisted. He might as well let his mother dangle in the wind for a while. Let her wonder if he was willing to come down to Charleston and start the rumors and talk all over again. The truth was that he wasn't looking forward to it, and that Aunt Lillibeth wouldn't have wanted it either. She'd been the one to advise him to leave and make a life somewhere else, where he could be himself.

"Fine. You'll do what you like," she huffed. "There isn't anything I can do about it, but at least think of what you'll put your family through."

"Fine, Mom. Is that all you called for? You told me the news and decided to rub salt into an open wound. Are you happy now?" JD got out of bed and pulled on a pair of sweats against the chill. He needed to clean up and knew he wouldn't go back to sleep, not after his mother's call. "If you're done piling on the guilt, I'm going to go now." She was his mother, but JD was coming to realize he really didn't like her much.

"I was just making sure you knew what happened." An uncomfortable silence settled over the connection.

"If there's nothing else, I'm going to go. I worked late last night, and—"

"I don't know how you can do that. A policeman, working with all those criminals. If you wanted to work in the law, you should have become a lawyer. You could have been very successful, but now…." The tsking sound was more than JD could take.

"Good-bye, Mom," JD said and ended the call. If he remained on the line, he was going to get angry and even more hurt. His aunt's passing wasn't unexpected. She'd been ill for some time with a heart condition and had been declining rapidly for the past six months. Still, it hurt that his mother had felt the need to call not only to tell him, but to make sure he didn't come home. The perfect way to start the day: a heaping helping of loathing mixed with a huge dollop of guilt.

JD sighed and tossed his phone on the bed, then retrieved it and fanned through the contacts for someone he could call to talk to about his aunt. But as he thumbed through, he realized, even with all the names, those doors were closed to him now. He placed the phone on the nightstand and turned away from it. Thank goodness he had to go to work. At least there he'd be around people who were less toxic than his own family. Hell, even the people he arrested were less poisonous to his soul than his own fucking family.

With a sigh, JD went into the bathroom. He brushed his teeth well, remembering the number of times his mother had told him to brush his teeth, always with a reminder of exactly how much, to the penny, they'd paid for him to have braces. JD ground his teeth at the thought and nearly swallowed a mouthful of toothpaste, which reminded him he needed to get to the store to get something better than the awful stuff he was using. Maybe he could find something cinnamon flavored. Spitting into the sink, he rinsed his mouth, shaved, and started the shower. Once he was done, he figured he'd do his errands before starting his shift.

ANDREW GREY is the author of more than one hundred works of Contemporary Gay Romantic fiction. After twenty-seven years in corporate America, he has now settled down in Central Pennsylvania with his husband, Dominic, and his laptop. An interesting ménage. Andrew grew up in western Michigan with a father who loved to tell stories and a mother who loved to read them. Since then he has lived throughout the country and traveled throughout the world. He is a recipient of the RWA Centennial Award, has a master's degree from the University of Wisconsin–Milwaukee, and now writes full-time. Andrew's hobbies include collecting antiques, gardening, and leaving his dirty dishes anywhere but in the sink (particularly when writing). He considers himself blessed with an accepting family, fantastic friends, and the world's most supportive and loving partner. Andrew currently lives in beautiful, historic Carlisle, Pennsylvania.

Email: andrewgrey@comcast.net

Website: www.andrewgreybooks.com

FIRE AND WATER
ANDREW GREY

CARLISLE
COPS
1

Carlisle Cops: Book One

Officer Red Markham knows about the ugly side of life after a car accident left him scarred and his parents dead. His job policing the streets of Carlisle, PA, only adds to the ugliness, and lately, drug overdoses have been on the rise. One afternoon, Red is dispatched to the local Y for a drowning accident involving a child. Arriving on site, he finds the boy rescued by lifeguard Terry Baumgartner. Of course, Red isn't surprised when gorgeous Terry won't give him and his ugly mug the time of day.

Overhearing one of the officer's comments about him being shallow opens Terry's eyes. Maybe he isn't as kindhearted as he always thought. His friend Julie suggests he help those less fortunate by delivering food to the elderly. On his route he meets outspoken Margie, a woman who says what's on her mind. Turns out, she's Officer Red's aunt.

Red and Terry's worlds collide as Red tries to track the source of the drugs and protect Terry from an ex-boyfriend who won't take no for an answer. Together they might discover a chance for more than they expected—if they can see beyond what's on the surface.

www. dreamspinnerpress.com

Carlisle Cops: Book Two

Carter Schunk is a dedicated police officer with a difficult past and a big heart. When he's called to a domestic disturbance, he finds a fatally injured woman, and a child, Alex, who is in desperate need of care. Child Services is called, and the last man on earth Carter wants to see walks through the door. Carter had a fling with Donald a year ago and found him as cold as ice since it ended.

Donald (Ice) Ickle has had a hard life he shares with no one, and he's closed his heart to all. It's partly to keep himself from getting hurt and partly the way he deals with a job he's good at, because he does what needs to be done without getting emotionally involved. When he meets Carter again, he maintains his usual distance, but Carter gets under his skin, and against his better judgment, Donald lets Carter guilt him into taking Alex when there isn't other foster care available. Carter even offers to help care for the boy.

Donald has a past he doesn't want to discuss with anyone, least of all Carter, who has his own past he'd just as soon keep to himself. But it's Alex's secrets that could either pull them together or rip them apart—secrets the boy isn't able to tell them and yet could be the key to happiness for all of them.

www. dreamspinnerpress.com

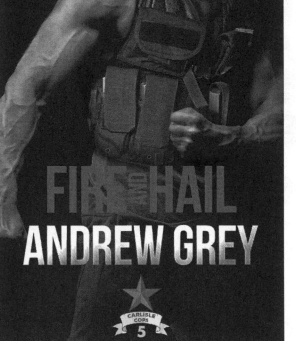

Carlisle Cops: Book Five

Brock Ferguson knew he might run into his ex-boyfriend, Vincent Geraldini, when he took his first job as a police officer in Carlisle. Vincent's attitude during a routine traffic stop reminds Brock why their relationship didn't last.

What Brock doesn't expect is finding two scared children in the trunk of a Corvette. He's also surprised to learn the kids' mother is Vincent's sister. But his immediate concern is the safety of the two children, Abey and Penny, and he offers to comfort and care for them when their mother is taken into custody.

Vincent is also shocked to learn what his sister has done. For the sake of the kids, he and Brock bury the hatchet—and soon find they have much more in common than they realized. With Abey and Penny's help, they grow closer, until the four of them start to feel like a family. But Vincent's sister and her boyfriend—an equal-opportunity jerk—could tear down everything they're trying to build.

www. dreamspinnerpress.com

FIRE FOG

ANDREW GREY

CARLISLE
COPS
6

Carlisle Cops: Book Six

Carlisle police officer Dwayne knows what Robin is doing the moment he lays eyes on the young man at Bronco's club. But he doesn't know that, like him, Robin also comes from a family who cast him out for being gay, or that he's still lugging around the pain of that rejection. Robin leaves the club, and soon after Dwayne decides to as well—and is close by when things between Robin and his client turn violent.

When Dwayne finds out Robin is the victim of a scam that lost him his apartment, he can't leave Robin to fend for himself on the streets. Despite Dwayne's offer of help and even opening up his home, it's hard for Robin to trust anything good. The friendship between them grows, and just as the two men start warming up to each other, Robin's sister passes away, naming Robin to care for her son. Worse yet, their pasts creep back in to tear down the family and sense of belonging both of them long for.

Will their fledgling romance dissipate like fog in the sun before it has a chance to burn bright?

www. dreamspinnerpress.com